KEITH LIVES!

Bodie Plecas

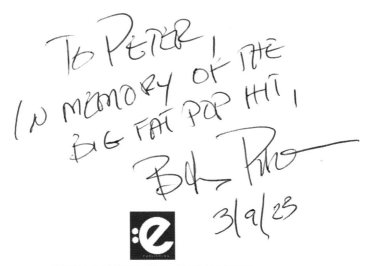

To Peter,
In memory of the
big fat pop hit,
[signature]
3/9/23

ELEMENTARY GROUP · LOS ANGELES

Paperback: 978–1-7379600-0-3
Ebook: 978–1-7379600-1-0

Library of Congress Number: LCCN 2022901920

First paperback edition September 2022.

Edited by Andrew Robles
Cover art by Juan Francisco Irusta

www.bodieplecas.com
Published by Elementary Group

For Hilda
With you is where all my best things start.

For Maja
You are my sweetest pop song
and my favorite story.

Contents

1. SO YOU WANT TO BE A ROCK AND ROLL STAR

The thundering is intense. The heavens rattle and shake. The sound echoes and rings in his ears.

"Keith! Keith! Keith!"

The packed arena pulsates like a living organism.

"All these people, all here for ... me?" he thinks.

A man emerges onto the stage. His broad smile pans the audience like a grilled high beam headlight as he approaches a microphone stand at the center of the stage.

"Are we feeling good tonight, Los Angeles?" he says in a voice drenched in the art of plastic cool. A mild response ripples through the audience.

"Back from a triumphant tour taking the sweet sounds he created right here in L.A. all around the world. Back like the conquering rock' n roll giant he is. Give up a big hometown welcome for your very own Keith Unger and His Hunger!"

The arena erupts. The sound is deafening. One rabid superfan, curly mop of blonde hair falling over his black-framed glasses, is going berserk at the front of the stage. His 'Feed the Hunger' tee shirt is already caked in sweat.

A figure saunters on from stage left with all the swaggering cool of a young gunslinger. He is stitched into his skinny black jeans, a loose-fitting bright red shirt hanging over his slim frame. A mop of unruly brown hair rolls well past the collar and falls down into his brown, soulful eyes. He has the looks that teenage girls crave – young, cute, and lost.

Keith Unger takes it all in. This is what he has dreamed of, prayed for. Now he is living it.

"Keith?"

It's a woman's voice calling his name. It seems to come over the sound system. Sounds familiar.

Keith looks stage left. There stands Candy Lamour – his girlfriend, his muse. The commander in chief of Keith Central. Without her, none of this would be possible.

Candy's frilly second-hand store dress drapes over ripped jeans. Her blonde, scraggly hair looks like it's at the point of no return on the road from mess to disaster. The bright red gash of lipstick screams an open declaration – I wanna destroy you. She is not classically beautiful, but there is something about her. She shakes her hair, head down, and looks up through her bangs with sultry eyes, in a well-rehearsed approximation of sexy.

"You kill 'em, baby," she mouths. He owes her so much.

Super Fan is leaping up and down, fists pumping the air in unison. "I Wanna Be Rad!" he screams. Keith points at him and smiles lazily. Superfan slides into nirvana.

"Keith? Are you there?"

Again that voice. It's an older woman.

I know that voice, Keith thinks, confused. He looks around. No, the voice doesn't come from the sound system. It's everywhere, like the voice of God, permeating all of creation, which in Keith's case is this arena.

He looks around the crowd. Clearly, he's not the only one who hears it.

"Keith! I said, are you there?"

The audience quiets. Some point at Keith, others laugh. The laughter builds.

His eyes are drawn down to where the audience is pointing. Keith realizes that he is standing naked, center stage, in front of 20,000 people. What the hell just happened? He panics as he desperately tries to cover himself with his hands, slinking backward on the stage, uncertain of where to go. Trapped.

"Keith, if you don't pick up that phone, I'm going to plan your birthday party all by myself, and you know what that means!"

"Mom?" utters Keith, like a little lost boy.

"Your *mother*, dude?" a fan leaning on the stage

yells. Laughter spreads like a computer virus through the crowd. "Mommy's calling the rock star. Did you wear clean underwear?"

The audience erupts in laughter, pointing at his stark nakedness. It's a collision of humiliations.

"Keith!!!"

2. TOWN CALLED MALICE

Keith sits bolt upright.

He is not in an arena, there is no crowd, and there is no band. There is no homecoming welcome, either.

Squeezed into a single bed in a bare, drab apartment, hands covering his crotch, he is confronted with reality. And this reality comes with a sucking sound, as his balloon of dreams painfully deflates.

Keith looks around nervously. He doesn't see her anywhere. Slowly he exhales with relief, leans back on his bed, and pulls the covers up. But he is abruptly hit in the face by a water-filled brush.

"Lennon!"

The young yellow lab has climbed up onto the bed and smothers Keith with sloppy, wet kisses.

"Dude, you freaked me out." Lennon puts his head in Keith's lap and looks up at him with adoring eyes. Keith reaches down and scratches him affectionately behind the ears.

"That was so freaky. I had a crazy dream. I was in

this arena, and I was getting ready to play a gig, a massive gig, and all of a sudden, out of nowhere, this voice yells ..."

"KEITH!!!"

Keith leaps to his feet. Lennon jumps off the bed and barks at the unseen malevolent presence as he circles in place, agitated.

"Keith Unger, I know you are there! Now stop avoiding me and pick up the phone this instant!"

The tiny studio apartment looks like a war zone staged inside a four-walled box. The single bed, a small TV, and a cluttered desk are somehow squeezed into this claustrophobic space.

Jumping off the bed, Keith rushes to the desk and pushes his hands through the pile of papers on top of it. A laptop computer suddenly appears. A guitar cable dangles helplessly over the edge of the desk. On the floor, in its general vicinity, is a beat-up black Fender Stratocaster guitar. An Orange Crush amplifier sits on a small hand truck next to the guitar, ready for motion.

"Honestly, Keith, why can't you have a cell phone like a normal person so I can text you instead of having to call?"

Behind the laptop, Keith's hand strikes gold as he pulls out a wireless landline phone, with a pair of underwear wrapped around it. He removes the obstruction and brings the phone to his ear.

"Mom?"

"Why didn't you answer?"

"I was sleeping."

"And why don't you have a cell phone like every other normal person? Really, Keith. Stella can just text her kids when she needs to, but I have to call! And leave messages that don't get answered. It's like you're living in the cave ages. So, why don't you have a cell phone?"

"Because I lost my job and didn't pay my bill, mom. Remember? You said you'd only get me a landline so I wouldn't lose it." Keith drops down onto the bed and leans against the wall.

"Well, don't expect me to give you any more money! Your father says you'll be 27-years old tomorrow, and you should be able to pay for your own bills. I'm not paying them. He said it's called helicopter parenting, and your father—"

"Reuben is not my father, mom. He's your husband."

"Now, that is just rude, Keith. He's my husband, and therefore he's—"

"Not my father!"

"Oh! You are so obstinate. Just like your father."

"Reuban?"

"No, your real father. And you know how that ended for him. Went and joined that stupid club. I told him not to, but did he listen? No. Hard-headed, just like you."

Keith looks at the wall above the desk. Collected like a family tree is his hall of heroes, the only decorations that adorn the bare walls. The pictures are of rock stars: Kurt Cobain, Jimi Hendrix, Brian Jones, Amy Winehouse, Chris Bell, Janis Joplin. All dead.

His eyes fix on the picture of the one unfamiliar face, which bears an uncanny resemblance to Keith. He is a young man with a slight beard who holds a guitar, a distracted expression on his face. A baby sits at his feet, looking up in awe.

"What did you want, mom? I have a show tonight." Keith looks at the clock next to his bed – 6:17 PM.

"Well, I want to know about your birthday. It won't be convenient for me to celebrate now. I'm going out of town with your father. To Italy. You know it's my favorite time of year in Abruzzo and your father, well, anyway we won't..."

"I'm not celebrating this birthday, mom."

"Now don't be silly, Keith, there is nothing ominous—"

"No."

"Your father's stupid decision doesn't—"

"Not this birthday, mom! And I don't want to talk about it. I gotta go. I love you."

"Well, that's just—"

Keith hangs up his end of the line. He exhales.

Lennon walks back over, and stands next to him on the floor with a look of concern. Keith gives him a warm pat on the head.

"You and me, Lennon, it's down to just us!" Lennon licks Keith's hand.

"Well, you, me, and Candy." Lennon utters a low growl at the sound of the name. "Lennon, that's not cool. She's like your mom." Lennon lies down on the floor, crosses his paws, and buries his head into them.

"I gotta get moving. Candy warned me not to be late."

Keith leans over and flips through the papers next to his bed until he finds a Staples bag. He opens it and pulls out a roll of tape and a stack of printed pages. Each sheet bears the same message: 'Keith Unger and Hunger, tonight, 8 PM at the Killer Klub, $15 entry, all ages welcome.'

He rises, walks to the desk, and dives back into the morass of papers. Like a blind man reading braille, his fingers wind their way through the pile until, miraculously, they find what his mind seeks – a slim, red computer flash drive. On the flash drive, in tiny letters, is scrawled 'I Remember You'. Keith kisses the drive and puts it into the pocket of a black leather jacket lying across the chair.

His feet deftly navigate their way through his jeans, avoiding the multitude of rips and holes along the way. Keith grabs a black "Death to the Pixies" tee shirt from the floor and pulls it over his head.

Black boots come on over bare feet. A wallet, attached to a silver chain, rises like a fishing line from the floor and is pulled into Keith's hand. He checks the contents: One hundred and thirty-six dollars. He links the chain to his belt loop and pockets the wallet.

The Strat is zipped into a soft gig bag. Then Keith places the Staples bag on top of the Orange amp and slips into the oversized, black leather jacket. The gig bag's strap goes over his shoulder, and he turns to the door.

Slowly, he opens the door and peeks into the hallway. Yellowed paint, with cracks from countless mini earthquakes, covers the hallway walls like modern abstract art.

The elevator is across and just down the hall, a short walk of 50 feet. Keith looks around intently – the hallway is empty.

Hurrying back into his room, he grabs the mini hand truck and begins to back out through the door. Once outside, he closes the door and cranks the key in the deadbolt.

"You are perhaps forgetting a small thing."

Keith turns abruptly. Standing before him is a small, elfish, older man with a balding head and glasses atop his shiny pate. His body slouches in at 5'6". Mr. Krajchik, the building owner, speaks in a thick Eastern European accent.

"You are owing two month rent, Unger. I don't not run boarding house for welfare peoples. You must to pay today, or maybe—" Krajchick slides his finger across his throat as if slicing it with a knife.

"You'll kill me?"

Krajchick looks at him aghast. "Of course no! What I am? KGB? No, you must move. You pay today or no more apartment!"

"I'm sorry for the delay, Mr. Krajchik, but don't worry, I have a big gig tonight. I've been advertising like crazy." Keith pulls a flyer from the Staples bag and proudly holds it up for Krajchik to see.

"You no use intranets?" asks Krajchik

"I'll have your money for sure by tonight. I promise."

Keith looks utterly sincere, and Krajchik looks completely disbelieving. He leans in and peers at the flyer. Then he shakes his head, turns, and walks away down the hallway.

"Tonight Unger! Two-month rent or apartment bye-bye." He disappears around the corner.

Keith exhales and slumps against the door. Crisis temporarily averted, he grabs the hand truck to continue his departure. But loud barks from behind the door stop him in his tracks. "Shoot!" Keith quickly unlocks the door, and a joyous Lennon rushes into the hallway. He leaps up and leans his body against Keith's.

"I'm sorry, dude," says Keith, rubbing the back of Lennon's ears. "They're kind of weird at the Killer Klub – no dogs allowed. But I'll be back right after the show, I promise, and I'll take you for a long walk. Cool?"

Lennon utters a low moan, looking up with doleful eyes, crushing Keith's spirit.

"C'mon, it's not my fault. It's just the way it is. I'll be back, I promise." Keith leads Lennon back into the apartment and closes the door quickly before he can change his mind, then runs to the elevator.

Keith exits his small apartment building's front doors, pulling the hand truck and amp behind him. The apartment building has a name, which was not uncommon in old Hollywood. This one is called the Garden, though it's anything but.

Parked in front, 20 feet down from the building, is a decrepit, old Dodge Dart. It has a midnight blue body, a white vinyl roof, and a meteor shower's worth of dings and dents. Keith loads his gear into the back seat. Then he slides himself into the front seat and fires up the engine. His right fist pumps down as the engine ignites and the car rumbles to life. Keith slides her into gear and gives the pedal a little gas.

The car bounces an inch forward, then roughly rocks back. Keith looks down. Yes, the emergency brake is disengaged. He tries again and gets the same results. He pushes down harder on the gas. The engine revs high, but Keith realizes this car ain't going nowhere.

A hand knocks on the passenger window. Keith looks up to see a guy wearing a backward baseball cap and scowl, looking at him through the dirty passenger window. The guy points to the rear of Keith's car.

"Your wheel, asshole."

Keith climbs out of the car and sees that a large,

bright yellow wheel boot firmly holds his car in place. Damn. Now for the first time, he notices the loose paper slipped under his windshield wiper. It informs him that his car has been rendered immobile by the City of Los Angeles for unpaid parking fines, to the tune of $932. Keith opens the glove box, and a cascade of parking tickets falls out. "Oh yeah," he frowns.

He removes from the car his equipment, plus the Staples bag, and pulls them onto the sidewalk.

"Got some spare, little brother?"

A black man is seated on the sidewalk, leaning against a building.

The man appears to be about 50 years of age. His skin is baby smooth, and his receding hair is fringed with gray. The big eyes are soft and wide but not innocent. The man's voice sounds like it's used to giving orders and having them followed. "No Name" is written on the name patch above his green army jacket's left pocket.

"What about it? Got some spare coin?"

Keith digs his hands into his pockets. Nothing. He looks at the man in the army jacket – a man on the street, without money, maybe an injured vet, no home to call his own, alone against the world.

Slowly, Keith pulls out his wallet and looks at its contents. He nods to himself, pulls six dollars from it, and hands it to the man.

No Name looks at Keith, not the money, measuring him seriously. "You need this?"

Keith shrugs. "I have a gig tonight."

"Ahh, musician. Gonna be a rock star?"

Keith nods uncertainly.

No Name efficiently scoops the money out of Keith's hand.

"Watch what you wish for, little brother. Just might get it."

Keith stands there looking at the man.

"Well, don't stare. This here is prime panhandling time, and I gotta make me some coins. Ain't no room for a crowd." The man shoos Keith away with his hands. "Go on."

Keith starts down the street but stops after a few paces to look back. The man shoos him away again. "Go!"

Keith continues down the street. But soon, he stops, pulls a flyer from his bag, tapes it to a wooden pole, then steps back to look at it.

"Can't miss that," he says to himself. But his confidence sounds fragile.

Working the sidewalk diligently, Keith puts flyers under car windshields, inside door handles, and into the hands of strangers. He unpeels a bit of the tape holding another flyer at a bus stop and then neatly attaches it to his, so they hang together in tandem. After a few blocks, his trail is marked by Hunger promos moving softly in the barely noticeable breeze.

Unseen by Keith and some 50 yards behind him, a young kid on a skateboard follows. The kid lands at every harbor bearing a posted Hunger flyer, pulls his own flyer from a slim backpack, and sticks it over the top of Keith's. Then he skates on to the next posting.

Where Hunger was once advertised, there is now posted: "Hip hop extravaganza! 20 DJs! Girls get in free! The Automatic, TONIGHT 8 PM!! 2 for 1 drinks! GIRLS FREE!"

Progress buries all in its wake.

3. YOU NEVER GIVE ME YOUR MONEY

"**N**o entry!"

A big, burly, biker-looking bouncer stands in the Killer Club's side door. "Can't you read?" He points to a sign on the door.

"I'm with the band. Hunger?"

The security holds out his hand without looking at Keith. "ID."

Keith pulls out his wallet and hands the man his driver's license. The bouncer checks it against his list, then hands it back.

"Happy Birthday."

"It's tomorrow."

As he enters the club, Keith is immediately hit by the strong smell of backed-up drains, old liquor, and scrubbed vomit. These smells are carpeted by an overdose of air freshener. It must be the same logic that led the French to invent perfume, he thinks.

The bartenders shine glasses and arrange bottles. Iron Maiden crashes out of the speakers as bar waitresses prep for opening.

"Tell your drummer to stop ripping off the beers," one bartender yells to Keith. "It's all getting charged to your bill."

Keith walks through an open-door entrance to the left of the stage. He walks through the short hallway to another door, which is cracked open, and enters.

"It's a Flying V, you moron. You know how long I had to work at my old man's shop so I could buy it? I'll kick your skinny ass all the way back to the Valley if you so much as look at it again."

Sly is pissed, his nostrils flared, and he is standing at his full height of 5'7", atop a chair, as he attempts to stare down Rami, who is a wiry 6 feet plus. In his hands, Rami twirls and taps a set of drumsticks, nervous energy relentlessly channeling through his body and into the sticks.

"Screw you, Kawasaki!" Rami smooths back the black pompadour atop his head with one hand.

"Don't touch my guitar, you hear me?"

Sly slips back down into his chair and resumes tuning his instrument. Once the guitar is tuned, his long fingers fly across the guitar neck in well-practiced scale forms, his eyes closed, finding the notes without sight.

"Hey," calls Keith. Sly nods without looking up. Rami drums his way over to the door and taps a few beats on Keith's head.

"Greetings, Unger. My money?" Rami holds out an empty hand.

"After the gig, Rami."

"Wrong answer," Rami responds. He quickly reaches into Keith's pocket and pulls out his wallet. Keith snatches it back.

"Come on, man," pleads Rami, his face weighted in pain, palms pressed together in prayer. "My little sister, man; you know I can't take her back to Dr. Nick until I pay on the bill."

Keith hesitates, but his resistance crumbles quickly. He pulls three $20 bills from the wallet. After a moment of thought, he takes two and extends them to Rami.

"Thanks, man," says Rami, as he takes the two $20 bills from the one outstretched hand while grabbing the third from the other.

Before Keith can pocket the wallet, Sly looks up.

"Man, I don't mean to bug you," he says in a low voice, "but we haven't made much money from these gigs, and I gotta show something for the work. Can you spare me 20, 40 bucks?"

Keith looks at his shrinking honey pot. Slowly, he peels two more $20 bills from the wallet and hands them to Sly.

"Appreciate it, Keith," says Sly as he pockets the bills, then returns to his scales.

"Hey, Juice," Keith calls out to a figure in the corner of the room.

Juice is seated cross-legged and straight-backed in a wooden chair, which is tucked into the back corner.

His long blonde hair, parted on the right side, hangs down nearly to the waist. Wire-rimmed glasses cling to his nose, which is buried deep in a paperback book. His Fender P-bass rests precariously against the top corner of a chair.

The paperback looks hefty, though its title is simple enough: *The Quantum Universe (Why Anything Can Happen and Does)*.

"Wow, that's a—" Juice holds up his hand without lifting his eyes, stopping Keith in mid-sentence.

Keith turns to Rami and Sly. "Have you guys seen Candy?"

"No, thank God," answers Sly.

Rami simply raises his drumsticks, forming the sign of the Cross, head turned in mock fear.

"C'mon, man. She's my girlfriend," says Keith.

"Sympathies, dude." Rami solemnly bows his head.

"She didn't pick out my outfit. I gotta get this okayed."

"Okay yourself." They all turn to Juice. He still sits in his Zen-like reading position, nose deep in his book.

"Stop staring at Stevie Ray Hawking! You guys are on in half an hour!"

Candy Lamour's body is a whirl of motion, vintage frill dress leaving a trail in her wake, scraggly blonde hair flying with every turn of her head. She sets a plastic wrapper with two limp flowers on a table next to Keith.

"These are from Harry. He said break a leg. He can't

make it. Some big meeting or something."

Scooping Keith's face into her large hands, Candy kisses him hard on the lips.

"How's my baby? Did you get an outfit?" Candy spins Keith around, looking at his attire. "Oh no, that jacket's too big! Shit, don't you have a pair of jeans with more tears in them? And where's the make-up kit?"

Rami and Sly turn their backs, hoping to avoid notice.

"Alright. Don't worry baby, mama brought her own," Candy exhales. "Those lights are bright. They'll bleach you out like a pasty, limp Jap."

Sly raises two middle fingers to Candy. Behind her back.

Candy stops and surveys the room. "Where's the beast?"

"Lennon?" asks Keith. "He's at home. No dogs allowed."

"Good," Candy breathes in relief.

Candy swiftly moves Keith into a wooden chair in front of a tiny, dirty mirror. She throws her bag onto the table and empties the contents: tampons, cigarettes, dollar bills, condoms, bottles of pills, rolling papers, a pair of rolled-up lime green underwear with red hearts on it. From inside a little black bag that falls out of her purse, Candy takes some make-up and begins work on Keith's face.

"You have to stand out. The stage is your mistress,

baby. Rub her until she's screaming, and she'll be yours all night."

Rami sticks his finger in his mouth and mimics gagging.

Candy's large and wide mouth is made more sensual and obnoxious by the lurid red lipstick covering it like a thick coat of cheap paint. It doesn't so much speak words as it forms them, like large hands mangling the metal of a car bumper. Extravagant shapes bring each syllable to life, making it hard to take your eyes from this moving red machine. Or to stop from imagining what else it's capable of doing.

Expertly adding a thick layer of dark eyeliner, Candy then pulls out a comb and teases Keith's hair, giving it height and drama. Kneeling down, she takes a couple of the rips in his jeans and enhances them by tearing the denim like a panther ripping flesh. Then she stands Keith up, thrusts her hand deep into his pants, grabs his little rock star, and moves it firmly to Keith's left. Pulling her hand out, Candy gently strokes the front of his pants.

"There you go, baby. Every rock star worth his salt dresses to the left – Mick, Plant, Reznor, Bieber. And Unger. Mama knows," Candy winks knowingly. Then she steps back to take in the totality of her new creation.

It all seems so forced, controlled, invasive – brutal, in fact. Yet the result is undeniable because Keith now looks like a top of the pops rock star.

The room is quiet for a moment. Sly has stopped noodling on his guitar, and Rami's nervous energy evaporates. Only Juice remains unchanged, still buried in his book. Sly and Rami stand mouths agape, staring at Candy and her Rockenstein creation. She looks back at them and tosses her hair.

"Hate the bitch, but worship the talent, peasants."

Candy walks over to Sly and feels the texture of his hair. "You need to cut that. It's dry and brittle. And too long. New decade, guitar boy."

From her purse, Candy pulls out four sheets of paper and hands one to each band member.

"Tonight's set list."

"Has it changed? No." Rami smirks.

Candy sees Keith's Orange amp on its hand truck.

"Why isn't that on the stage?" She opens the door and grabs the first person she sees walking through the hallway, a Hispanic dishwasher. She pulls him in and points to the amp.

"Take that to the stage, Jose, got it?"

The dish washer looks confused.

"Tomas este amplificador a la etapa. Comprende pinche cabron?"

Candy spits out the Spanish words like their hot chili peppers. The dishwasher nods his head, looking at her in abject fear as he quickly grabs the hand truck, rushing the amp out of the room.

"Have you talked to Harry about the label?" asks Candy as she turns back to Keith.

"No, I ... I figured he'd be here tonight."

Candy pats Keith's face like he's a slow learning child. "Don't figure anything. He's your manager. If you don't push his ass, he ain't gonna plow any fields for you. We wanna go to the top, right? To the very tippity top of the top, right?"

Keith nods.

"We want to be filthy rich, play festivals in Europe and Colorado, have a house on the beach in Malibu, hang out with Beyoncé, Kanye, and that guy from Coldplay, right?"

"Well, I'm not really a fan of ..."

"Keith!"

"It's just that they're not really rock and ..."

"Stop whining! This is my damn dream!" She softens and smiles at Keith. "OUR dream, isn't it, Keithie? Right, baby?"

He nods his head uncertainly. "I guess so."

Keith doesn't notice that Candy has pulled his wallet out until she's holding it in front of him. She pulls the remaining bills from inside.

"Good. So you gotta pay attention to detail, keep your eye on the ball. Find out when your lame ass manager is signing that recording deal with Massive Records. Okay?"

Candy pockets the bills.

"Good boy. Now, let's get this show on the stage!"

The lights on the Killer Klub stage are hot. The speakers seem to heave under the weight of the full discharge of the sounds emanating from them.

Sly flops to his knees, the center of the Flying V body cradled over his thigh as he tilts his body back, fingers obliterating the strings on the guitar's neck. Rami is a whirl of perpetual motion, dancing over the drums in full frenzy, eyes never straying from the bass player. Juice's hair makes perfect sense now as it flies in a coordinated, circular motion, whipping from side to side like an insane pendulum, as he expertly navigates the neck of his bass. These are good players, and it shows.

At the center of the stage, Keith thrusts and stabs harsh rhythmic chords across the Strat's strings. His hair has lost its prior drama and now falls hard over his face, eyes buried beneath the brown fringe. His mind is transported, caught up in another world, while his body vibrates to invisible sonic waves.

But it's a lot of effort and talent wasted on one of the simplest songs ever played on this decrepit stage. When Keith opens his mouth to sing, he services lyrics so insipid that calling them crap is a mercy killing.

"Oh baby, I feel so bad. I don't know, but I think you're mad. I can't help feeling sad when all I want is just to be rad."

But Keith delivers them with enough power and charisma that even the jaded waitresses stop and take notice of the guy at the mic.

The audience is alive, one with the band, gyrating

to the beat, flailing about with reckless abandon. It is leaping, turning, spinning, burning a trail across the floor, mouthing along to the empty lyrics, blissfully unaware and soullessly uncaring of their pointless nature. Lost in a whirling dervish frenzy, it belongs to the band entirely.

Unfortunately, the audience consists of one.

Superfan wears his 'Feed the Hunger' tee shirt. Droplets of sweat stream down the glass of his black-framed spectacles. Danny Wallburger doesn't even try to contain his natural exuberance, and he couldn't care less that he's the only person who recognizes the genius of Keith Unger. He is John the Baptist, and Keith is his own personal Jesus.

A bartender hits on a waitress, proving his rock knowledge by dissing the band as "pop tarts." As the last strains of the closing chord reverberate through this black hole of a club, the sound abruptly dies, and the waitress targeted by the musicologist barkeep is caught screaming at the top of her lungs, "Yeah, but the singer's cute."

"You're lucky this ain't pay-for-play like a lot of other clubs," Big Sid says as he slides the last greasy, creased dollar bill into Keith's hand. He is seated at a table in a backroom office of the club. A portrait of Bill Gazzarri sits on the wall behind him.

Sid has earned his name the honest way – he's a

giant of 6'4", weighing in at over the 300-pound mark. His grey hair rises like a curly mushroom above his head. He chomps hard on the cigar in his mouth, which moves in effortless rhythm with his teeth as he talks.

"You know the Whisky charges, right? Roxy too. This ain't Jim Morrison's Sunset Strip no more, and you ain't no Jim Morrison, buddy boy. I knew Jimbo, and he never disgraced himself like that. He'd a found some new creative ways to do it."

Keith looks at the small wad of money in his hand.

"That doesn't seem like ... enough, Sid."

Sid's eyes rise slowly and contemptuously. "Enough?"

Keith quivers as Sid stands up and towers over him.

"Well, let's do the math here, Einstein. You get $100 for playing an hour, and your guest list gets deducted. You only had one guest, that curly-haired freak, so that brings you to $80. You didn't bring any girls in. You know how many girls there were at that Hip Hop show at Automatic tonight?"

Sid leans into Keith, who unconsciously tilts back on his heels.

"Me neither, but it was a lot! Girls bring guys, guys buy beers, beer sales make money, and money pays for musicians. It's simple math. You didn't sell no beers, but your hood rat drummer boy clipped six at 7 bucks a bottle, so that's 42 bucks." He points at Rami, cowering at the back of the group. "I see you, pal."

"And my accounting fee," says Sid, as he takes

another $5 bill from Keith's wad. "That leaves you with $33. Still better than pay-to-play."

Sid turns and lumbers out, leaving Keith staring at the money in his hand and the rest of the band watching another rerun.

4. HIGH AND DRY

Aglum and defeated group is seated around two tables at Coffee a Go-Go, a coffee shop on Hollywood Blvd. Keith counts money.

"So $33 divided by 4 is—"

"$8.25," says Juice without looking up from his book.

Keith hesitantly counts out $8 for each band member, leaving one lonely extra dollar bill. He looks around the table.

"Keep it," says Sly.

Rami nervously empties sugar packets into his coffee saucer, creating a large mound. Sly strains his tea bag into his cup without looking up. A Hunger flier lies on the table.

Keith is dejected for more reasons than he can even begin to recognize, let alone list. Candy looks around the dismal table, which is as solemn as a funeral. She smacks the table hard with her hand.

"Okay – so what?" she blurts. "It's just one show. Yeah, a really, really bad show, but just one damn show. Like the man said, it's a long way to the top if you wanna rock the roll!"

"Rock AND roll," corrects Sly.

"Whatever. Boy, you gotta carry that load a long time! What if the Beatles quit after Abbey Road? Or if Elvis never ate at Sun? What if the Stones never put out Goat's Head Soup? Yeah, that's a dose of some reality." She nods her head. "So, it sucked that we only had one person in the audience tonight, and he was a freaking nerd super fan who has nothing else to do with his pathetic life—"

"Thanks for coming, Danny," Keith whispers to Danny Wallburger, who sits at the single table next to them.

"You guys are the freaking best, Keith!" says Danny, barely containing himself. "Did I show you my new tee shirts?" Danny pulls out several tees, one featuring Keith's face with text that reads: "Hunger for Rock!"

"Can I finish here?" Candy says, giving Danny the evil eye.

The coffee shop waitress walks around the table with a coffee pot, checking if anyone needs a refill. She is cute, with her brown hair cut in a bob, lean figure, no make-up, and calm demeanour. Keith looks up at her from under his brows, hoping the look doesn't get noticed by Candy.

"Can you beat it, Sorority Susie? We're having a business meeting here!" snarls Candy. The waitress doesn't react. She just fills the next cup then goes back to her table. She sits down and picks up an open book lying on the table, then resumes underlining passages.

"Nice tee, Danny," Keith whispers under his breath. Danny pants like a puppy dog.

Juice lays down his book, puts a bookmarker between the pages, and folds it shut. He places his wire-rimmed glasses on the book, his elbows on the table with palms pressed together, and leans his chin against his hands. The entire table turns to look at him, surprised by the sudden motion.

"Here's the deal. You're a great guy, Keith. I really like you. I think you have talent, but I think you haven't figured how to dig it out yet. Your songs don't reflect life in any meaningful way, nor with any depth or insight. The lyrics are like this bookmarker – just holding a place. Because while your lyrics are lame, your melodies are nice, catchy, sticky like taffy. You sing well, and you have an untapped charisma."

Everyone stares at Juice. Not a sound is uttered.

"The problem is, I don't know if you can ever make it. Because you've got this shrew of a girlfriend—"

"Asshole!" Candy injects, giving Juice the finger.

"—who controls and dominates you because you won't control and dominate yourself. The deal is – life is short, you blink, and it's gone. Until you figure that out, you'll keep wasting your time. I can't afford that. I have a wife and two kids to support, and ..."

Juice picks up his $8 share, then releases it, letting the bills flutter back down onto the table like green paper rain. "$8 a night is just not going to do that. So I wish you the very best of luck and a wonderful life, but I'm leaving the band."

Juice nods his head to the group. Then he rises with his book, his gig bag, and walks out of the coffee shop.

Stunned silence rests like a stalled, pregnant rain cloud over the table of four.

Rami leans back in his chair. "Wow," he says. "That's heavy." Sly stares into his teacup. Candy looks over the group.

"What? That weasel leaves, and you guys get all panicky? Who needs him, the traitor. He's just a stupid bass player, dime a dozen. You know what you throw a drowning bass player? His amp! Let that book buying, Dickens reading loser drown. Who needs him!"

"I do." Eyes turn to Rami. "Juice is the best bass player I've ever played with, man. My timing is crap. To be honest, the only reason I stayed in the band is because of Juice – he keeps me in the groove. Rock is dead, man, nobody listens to that shit anymore. It's all hip hop, electronica, pop. That's what everybody wants."

Rami rises. "Sorry, man, but I'm outta here, too." Rami walks out the door, looks left, then right, and calls out, "Hey Juice! Wait up!"

Then there were three.

"Feels like the last man on the Titanic." Sly looks up from his cup of tea.

"No, not you too, Sly?" Keith's face pleads.

"Dude, I don't even like those other guys. I like you. But a guitar player and a singer ... that's not a band, man. It's folk music. And I hate folk music."

"We could get some other players. Your leads give my songs their hooks, Sly. Without you, they don't stick."

"I appreciate that," Sly nods. "But you don't need my hooks. I'm just playing what's on your demos, man, and the only reason I play them is you don't have the confidence to do it yourself. We've got a bad reputation for making no money and drawing no crowds. We're not going to get anybody good to play with us."

Keith deflates with great speed as he senses what's coming.

"Everything's got its shelf life, K. Sorry." Sly turns to Candy solemnly. "Look, I know you've been a jerk to me, called me every racial slur in the book, put down my playing, and bitched about my clothes. But now that it's the end of the road, Candy, I have to be honest and tell you – you're a disgusting, controlling degenerate jerk and I hope you rot in hell."

Sly grabs his gig bag and hurries out the door calling over his shoulder, "Good luck, Keith!"

It is now utterly quiet. Even Candy is stunned. Keith looks as though a sledgehammer has hit him upside the head.

"Some more coffee?"

The waitress hovers over Keith's shoulder. He

doesn't respond, so she turns to walk away.

"What about me? Maybe I might want some coffee? Or are you just trying to pick up on my boyfriend?" demands Candy.

Keith turns to calm her down. "Candy, she was just—"

"Shut up, you incompetent no talent!"

The waitress has finally had enough.

"Why don't you just leave him alone. You are a mean, mean girl. I can't imagine why anyone would want to spend any time with you."

Candy suddenly grabs her coffee cup and violently flings its contents at the waitress, who easily dodges the liquid. However, it splashes directly into Danny's face.

The waitress walks to the counter. Candy turns to Keith.

"You are such a waste of space and time. You know how much I've done for you, how much I've sacrificed for you and your stupid dream? Primping, pushing, advising you, sleeping with you. For what? FOR WHAT? You're a pathetic loser! I tried to mold you into a star, but you can't mold a turd into art. You're just another asshole guy, just like my old man."

Candy stands and looks down at Keith with a snarl.

"You think I can't move on from you? Watch me. I've spent my whole life moving on. You're just another stop on the rocket to my dreams, but your stop is a dead end. I'm gonna find a rocket that goes straight through to Beyoncé, Coldplay, and Malibu. And that rocket is gonna be huge!"

Keith is in full panic attack mode. "Candy, please ... you can't. I need you. What am I going to do?"

"Figure it out for yourself because it ain't my problem. Me, me, me, that's all you care about. Well, what do I get? Huh? What about me? Nothing!"

Suddenly, Keith remembers. He reaches into his pocket and pulls out the slim red flash drive as Candy gathers her things.

"Wait! I did get something for you. I wrote you a song, it's a great song, and it's for you. About you."

"A song? For me?" Candy utters in a sickly-sweet voice. Then she slaps Keith across the face. "Wake up! What good is a song to me? Is that going to buy me a vacation or a yacht? No!" Nevertheless, she smoothly takes the flash drive into her hand. "I need something concrete, not bullshit."

"I poured my soul into it. It's called "I Remember You" and—"

"Oh, you'll remember me. But I'm about to forget all about you."

Candy reaches down, picks up the nine remaining dollars on the table, and then scoops up the eight that Juice dropped and stuffs them into her dress.

"The least you owe me is cab fare."

With that, Candy spins around, opens the door, and storms out. But on the way out, her frilly dress gets caught in the handle. She tries to release it, but it won't budge. As she struggles, the waitress walks over and calmly pulls the fabric of her dress from the handle.

"I could've done that, bitch," spits Candy, as she exits Coffee a Go-Go like a puff of bad-smelling big black smoke.

Now, with Candy's departure, the shop is eerily quiet. Keith sits staring ahead, shell shocked. Danny looks around, uncertain. The waitress hands Danny a towel, then goes back to her table.

"Wow," Danny whistles as he wipes off his face. "That was like a movie. Think she'll come back?"

Keith doesn't respond.

"Just a bump in the road, man. You're the star, they're your songs. 'I Wanna Be Rad' is gonna be a huge hit, man, you wait and see."

There is no expression on Keith's face. Danny looks around uncomfortably. Finally, he rises.

"Yeah, I get it, man. You gotta process and all that stuff. No worries. Maybe we can do something, like hang out, you know, now that Candy's not around?"

Keith flinches.

Danny begins to back up towards the door. "So, I'll hit you up—okay?" When Keith doesn't respond, Danny steps out onto the sidewalk. He walks down the street slowly, looking in through the shop window.

A flood has engulfed Keith, a torrent of toxic emotions, and he is being pulled down under it. His mind rolls and spins, punished by the currents of shame and betrayal, sucked into the dark brackish waters of misery.

"What an—unpleasant person."

Keith looks up. The waitress is cleaning the table around him.

"I'm sorry, that was rude. I shouldn't speak ill of someone, especially someone I don't know. I'm sure she has issues she's dealing with, but—she really is a very, very—unpleasant person. Do you know her well?"

"She's my girlfriend."

"Oh." The waitress hesitates at her faux pas. "I don't mean to be insensitive. But I think you can say she 'was' your girlfriend. At least from what I just heard. Do you want some more coffee?"

Keith shakes his head.

"Okay. Here's your bill. Let me know if you need anything else. No hurry."

The waitress places the bill on the table next to Keith, and walks back to her seat.

Keith looks around the table: Empty coffee cups and plates. Plates and cups that once bore the sweetness of life, now empty and barren like the core of his soul. He nods. That's not bad, he thinks, I should write it down, use it in a song. No, I'll remember it. But then he remembers another thing – he has no band, so what good is a song?

"Are you in a band or something?"

The waitress is looking at him from her table, concerned.

"I was."

"You have to stick to your dream," she says. "My dad taught me that. If one path closes, you find another one. That's what he said. He's brilliant, my dad. There's always another path if you don't give up. Just a thought."

Keith nods. I'm screwed, he thinks. He looks up at the clock on the wall. After midnight. My birthday. 27 with a bullet.

He picks up the bill. Four coffees, one cinnamon roll – that was Rami, he's addicted to sugar – and two donuts. The donuts were Candy's. How does she eat so much and stay so thin, he wonders?

$19.62. And a smiley face drawn in blue ink.

Keith does the obvious, knowing in advance the result. His wallet is empty. Could humiliation go any deeper? Yes, he thinks as he sheepishly lifts himself from his chair and walks to the waitress.

"I'm sorry. I have a problem. My, uh ... friends left me with the bill, but I ... I don't have any money."

He scrunches himself up, waiting for the explosion, the same one he gets from Candy or his mother when they are met with something they don't like from him. And what could you like less, if you are a waitress, then a broke customer with no way to pay his bill, or leave a tip?

"Don't worry. I'll cover it. You just pay me when you have the money." Then she lifts her head and smiles at him. "Or not."

Keith is stunned by her generosity. "Thank you"

seems like such a small and insignificant thing to say in response. But it is all Keith can muster. The waitress smiles, nods, and keeps reading.

For the first time, Keith takes note that she has been working on her books diligently the entire time he's been in the shop. He determines to ask her what she is doing because it must be important. But the words never come.

Instead, he becomes consumed with figuring out his next step because he desperately hopes there is a next step. There has to be another step. Usually, Candy tells him what it is.

He gets up and walks absently out the door. It's night, but in this part of Hollywood, night and day have no clear demarcation. The action of the street is non-stop. Only the players are replaced, like factory workers changing shifts.

"Hello! You forgot your stuff!"

Keith turns to see the waitress at the shop door. She pulls out his hand truck, with the Orange amp and the gig bag holding the Strat. He walks back, takes the hand truck from her, throws the gig bag over his shoulder, then turns and starts down the street.

The waitress watches him walk away, a lonely figure. She feels sorry for him. He seems lost and adrift, with no clear path home. She wishes she could help because she is the kind of person who likes to help. But people have to help themselves first. That's what her dad says. So she returns to her books inside the shop, knowing her dad is always right.

As he walks, Keith looks at the homeless people, sheltered under the building eaves, seeking a safe harbor for a night's sleep. All these people, all alone, no one to watch over them. Just like Lennon and me.

Lennon!

In his self-absorption, Keith realizes he's forgotten entirely about the only living being who loves him unconditionally, who would be there for him no matter what, band or no band, dream or no dream. His most loyal friend was left to fend for himself, alone in that dark apartment.

Keith spurs into action as his feet pick up steam. Maybe there is a way out, he thinks, instinctively holding onto a shred of hope. But his dark thoughts don't let up the entire walk home.

He is surprised to find Lennon in front of the door to his apartment, head resting on his paws. Lennon leaps to his feet and jumps up to reach his friend. But he is yanked abruptly back by his leash, which is attached to the apartment doorknob.

Keith quickly realizes that all his belongings are stacked outside his door: computer, clothes, books, rock star pictures.

"What are you doing out here, buddy?" asks Keith, trying to comprehend.

Keith pulls the apartment key out of his pocket and

puts it into the deadbolt. But the key doesn't turn. He pushes some more—still nothing. Keith looks closer at the lock and realizes it is not that old, scratched-up one that used to occupy this space, but rather a shiny new lock. And for the first time, he notices above the lock a slip of paper taped to the wood.

It is an eviction notice. The notice is stamped with a court number and address, along with other stuff he doesn't recognize. But there's no need to because he knows – Mr. Krajchik has evicted him for failing to pay his rent.

It's a moveable feast for that bitter lady reality. Homeless, car-less, band-less, love-less, money-less—that's a lot of less to end the day on.

The darkness is back, and his world resumes its spinning. The churning waters of despair pull him down where no light will shine. He searches for something to stop the dizzying motion in his head, something to hold him up and stop him from drowning here on this Hollywood carpet, on this cursed day, his birthday. Some driftwood ...

Harry! Of course. Harry Chukstein, his manager, his mentor, his friend. Harry could help.

Harry always has the answer, the right piece of advice, the perfect solution. For Keith, he is kind of like a Dad, and the waitress said her dad was always right. Maybe Harry had news from Brad Rossi at Massive Records. A recording contract would solve everything, bring back the band, reunite him and Candy, not to mention pay his rent and parking fines.

Keith quickly takes his computer and shoves it into his gig bag, under the guitar.

Harry is his last chance. And Harry stays up late.

5. SENSES WORKING OVERTIME

Opposite the north corner of Franklin and Sycamore, in Hollywood, sits the Highland Gardens Hotel. In an earlier incarnation, it bore a more appropriate honorific – the Landmark Motor Inn.

Here, on October 4, 1970, Janis Joplin was found in her room, lodged firmly between the bed and the dresser, face down, implanted in her own vomit, dead from an overdose of an exceptionally pure and potent batch of heroin. She was 27. You can rent her room for a night or more and share that small space with whatever spirit of hers still resides within. Dead rock legends command that kind of devotion. The heroin is extra.

On Sycamore Avenue, half a block down, Bobby Fuller, the Texas-born singer of *I Fought the Law*, was found dead in his car on a hot July day in 1966, with a can of gasoline and a rubber hose. It was officially ruled accidental asphyxiation. But by popular opinion and the facts, Bobby is forever after remembered as young, talented, and owner of a hit record with a bullet on the day he died.

Death is everywhere, thinks Keith as he passes Sycamore. This is one depressing trip. It is no small relief when he finally sees the giant, vertical white buoy rising up from the ground before him.

Harry's building rests at the terminus of the Sunset Strip. Sleek, white, tall, and clean, it clings confidently to its steep slant on the last bit of the Hollywood Hills that tumbles below Sunset Boulevard into the flats of West Hollywood.

Though he's never seen him before, the building's night doorman doesn't flinch when Keith approaches. The doorman is well accustomed to the sight of musicians in ripped jeans and distressed hair. People in the know, know it can be hard to tell a multi-millionaire pop star from a homeless dude.

"I'm here to see Harry Chukstein."

"Is Mr. Chukstein expecting you?"

"I don't think so."

"Your name, please?"

"Keith Unger."

"And your companion," asks the doorman, looking down at Lennon, who sits patiently next to Keith.

"Lennon."

The doorman nods, picks up his phone, and waits.

"Mr. Chukstein, there is a Mr. Keith Unger and a Mr. Lennon, here to see you ... Yes ... Yes, they are." The doorman strains to look at the backside of Keith. Though he has no idea what the man is looking for, Keith obliges by turning slightly to accommodate him.

"No, it does not appear so, not that I can tell."

The doorman looks at Keith as he speaks. Keith tries hard not to look too desperate, which he assumes is a losing cause. However, it doesn't affect the outcome because when the doorman hangs up the phone, he motions to the elevator and asks, "Do you know the way?"

A few minutes later, Keith is standing in front of Harry's condo door. He barely raises his hand to knock when it opens. Harry Chukstein is walking away from the door, into the apartment, with a phone in his hand. He motions grandly for Keith to enter without looking at him.

"I really don't appreciate this, Ira. Is this how you treat your friends?"

Harry stands a deceptive six feet tall. His crow's nest of grey flecked hair looks like a mangled art project, rash and unruly, stray strands flying everywhere, thinning around the front and on the crown. In contrast to his disappearing hair, his paunch is in expansion mode, and his rumpled suit looks like he's already slept in it at least one night. He talks from the side of his mouth as if the other part of it has been struck down by stroke.

Patently untrustworthy, yet perversely lovable, Harry is like the rogue friend who rips you off over and over again, but to whom you keep loaning money, against your better judgment.

"Do I really need to remind you of that night with the F.O.K.E.R.S. at the Kibitz Room ... Well, I refuse to bend, Ira, my clients, are sacred to me, and their best interests are always foremost in my mind."

Harry holds his hand over the phone, winks and nods to Keith.

"Well, then I guess this is to be continued. Au revoir, Ira, my greetings and salutations to Trudy." Harry sets the phone down on the glass end table and then sits down on an oversized, brown velvet couch. Worn out by the effort, he looks up at Keith.

"Welcome," Harry says in his trademark, deadpanned style.

"Sorry to bother you so late, Harry."

"Don't mention it, don't even give it a thought, mi casa es tu casa. My man!" Harry stretches out his hand, and Keith fist bumps him. "So, what brings L.A.'s soon-to-be most famous rock star to my ever so humble door?"

Keith struggles to find an appropriate way to express his feelings and fears. He's worked for hours to shore up his emotional defenses, to find that glimmer of hope in the dark waters of doom. But now, the weakened walls of denial finally spring a leak, and a violent shot of today's bitter bile bursts out.

"Oh Harry, it's been a horrible, terrible, ugly day. I mean, it started okay with a great dream. I was a rock star playing at the Staples Center."

"Nice."

"And then my mother called my phone, on stage ..."

"Ouch!"

"Only I wasn't at the Staples Center, I was in my apartment, and she reminded me of my birthday."

"Happy Birthday, pal!"

"Then my landlord threatened to evict me—"

"Capitalist pig! I told you, vote Socialist. Even the Democrats have gone corporate."

"I know. So, I went to the show, and then the band quit on me ... "

"Traitors!"

" ... Candy dumped me, and when I got home, I was evicted, all my stuff was in the hall, and Lennon was tied to the door handle outside my apartment!"

"We'll call PETA. They know how to deal with this animal cruelty stuff."

"All I could think of was coming here, that you'd know what I should do. So ... what should I do, Harry? I'm 27, and I'm not famous, and you know what that means. You know, my dad and all, and the sins of the father, and—"

"Whoa, whoa, whoa!" Harry stands and raises his hands high in the air, palms out. "Just stop. Stop right there."

"—they booted my car."

Harry leans in and presses his finger against Keith's mouth, then gently pushes him down into the fuzzy armchair opposite the couch. Keith feels himself sinking back into the womb. It's warm, comfortable. Lennon lies down at his feet.

"Silencio. Close your eyes, take a deep breath. Good. Push the chest out with your inbreathe, and count backward from ten with each exhale. Now repeat after me—Nam-myoho-renge-kyo."

Keith opens one eye. "You know, we're Methodist or—"

"Fine. Repeat any mantra you like. Try 'I am a brown haired rock god.'"

Keith closes his eyes and breathes. His chest expands and retracts in rhythm to the breaths. "I am a brown-haired rock god. I am a brown-haired rock god."

"That's right, but to yourself. Now, I am your manager, your mentor, and everything will be alright. Everything will work out fine. All minor details of today will remain minor. Keep your eye on the big prize, a recording contract."

Keith's eyes pop open. "That's exactly what I was thinking – the recording contract. Did you talk to Brad?"

The side of Harry's mouth freezes.

"No, I have not talked to Brad. You were supposed to call Brad. Did you call Brad?"

Keith tries to think, but the currents of his mind are once again crashing against the walls of denial. His breathing quickens. Big scary waves batter his mental fortress, breaking it down, rock by rock.

"Well?"

Harry sits on the couch, opposite Keith, leaning forward on his elbows.

"Now, this isn't hard. You were supposed to call Brad yesterday to ask what Massive thought of the demo."

Keith tries harder. He is so confused. The fortress is chipping under the pressure of the waves; rocks fall from the top of the walls of denial. Memory flickers, Keith sees a phone in his hand. He shakes his head.

Harry smiles empathetically. Warm rays drift out of the lazy corner of his mouth.

"It's okay, we're in this together, manager and artist, father and son. Did Brad want to develop you, see you live?"

The walls of denial crumble under one brutal wave, which pushes far up into Keith's consciousness. That bitter bitch reality shoves her ugly face into his head again screaming "I don't like it!"

"He said no."

Harry's smile freezes. "What?"

"Brad said no. I wanted to forget. He said no. He said the music was juvenile and meaningless – that could be a compliment, right? Oh, and it doesn't fit today's market. No group yells or thumping, programmed drum beats. It's like classic rock, he said. I think that's bad. Oh, and I sang. He said no one wants to hear singing unless it's perfect pitch. That's what he said."

Keith exhales.

"Wow, I do feel better. It was horrible holding that in. It's such a relief to let it out. So, what's the new plan?"

Harry sits back onto the couch, air silently escaping his lips.

"Should I do a showcase or something?" Keith looks at him, still broken but hopeful. "Send out new demos?"

"You ... you ..."

"Harry?"

"... you little piece of shit. You little, insignificant, unimportant tiny speck of dark brown shit!"

Harry jumps to his feet.

"All you had to do was make a demo decent enough to get Brad Rossi's ear. It didn't even have to be good. He doesn't have a clue about music. He was in used auto parts before he came to Massive Records for Chrissakes. He'd sign Hitler reading the Torah if someone told him it would sell. Just one reasonably good song. But no—"

"I don't understand. You said you liked my songs, Harry."

"Don't tell me what I said, you pea-brained turd. I say whatever I say!"

"But what do we do now?"

"We? What are WE going to do? WE aren't going to do jack shit, buddy boy, because you're on your own. Brad Rossi is my last connection for you in this business. This highway to hell ends here for me."

Harry sits back down and tries to calm himself. Any calm Keith had achieved is now dashed.

"But there must be another way?"

Harry looks at Keith as though he is crazy.

"Listen up, Phil Collins – it's over. Done. Kaput. Finished. End of the line. That was your last shot, and you blew it. Where's my vodka?"

Harry gets up and walks to the kitchen. He picks up a Scooby-Doo glass from the kitchen counter and takes a mighty swig of its clear liquid. Then he downs the remaining half glass in one mind-splitting gulp.

Keith sits in the chair as the room fills with water. In his mind, the sea is rising fast, and he is slipping under, battling for air.

"You might as well go down to the Guitar Center and try to sell equipment to some real musicians."

The Guitar Center stabs downward into Keith's chest like a broadsword. No, not Guitar Center!

"But I'm 27 today, Harry."

"So kill yourself. What do you want me to do about it?"

Kill yourself. That's what Keith's dad did. No, they didn't call it a suicide. His mom said it was a gardening accident gone horribly wrong. But Keith knew the truth. His dad chose those gardening shears, just like he'd chosen the path of legends. The sins of the father must be paid—27 with a bullet pointed down.

Lennon barks.

Keith struggles for air, but the water that surrounds him pulls him down. His whole world has convulsed; he is an island in this ocean, swallowed up by the surrounding sea.

Like the Titanic's iceberg, reality has crushed a monster hole into the hull of Keith's world. There is nothing left for him but to go down into the turbulent waters, the light of the sun a fading shimmer as all grows dark. His last remaining air bubbles stream up past his eyes. Just take a breath, suck in the water, and accept the cold embrace of life's twin sister, and then forever—

Smack.

A sharp pain on his face interrupts the watery comfort of drowning.

"Snap out of it! Yo? Are you having some kind of seizure or something?"

Harry is sitting on the couch, leaning forward, hands pressed together in front of Keith's face. Keith finds he is back in Harry's condo, but nothing else is the same. All paths have narrowed to one, and that path has a big blue sign pointing the way.

"If you puke on this rug, I'm going to sue your sorry ass all the way to Iran so you can buy me another one. Do you hear me? If you gotta puke, do it in the bathroom."

A big blue sign on the wall reads 'Bathroom' and is helpfully accompanied by an arrow. Keith slowly lifts himself from the armchair, struggles to his feet, and like a wounded movie zombie, he shuffles off in the direction of the sign, turning with the arrow.

"If you puke in the sink, clean it up. Rosario doesn't come until Wednesday, and I don't do bathrooms. You hear me?"

Keith stumbles down the hallway towards the door at the end. When out of the blue, like a bat out of hell, Harry passes him. He stops in front of the doorway, arms up, blocking the entrance.

"No! Not here! You're not puking in my bedroom!" He points to the door on Keith's right. "Use the green towels. I was going to get rid of them anyway."

Once inside the bathroom, Keith closes the door, accidentally depressing the lock as he does. He drops to his knees in front of the porcelain toilet, opens his mouth wide, and belches. Loudly. But no vomit comes forth. He rests his head on the toilet seat. His mind is still woozy from the storm and the waves.

He slowly stands in front of the sink. The person in the mirror looks pasty white. The giveaway is the eyes – they are dead pools, without emotion or any sign of life. The path forward is once again clear – there is no path forward.

"Don't use the toothbrush!" Harry calls from outside the door. "That's how you spread germs, and I don't need any failure germs in my mouth."

Keith looks around the bathroom. He sees Harry's bathrobe hanging from a hook on the door. Its extra-large size is perfect to fit comfortably over Harry's ample frame. Keith pulls the cloth belt from the two loops that hold it to the robe.

Stepping into the bathtub, Keith ties one end of the belt to the pipe connecting the shower head to the wall and binds off the other end, forming a loop. He puts his head into it. Then he tightens the noose, making sure the distance from his neck to the pipe is short. If the end is nigh, let it be quick. The eyes of the Buddha in a picture on the opposite wall stare accusingly at him. Keith pulls the shower curtain shut.

"Did you puke? Or are you dry heaving? Jesus, I just redid the tiles in there."

Mother? She won't miss me. Lennon? He'll be better off without me. It's meant to be, preordained since the day dad left. Don't think, do.

And with that, Keith pulls his legs up under him, and his body drops hard. But it's a short drop. His full weight comes to an abrupt stop at the bathrobe belt's end. It jerks hard, tightly constricting his neck. The remaining air thrusts out of his lungs like a speeding locomotive until nothing remains but the visceral pain in his neck. His head tingles as consciousness closes out. He sees a light and hears the sound of the big—

CRACK!

With a loud crunch, the pipe breaks, and Keith comes crashing to his knees in a spastic flying knee drop, his hand pulling the shower curtain down with him. A torrent of water comes roaring out of the broken hole in the wall, where the showerhead pipe used to be. It gushes over Keith's body, and in moments, he is soaked.

Lennon is barking outside the door. The handle jiggles vigorously, then violently.

"What the hell is going on in there? Open the door, Keith! You hear me? Open the damn door!"

Then with one loud smash, the door crashes open, and Harry comes tumbling in. Lennon runs past him to Keith. He licks water off his friend's face.

Harry stands and looks at the broken pipe and the river of water pouring relentlessly from the wall. He doesn't look at the soaked, damaged musician on his knees in the tub. Instead, spinning abruptly, Harry rushes out of the room and towards the kitchen.

"Now you did it, you stupid sonuva—" Harry is yelling from the hallway. "Now you did it! How in the hell do I stop this, Noah? Dammit, where's that water shut off? Shit shit shit! The sink!"

Keith slumps and rolls over in the tub. He is now lying facing up, increasingly underwater.

Rushing back into the bathroom, Harry falls to his knees in front of the sink. His knees crack under the strain. He swings open the small cupboard under the sink, reaches his hand in, and searches blindly with his fingers. The tub is now full, water spilling onto the floor. Finally, Harry's hand finds the handle. He stretches his arm to its maximum as he strains to turn his hand sharply to the left. Mercifully, the water stops pouring from the pipe.

Harry turns, leans his back against the cupboard and exhales. Keith lies in the tub, eyes open, staring blankly at the ceiling. There is silence.

After a few moments, Harry rises slowly. He uses his hands to lift himself up from the ground, then leans against the sink, surveying his bathroom.

"Jesus, if I wanted a damn Jacuzzi, I could have bought one. Who's going to pay for this?" Harry looks at Keith without a shred of pity. "You?"

From the outside, it's hard to tell if there is still any electrical activity percolating in the circuits behind Keith's dead eyes. But on the inside, the drama and commotion have done nothing to sober his mood. Another failure, he thinks, another screw-up by Keith Unger.

"Were you trying to kill yourself?" Keith doesn't turn his head. "Do you hate me or something? Wasn't I good to you? Didn't I keep my end of the bargain? I worked my ass off to get you a record deal, and you pay me back by, what, destroying my bathroom? Or do you just have a problem with plumbing in general?"

"Sorry. I ..."

Harry is furious. He stomps out of the bathroom. When he comes back moments later, he is brandishing a revolver, waving it recklessly in the air at Keith. Dead-eyed, Keith slowly raises his hands in surrender.

"You, you ... bathroom destroyer! Get out of my tub."

Keith slumps back down. "Shoot me."

"Shoot you? And get a murder rap? How far does your hatred of me go? You shoot you!"

Harry checks the safety, turns the gun around, and puts the handle into Keith's left hand. He loops the pointer finger around the trigger and points the gun up to Keith's temple.

"There. Do it. You wanna kill yourself, do it right, no mistake. Just pull the trigger, and poof – you're gone. And my life is back to normal."

Keith holds the gun for a long moment. Then, slowly his fingers begin to tighten. His face scrunches down in supreme effort as he screams and pulls the trigger.

But at the last instant, Harry grabs the gun out of his hand. In the commotion, the gun fires with a loud bang. The bullet ricochets off the metal framing around the window, changing its trajectory. It flies across the narrow bathroom, driving through the Budda's smiling mouth, lodging itself in the wall behind the picture of the former Siddhartha.

Keith is dazed. Harry jumps back and nearly slips on the wet tile floor. Then he pulls the Buddha picture on the wall aside, examining the bullet hole behind it.

"Why did you do that?" Keith hears his voice in a slow, somnambulistic tone.

"Because with your luck, you'd miss and shoot me. Or you'd splatter your blood all over the walls of my bathroom, and like I said, Rosario isn't here until

Wednesday. Not to mention I could lose a ton in resale off this place."

Harry roughly grabs Keith by the elbow and pulls hard to lift him up. But Harry hasn't worked out in over twenty years, so he nearly falls in on top of Keith. Instead, he gives Keith a direct look.

"Remove yourself from my bathtub." Then Harry turns and walks out.

Keith's faraway eyes stare into a world of his own, a world where one voice keeps talking, stuck in mind-numbing repeat: "Failure, failure, failure."

Slowly he rolls to his knees and lifts himself to his feet, water splashing out of the tub onto the tiles. Lennon licks his waterlogged boots as Keith walks to the kitchen.

Harry is at the kitchen counter, scribbling on a piece of paper. When he's done, he rips it from the pad and shoves it into Keith's hand.

"You want to kill yourself? Do it the sure way. Go to Deep Canyon. In Malibu. Follow the sign to the overlook, stare out at the ocean, and jump. If the fall doesn't kill you, the rocks will. And if the rocks don't kill you, you'll drown anyway. Either way, morning tide will wash you out of my hair and out of your misery."

Keith takes the paper and looks at it.

"Take the bus," says Harry, as he takes a couple of dollar bills and shoves them into Keith's jacket pocket. Then he puts his hand on Keith's shoulder.

"I think this is for the best. You've made a wise

choice." Harry moves to give him a hug but realizes Keith is sopping wet. So he pats his shoulder instead. Then he pushes him towards the door.

As Harry opens the door, Keith turns and looks at him.

"Are you still my manager, Harry?"

"Are you kidding?"

"Please."

With slumped shoulders, beaten down face, and soul-dead eyes, Keith looks like he is already in his own hell.

"You have any other demos?" asks Harry.

"In my computer." Keith points to the gig bag leaned against the wall.

"Passcode?"

"Hungry4rock."

Harry looks at the bag, then back at Keith. He nods.

"If by some miracle, and contrary to all your efforts to destroy me and your career, any of your songs should make some money after you are gone, I, Harry Chukstein, promise that I will collect any and all money owed, pay my managerial cut, as well as cover all bathroom repairs. Then I'll pass the rest on to your mother."

Keith nods.

"But I am not, nor will I again be, your manager. Ever. Clear? You'd have to die and come back as a rock star to even begin to make that worthwhile. Not gonna happen."

A female voice calls from the back of the condo.

"Good luck," Harry says to Keith, then gives him a quick shove, closing the door behind him.

Harry stands for a moment and stares at the closed door. He shakes his head.

The kid sure does have a flair for drama. That could have made some money if he'd been able to channel it. Instead, it's going to cost a pretty penny to fix the bathroom. The female voice calls again.

"Alright, I'm coming! Hold your knees together." Jesus, he thinks, I'm like a damn wet nurse.

On the other side of Harry's closed door, Keith is desolate, a small puddle collecting at his feet. The smooth surface of the paper rests against his palm. Lennon sits at his side, looking up.

This feels like the end of the last chapter of a short book, he thinks. Or "The End," which closes out *Abbey Road*. Except that *Abbey Road* was a legendary record, and there is nothing legendary about Keith's short life.

The directions are simple - a bus ride, a short walk, another bus ride, a dirt path, and finally, a long drop down into oblivion.

Deep Canyon. Keith had never heard of the place. He knew most of the beaches. He had a surfer girlfriend in high school who was from Malibu. They used to go to the beach to surf. Well, she surfed. Keith was afraid of the water. And he couldn't swim. Which makes this plan perfect, he thinks.

It is a lonely feeling as the bus pulls away and leaves Keith standing on the side of Pacific Coast Highway. There are no other cars in sight.

He and Lennon cross the road and start down a worn dirt path. Soon the path opens to a spectacular panorama of the vast, endless Pacific Ocean. The tranquil band of blue stretches across the early morning sky to the horizon and beyond. You can walk right out to the edge of land here and look out over the cliff, no guardrails to protect you from yourself.

Light is slowly rising. It must be six in the morning, Keith thinks.

A solitary tree grows in a space some 20 feet from the cliff's edge. Keith walks tentatively to where terra firm drops abruptly into the void. Since he is deathly afraid of heights, the view causes his head to spin and his knees to wobble. He shows considerably more care for safety than one would expect from someone preparing to fling himself from this cliff.

It is a very long way down, he thinks. Big rocks are scattered in the water below, white, foaming waves crashing hard against them. A riptide is pulling out to the sea, its dappled water forming a line perpendicular to the horizon.

Harry was right - if the rocks don't kill you, the drowning will.

The long drop, the big rocks, the deep sea, the vast unknown all collide together in Keith's mind. He wavers in his commitment to the mission. But that persistent voice in his head responds with vigor: You chicken shit! Are you going to mess this up, too? What's left? You're nothing but dead weight, a burden to everyone. You're better off dead.

Lennon's bark cuts through his thoughts. Something is wrong, and the dog can tell. Keith looks down at him, tears forming in his eyes. Leaving Lennon, not the waiting, that's the hardest part. He kneels down, and takes the dog's head into his hands, and cradles it close to him, tears streaming down his cheeks. Lennon tries to lick them.

Just do it, says the voice in Keith's head. Lennon's life is misery tethered to your useless existence.

Without giving himself any more space for thought, Keith quickly leads Lennon to the lonely tree and ties the leash around it. From his pocket, he pulls out a piece of paper and pen, which he always keeps on him in case inspiration strikes. The paper is dried from its soaking but somewhat rumpled.

He quickly scribbles his parting words to a world that no longer needs nor wants him. He slips the paper into Lennon's collar, making sure it is snug.

Keith gives Lennon a last passionate hug, a kiss on the forehead, then walks to the cliff's edge. He looks down into the ocean again. I wonder if I'll pass out before I hit the water, he wonders.

Lennon barks. Keith turns to look at him. He struggles to hold back the tears.

"I'm sorry, buddy. You'll be better off."

"What are you thinking?" Lennon barks. "This is crazy. It's your only life, your greatest gift. Don't throw it away! You still have me. As long as you have a friend, there's a way out."

"It's no use. This is the only way," says Keith, incapable of determining if the dog is actually talking or if it's all in his head.

Keith is crying. He looks down at the ocean. Gosh, it really does seem such a long way down, he thinks. And those rocks look awfully hard.

"Please don't do this!" barks Lennon. "I love you. We can figure this out. Remember what the girl said."

Keith pauses, then turns. "What girl?"

"The girl. The waitress, at the coffee shop. She said to keep taking the next path, and when one closes, you find the next one, on and on, until you get to where you're supposed to be. It's like hiking."

Keith remembers the waitress, her brown hair, the cute nose that seems to take a slight lift at the end, and her big eyes. Funny, he only now realized her eyes were green. He also remembers how she kept working on something at her table. What was she working on, he wonders? He sure would like to find out. She seemed so disciplined.

But the voice in his head is persistent, uncompromising. It offers no mercy: Do it!

Keith looks down at the angry blue ocean, waves crashing into white foam against the rocks. He looks back at Lennon, his pleading eyes, neck-straining hard against the collar around his neck. And he wonders.

He wonders if maybe there is one more path, one path he had somehow missed. Maybe Candy got home, heard his song, changed her mind. Or maybe Harry would take him back, find one more possible deal.

But mostly, he looks at Lennon and wonders if he should take him for another walk, roll around on the floor together, share a package of Girl Scout cookies. And that's when he knows - you don't desert your friends.

"Maybe there is one more thing we could try, buddy, something I missed. Maybe my fate isn't jumping off this cliff, maybe my fate is—"

But sometimes, fate and paths take long, winding, and circuitous roads. And the turns can come unexpectedly.

Because at that very moment, the ground beneath Keith's feet tickles, like a foot massager. He looks down to see that it isn't a foot massager he is standing on. The ground around his feet is shifting and cracking. The edge of this little part of the cliff that he stands on is giving way, crumbling. Keith looks up with terror in his eyes.

"Lennon!" he screams.

And as he does, the dirt beneath him finally gives way, and the tip of the cliff he occupies plunges straight down into the ocean, the rocks, and the riptide, carrying Keith with it, to death and oblivion.

And just like that, Keith Unger is gone. Here one moment, breathing, yearning, thinking, dreaming. And in the very next, he is no more.

Lennon barks and pulls furiously against the leash that chains him firmly to the tree, desperately trying to rescue his friend one more time. But no bark can save Keith Unger now. He is gone.

6. WAKE UP THE NATION

"**N**ow, fifty years later, Milo Wilkins is keeping that promise. Today twelve precious, little kittens have come home with Milo to this quiet street in Palms, a special anniversary surprise for his wife Delores, and a debt finally fulfilled. Now isn't that cute?"

The blindingly bright, hot white smile of Los Angeles' favorite morning human interest reporter switches on. Her blonde hair is coiffed to perfection, and her larger than average head floats blissfully atop her tightly toned body. There is just that little bit of squeak in her voice that screams "cute" to not only men, but also the great multitude of female fans she has around the city.

"I'm Vondy Wells for KNLA, and now back to you, Chris."

The video camera switches off, and Vondy's cameraman, Skip Lester, sets it down on the ground and begins gathering up his equipment.

Vondy gives Milo Wilkins a hug. The 90-year old

subject of her feature piece is dressed in his Korean War uniform.

"Thank you so much for opening your home to us, Milo," she squeaks, "and for sharing your beautiful story."

"Can you take one of these damn cats with you?" Milo responds, his smile turned upside down. "Delores is real pissed off. I gotta get rid of 'em fast."

Skip loads the equipment into the news van whose KNLA News logo is prominently displayed on the side panel. He wraps his last cords as Vondy walks up.

"What's next, boss?"

Vondy pulls a lighter and a pack of Marlboro reds out from inside the van's passenger side door and thrusts a cigarette in her mouth. She lights it up, inhales deeply, then lifts her chin and exhales a massive plume of smoke.

"If I have to do one more human interest story, my brain is going to explode." She slumps against the side of the van and takes another drag off the cigarette.

"They're out to get me, Crumbs. Anything to keep a good woman from rising to her rightful place. But they didn't stop Barbara."

"They did not," affirms Skip.

"And they didn't stop my girl, Katie."

"No, siree."

"She didn't take 'no' for an answer. She did anyone she had to, lied to everyone she needed to, and ripped off every great story she could get her hands on. And look where it took her - top bitch in news."

"She's no better than you, boss."

"You're damn right she's not! But she's hot, and I love her. She's my north star. I just need that one story that I can ride like a bullet train, straight to the top, to my anchor. And then I'll be the top bitch in news. Maybe I'll have lunch with Katie."

"She'd be lucky to share sushi with you."

Vondy climbs into the van while Skip slides into the driver's seat. "Where to?"

Vondy flips on the police scanner and lets it oscillate between police frequencies. The static is periodically interrupted by conversations between cops and dispatchers or cops and cops.

"We're on our own. Let's see what's going on."

Skip nods as he takes a Starbucks bag from the dashboard and pulls out a half-eaten maple-covered scone. He takes a big bite, and the scone crumbles in his mouth and onto his shirt, pieces resting in the creases over his belly.

Vondy sucks on the cigarette. This was not how she expected things to work out when she moved west. Things had started so well after college. She screwed the station manager at WLAL in Raleigh and promptly got the morning show hosting spot.

When an L.A. news producer came through town, she knew she had to up her game if she was going to have any chance of moving up to the big leagues. The Kama Sutra had nothing on that flesh tsunami I laid on him in his hotel room, thinks Vondy. She knew she'd done good when the jaded L.A. news guy stayed over an extra night. Good enough, in fact, that he decided he needed to bring her back to L.A. with him and give her a job as a field reporter on the morning news show. The job also came with an apartment far from his wife's prying eyes.

Chuck was gone now, gone to that big news station in the sky following a San Andreas-sized heart attack twenty minutes after leaving Vondy's apartment. But his replacement, Bill Daily, was just as pliable, and she'd managed to figuratively suck every benefit possible out of him. The station now let her do all her live shots remotely without interference, and she got the liberty to choose what stories to do.

And why shouldn't I, she thought, I'm the most famous reporter on Los Angeles morning T.V.

But that wasn't what Vondy wanted. What she wanted was prestige, fame, and much more money. She wanted an anchor job at a network. No, not Fox. They already had a full complement of blonde news jobs. MSNBC sucks, thinks Vondy. No one watches that clown car. Rachel Maddow? Please. CNN might work, though.

Vondy looks into the mirror and pouts her lips. Then she turns slightly to each side, appraising her profiles.

"I am so hot."

"The hottest, boss," adds Skip on cue.

Skip is her lapping puppy dog, the consummate ass kisser, her personal 'yes' man. And a hell of a good veteran cameraman to boot. She isn't deluded by his compliments - it isn't because he loves her. Oh yeah, Vondy knows he'd jump at the chance of putting sour cream in her burrito, but then what semi-straight male (and more than a few females) over the age of 14 wouldn't want a piece of that princess pie? No, Skip's aims are pure.

Skip wants to ride the rocket to the top with her when she gets her big break. Crumbs dreams of working with the big boys and making the big money, so he can bury himself under bigger gourmet crumbs.

Are those roots showing?

Her thoughts suddenly slam on the brakes. She looks closer in the mirror at the hairline on the crown of her head. Damn, that looks like a little bit of brown coming up under the blonde. Shit!

She would have never gotten that job in Raleigh if they'd known Vondy Wells was, in reality, Carlita Garcia. Blonde dye, applied artistically and thoroughly, covered a lot of past tracks. She learned in Raleigh that you have to spread that color shift south of the border, as well as to the north pole.

Of course, being a Latina wouldn't have mattered in Los Angeles. It probably would have been an asset. Now it would even be an asset in Raleigh. But the dye was cast, so to speak. A reporter doesn't want to be found out as a liar, even though most are.

Racist Anglos, she thinks, sucking hard on her cigarette. Forcing me to deny my heritage just so I can get a leg up in this business. But they'll see - you can't keep a strong, Latina woman down.

"What was that?" She quickly turns up the police scanner and locks it into its current place. "Did he say a *187* or a *10-56* in Malibu?" That meant either a homicide or a suicide in rich beach.

A dog was found tied to a tree in Malibu, a suicide note attached to its collar. Choppers called in to search the waters below, a possible jumper.

"Note is from some rock and roller cashing it in because he can't hit the big time? Is that what he said?" asks Vondy.

"That's what he said," Skip confirms.

"Oh, now that's juicy." Vondy imagines the scene and adds her own colors. "Young kid trying hard to make it in the brutally hard world of music, playing a dying art form. Squalid living conditions, barely enough to eat, sharing food with the dog he ended up leaving behind, tied to a tree."

She looks over at Skip. "Maybe they shared dog food? No, it has to be something punchier."

Go for the gut. She knows that's the play. Knock the audience down and don't let them up.

"Emotionally raw artist, caught at the end of his ropes, pushed to the limit by the cruel and unfeeling world that has rejected his desperately beautiful artistic pleas, decides to take the big plunge into the cold Pacific Ocean, washing away the world's indignities, ending his meaningless life and entering into the annals of rock and roll Valhalla."

Yes, that's better. Vondy nods her head as her mind races. Did I say juicy? It's downright delicious!

"Where's Deep Canyon?" she looks at Skip.

"Oh, wow, well, let's see ... it's in Malibu, and it's south of Zuma, just off of the PCH. It'd be a great surf spot, except you'd have to paddle in, no beach access. Unless you make a straight drop in from the cliff."

"That's our story."

And a hell of a story it'll be by the time she gets her nimble hands on it. What really happened doesn't matter because Vondy will give the public the story she knows they want. And this one will be gut-wrenching.

The drill plunges straight into his tooth, slamming down hard into the red hot, inflamed nerve beneath it. The sound of the drill needle spinning comes in bursts, punctuated by brief respites. But the pain is relentless.

Make it stop! Make it stop!

Harry wakes up in a sweat. It is dark. Very dark. Must be midnight. He looks at the clock. 11:32 - AM. He looks over at the windows and remembers the black-out shades he had installed when they painted the bedroom dark blue. He hears light snoring, feels around with his hand, and finds a solid form. His hand works its way up the form. It's a leg. A long leg which elicits a moan when touched.

Oh yeah, he remembers.

There's that damn drill again! But it's not coming from his head, it's coming from the living room. Harry gets up, opens the bedroom door, and steps into the hallway. It's no drill - it is the doorbell to his condo.

Harry walks up to the door and looks out the spy hole while cursing Manny for bothering him so early in the morning. But he jumps back in shock when he sees that outside his condo door is not the solitary daytime Mexican doorman, but at least a dozen strangers. Some carry video cameras, others SLR cameras, and they all look hungry, like sharks in a fish tank at feeding time. Harry flips from the door and plants his back firmly against the wall.

Reaching over, Harry grabs the intercom off the wall and presses the call button. He warily backs up in the direction of the bedroom, staring at the door. Someone comes on the other end.

"Meester Harry?"

"Manny," he whispers into the phone as he grabs his robe from the bedroom. "Who are those people outside my door, and why the did you let them come up here?"

"I'm sorry, Meester Harry, they come like army, come into lobby, they don't listen to Manny, they go into elevator. Es muy loco. I try call you, nobody answer."

Harry slips into the robe and ties the front, juggling the phone on his shoulder. He walks up to the door and looks out through the peephole again. Still there.

"What do they want?" he whispers into the phone.

"I don't know. They say comment, but they no say what comment for. I think they from T.V." Harry hangs up.

News media? Okay, if the news wants to talk to me, it can't be bad. Right? He looks into the little mirror on the wall, the one with the teak wood frame and the Hindu god of something carved into the wood.

Harry adjusts his robe. He runs his hands through his hair, trying to corral it. Then he swings the door open, and the crowd erupts.

"Ladies, gentlemen. I am sorry, you seem to have caught me fresh from the boudoir. Please ask your cameras to be kind."

One dishevelled-looking young guy in a tee shirt with "It's news, dude" emblazoned on the front shoves a microphone into his face.

"Do you have any comment on Keith Unger?"

"I'm his manager," Harry replies. "Unless he killed somebody."

"Did you have any idea? Or did it come as a surprise?" asks a girl with a video camera, her eyes glued to the flip screen.

"What kind of problems was he having?" "Did he tell you?" "Is it true he was just signed by Massive Records?" "Was he really getting ready to come out as gay?"

The questions come fast and furious, barely a breath between them. Harry, who still has one foot in the bed, can't keep up or comprehend. Why the interest in Keith Unger?

"Haven't you heard?" asks the girl with the video camera as she zooms in tight on Harry's face.

"Keith Unger is dead."

The expression on Harry's face must not be priceless because the cameras click into action to capture it, and they only do that for profit.

Harry numbly closes the door on a cacophony of questions. He turns to the living room, picks up the remote control on the glass table, and turns on the morning news. Vondy Wells appears onscreen, in a medium close-up.

"Police sources close to the investigation are being tight-lipped," says Vondy, "but apparently Unger was disillusioned, and depressed, his dreams of rock stardom in tatters on the cold streets of Hollywood. With no place to turn and no soft shoulder to lean on, he saw only one way out, leaving his one remaining friend with an uncertain future."

Vondy shifts to look behind her. Lennon lies on the ground, paws crossed in front of him with his head laid across them, motionless while the police move behind him.

"Holy shit, he really did it." Harry slumps onto the couch. He is transfixed by the T.V. Oh, the dog is a nice touch, he thinks, that'll get sympathy.

"Do we know anything about next of kin, or anyone related to Keith Unger, Vondy?" interrupts the well-modulated voice of Chris Miller, the morning news anchor, who appears onscreen.

"We know very little, Chris. His mother left the country this morning for a European holiday and is in transit, unavailable for comment. His manager is a—" Vondy looks down at a sheet of paper in her hand. "—Harry Chuckstein. We have a reporter at Mr. Chukstein's residence, and we're waiting for a statement."

"I think we may have that film coming up right now," says news anchor Chris Miller, a layer of gel reflecting light off the top of his smoothed black hair, as he faces the camera with grave solemnity.

"This is a tragic story, and certainly not one we like to start your day with. Our news crew was at Mr. Chukstein's home moments ago, and we have raw footage coming in—"

The sound of the central riff of the Beatles' Day Tripper plays and then plays again. Harry walks to the kitchen counter and picks up his cell phone. He looks at the caller I.D., then answers.

"Yeah, Brad ... I'm watching it now ... No, I'm completely in shock ... I had no idea. I mean, he was pretty depressed after he talked to you ... I'm not blaming, just saying ... well, as Keith's manager, I have a contractual obligation to continue signing deals on his behalf …"

Harry smacks himself on the head and begins desperately searching around the apartment for something.

"… I'm glad you've come to your senses … Yes, I can do tomorrow. But I have to tell you, Brad, the price has gone up … I agree, let's not waste time, strike while the iron is hot … Okay, but make it one pm. I'm not an early riser."

Harry hangs up the phone and slaps his hands together in glee.

"Sonuvabitch did it! He really did it!" Harry cackles while doing a little jig. "We're gonna be rich, we're gonna be rich! Sorry, you won't be around to enjoy it, Keith, but you can't always get what you want. Now, where did he say those demos were?"

Flopping onto the couch, Harry retraces his conversation with Keith. But nothing comes to him. It's going to be a limited pot of money if I can't remember where those demos are, he thinks.

The sound of the bedroom door opening is followed by the padding of footsteps on the condo's stone tile floors. Out from the darkened hall emerges a ghostly female figure, wrapped in a pale blue sheet, clutched loosely around her breasts, and gathering around her feet at the floor. The dishevelled bleach blonde hive of bed head falls over her face, while remnants of red lipstick tattoo her lips.

Candy looks at Harry through sleepy eyes and yawns. "Is it early?"

"Keith's dead." Harry's face betrays no expression. Candy scratches her head and yawns again.

"Uh-huh."

"Jumped off a cliff in Malibu."

Candy nods. "I hope he took that stupid dog with him."

"He didn't."

Candy stretches, and the blue sheet falls to the ground, revealing her long-limbed, lean figure, small mounds on her chest, translucent skin.

"You coming back to bed for another round?"

Harry takes in a deep breath, lets it out slowly. He rubs some sleep from his eyes.

"Yeah. In a bit. I wanna have a look at Keith's contract first."

Candy turns and sleepily pads back down the hallway to the bedroom. "Hurry up," she calls over her shoulder, "I'm wetter than a bag of paint."

Harry slaps his hands. "The gig bag. They're in the gig bag."

"In a sign of the pace at which our modern culture now moves, the story of Keith Unger, the disillusioned rock musician who tragically took his own life, a story

I reported on just this morning, has exploded across the internet."

Vondy talks directly into the camera. Her sincerity is undeniable. She stands in front of the Garden, Keith's apartment building.

"The story of this young man, and his forlorn dog, lost in a modern world where art is commerce and music holds little value, has struck a raw nerve with the public. They may not buy records, but they certainly like to hear about the people who make them. And their dogs."

Vondy turns to her right and is seen from a new camera angle. A picture of Keith and Candy appears in a box in the screen's upper right corner. They both look morose to the extreme,

"Keith's girlfriend, Candy Lamour, pictured here with the singer in happier times, has been left to cope with an unbearable loss. I spoke with her today as she left the home of Keith's manager, Harry Chukstein, where she had gone for consolation."

Candy appears onscreen with Vondy in taped footage outside Harry's apartment building. She wears the same crumpled dress she wore last night but has improved her lipstick since this morning. Her eyes are hidden under oversized dark sunglasses, and she wears a black colored scarf over her head, tied under her chin.

"I'm devastated, Vondy. We were so close." Candy dramatically wipes another invisible tear under her sunglasses. "Now, I'll have to raise our dog Glennon by myself."

Candy looks directly into the camera and strikes a pose that strives for sad and sexy at the same time.

Harry is sitting on a couch in his living room. He eats popcorn from a bag while watching this all on T.V.

"You can't buy this kind of publicity."

Onscreen, Vondy continues. "I also spoke with Harry Chukstein, Keith's manager, today at his apartment in West Hollywood."

Harry rubs his hands together in anticipation.

In the T.V. footage, Harry appears in his apartment, seated just as he is now, silk sleeping robe draped over him, tied neatly at the waist. He is reclining on the couch with a look of studied resignation, hand at his forehead.

"He was like a son ... like a little brother to me. He would sit at my feet, right there." Harry points vaguely to the space in front of him. "Last night, I pleaded with him, desperately blocked the door with my body. But it was of no use."

Onscreen, Harry's face goes into his hand. "Now he belongs to the ages."

Vondy again appears onscreen alone. She looks moved by the segment with Harry.

"Mr. Chukstein, in an exclusive to me, confirmed there has already been an illegal release of a Keith Unger demo recording on the internet. He confirmed that as Keith Unger's representative, he has hired the highly regarded law firm of Emerson, Spicer, and

McLenon, to vigorously pursue legal action against anyone who might try to profit illegally from this release."

"You bet your ass I'll sue!" Harry yells at the screen from his couch in his living room. "Those dollars are mine!"

7. IN THE STREET

"Nina!"

Up to her knees in the water, Nina looks up. "Yes, momma."

Nina's mother, long and attractive, with dark hair and a nervous look, is stretched out on a blanket. She motions to her daughter.

"Don't go out so far. You do know there are sharks out there? They come close to the shore and jump up out of nowhere. You'll be gone before I can call your name, and then what? You'll be a bloody mess in the water with nothing to bury."

Ten-year-old Nina rolls her eyes at the absurdity of her mother's fears. They studied the world in fifth grade, and like any other well-adjusted Angeleno kid, she was pretty sure she had a better grip on it than her silly mother did.

"Nina!"

"I'm right by the pier, mom!" Nina points to the Santa Monica pier, a mere 100 feet away. "There are no sharks this close to the pier, everybody knows that. Don't be such a—"

Suddenly a dark figure shoots up from the water, right next to Nina, white teeth glinting in the sun, one crazed eye pointed skyward, its body twisting to its side. Then it crashes back into the water and disappears.

Nina screams and runs the few feet to shore. She falls into her mother's arms, confused and terrified.

The thing appears again as the wave recedes back into the ocean. And then, like the primordial fish that some say came out of the sea, walked onto land, and evolved into modern humans, this thing begins to crawl. It uses arm-like appendages tucked back into its body and drags itself up onto the sandy beach until its head is out of the water. Then it lies down, motionless.

Nina is terrified, her mother much more so. But as the thing lies on the ground, Nina's fear begins to fade, and that cat killer, curiosity, begins to take control. Breaking from her mother's arms, Nina walks to the creature.

"Nina! Get back here!"

Nina looks closely and realizes the thing has a head and face, with eyes, nose, and mouth. Suspicion graduates to certainty as her ten-year-old eyes recognize the obvious.

"It's a man," Nina yells to her mother.

On cue, the man belches, and a gush of water exits his mouth. Nina's mother, coming to her senses, rushes to her daughter and takes her by the arm.

"It's rude to stare, Nina. Even at drunks on the beach. Let's go!" She gives her daughter a push on the tush, and Nina starts walking up the beach. The mother turns back to the man.

"You should be ashamed of yourself, making a scene at a public beach in front of children! Do your drugs at home like the rest of us!" With a huff and a dramatic toss of her head, she follows after her daughter up the beach.

Keith raises his head and slowly looks around, taking in the terrain. He lifts his hand to his face and wipes. He is dulled and drained of life, and his eyes are blank - the lights aren't on, and no one is home.

He slowly lifts himself to his knees, then even more slowly to his feet. He is wobbly as he tries to balance himself on his newfound legs, battling gravity as if for the first time.

Then, without thought or purpose, he begins to move up the beach away from the ocean, his feet dragging in the sand. As he passes two girls lying on their stomachs sunbathing, he accidentally sprays a little sand across their backs.

"Hey, watch it, loser!" hollers one girl as she sits up and wipes away nearly a half dozen grains of sand from her arm. Her friend lifts her head lazily and looks at Keith's form, which is moving past them like it's trudging through sludge.

"Damn homeless. Shouldn't even be allowed on the beach."

Homing pigeons use low-frequency sound waves, which emanate from nearly everything around them, to map their world. Then they use these maps to find their way home.

In his current state, Keith couldn't find a map, let alone read one. But somehow, like the homing pigeons flying somewhere above his head, he continues walking, winding his way through the patchwork network of neighborhoods, the abstract art of arteries represented by freeways and byways, roads and boulevards. And in that way, Santa Monica gives way to Culver City, which crumbles into Beverly Hills, then melts into West Hollywood, until finally, inexorably, like liquid in a glass, his water finds its true level – Hollywood.

His face is a blank canvas. The ocean has tangled and tossed his hair like a creative angel hair pasta, leaving it falling over his face. His shoulders sag, as do his eyes and mouth, and his clothes are a ripped mess. He is unrecognizable from his old self.

People move to make way for Keith, but it's instinctual as few actually notice him. If they did, the vacant look on his face might give them pause and cause for concern.

Keith's aimless movement brings him to the door of a plain, indistinct storefront with shuttered windows. A cluster of men stands out in front. All wear beards, and many have little beanies over their heads. Keith is drawn to the crowd.

The trauma of the day has disconnected his mind from its traumatic events. He's like a newborn baby, a blank slate. Standing in this crowd feels good. It's comfortable being part of a group, anonymous yet acknowledged.

As the men begin filing into the storefront, Keith follows. Inside is a small lobby, separated from a larger room which is bare and nondescript. In this room, Keith can see men on their knees, in rows, on a carpet, bobbing up and down, bowing to the ground with their heads, then lifting themselves back up. It's hypnotic, especially with the exotic chanting.

Keith's mind is too numb to work, so his body takes over. He begins to bob back and forth, bending at the waist, imitating the motion of the other men. But he starts to feel dizzy, so he stops. Some of the other men look at him suspiciously.

He notices that men are removing their shoes as they enter the foyer. Along the lobby wall, rising about four feet off the ground, are rows of cubicles, each big enough to hold just one pair of shoes. All are full. Scattered on the ground in front of the cubicles are more shoes, left as if the owners had just stepped out of them and into another world.

Keith's eyes land on a pair of blue running shoes, with orange trim, lying on the floor. They look so lovely and inviting. Keith looks at his own bare, dirty, bloody, and bruised feet, then at the running shoes. His feet hurt so bad. So he slips them into the luxurious comfort, the soft padded pampering, of the running shoes. He walks around, rejoicing in the new spring in his step.

To get more space, he steps outside. Once out of the storefront, Keith begins to walk briskly, caught up in the feeling of the shoes. He is absorbed in their bend and flex.

Keith's absorption is interrupted by a loud rumble of voices. At the doors of the storefront, several heavy-set men are talking animatedly. One is gesturing wildly, pointing to his bare feet. The voices rise to a crescendo. And then they see Keith. The shoeless man points at Keith's feet. Keith looks down at his new shoes, then up at the men, who are now running towards him.

Keith finds he has more energy than he expected as he races ahead of the group of men. He rushes blindly through streets, down alleyways, but they are still behind him. The men are gaining on him, and Keith is scared. Desperate, Keith turns around another corner, with the men temporarily out of sight. Suddenly a hand abruptly grabs his collar and pulls him into the doorway of a shop.

A hand goes over Keith's mouth. He is confused and disoriented. He can see that he is in a tourist shop. The shop owner, a South Asian man, rises from behind the counter and eyes him suspiciously. The hand on his mouth relaxes, and Keith turns. He sees that the hand that pulled him in is connected to the giant frame of a familiar-looking black man. No Name scratched across the name tag of his army jacket, the big man raises his finger to his mouth for quiet.

Before Keith can further examine his surroundings, the group of men comes running down the street and stop directly in front of the shop. They are large men and out of breath from their effort.

Free of No Name, Keith fearfully sinks back into the shop wall, which is covered with hanging tee shirts. His heart is pounding, and he can feel a trembling in his limbs. The owner glances at him, then at No Name, who is also looking out the large doorway.

The group of men talks angrily in a foreign tongue. They gesture broadly with their hands and arms as they look in every direction.

The shop owner quietly reaches under the counter in front of him as he keeps his eyes steady on Keith and No Name.

After a few minutes, most of the men turn and begin walking back the way they came, leaving only the former owner of the blue sneakers yelling at them, clearly frustrated they are giving up the hunt. Finally, even he starts back in the direction they came from, angrily complaining as he does.

When Keith turns, he sees the shop owner is now holding a large, fat, metal rod. He is looking right at Keith as he raises the rod, ready to strike.

But No Name smiles, steps between Keith and the owner, and calmly raises his empty palms. Then he bows slightly at the waist and speaks in a low, gravelly voice. "*Boht boht shukriya, dost. Sukoon.*"

The shop owner hesitates, confused. No Name then turns and exits the shop door, leaving the owner frozen, holding the metal rod in the air.

With a glance at the shop owner, Keith also steps out onto the sidewalk, He looks down the street where the men went, but they are gone. He looks in the other direction, but there is no sign of No Name – it's as though he has evaporated into the dry Hollywood air.

So Keith resumes his walking, moving slowly and aimlessly. The rhythm of movement is all he knows. The beat of his steps is his only direction. The sun is going down and with it, the temperature.

An entire day separates Keith from his fall from the cliff. How long was he in the water, and how did he survive? He doesn't know because he can't allow himself to think of it. All he knows is to keep moving, so the thoughts chasing him don't catch up.

Restaurant windows along the walk are like large-scale T.V.s, each playing its own show. Keith stops in front of one showing the dramatic scene of a couple seated in an inviting, cushioned booth. They are arguing animatedly. The man gestures wildly with his hands, and the woman cries.

A waiter interrupts them as he sets two large plates of food on the table. Keith drools at the sight of the food. The man begins to load spaghetti onto his fork, shovelling it into his mouth, tiny bits of pasta launching like projectiles as he continues to rant. The woman's vegetables sit untouched. The waiter returns with a bottle of wine. He looks up and eyes Keith sternly. The man and woman follow his gaze.

No longer the voyeur, but now the subject, Keith quickly begins to walk away. He passes homeless people, huddled under blankets, tucked into doorways, some in tents, sleeping on the treacherous streets of night.

Keith's leaden legs can barely move. He finally surrenders to his body's demands, steps into an unoccupied doorway, and sinks to his knees. He slowly lies down on his side and huddles into a fetal position—the cold of the concrete chills through his skin and lodges in his bones. I'll freeze before I wake up, he thinks. But he doesn't care.

His body responds to no commands as it slowly curls in on itself. His mind grows fuzzier as his eyes close. He hears a car screech to a stop and a door open, but he cannot lift his head or even open his eyes to investigate.

"Get back in the damn car, Julie!" he hears a man scream.

"Stop being such a selfish pig, Barry, can't you see he's freezing," a woman's voice responds. Keith hears steps approaching him. Then he feels fabric fall across him, warm and fuzzy. Hands tuck the fabric under his body, forming a thin barrier against the stone ground.

"I'm going to leave!" screams the male voice.

"Then go," Keith hears the woman say. In a lower voice, she whispers, "Stay warm. God Bless you."

"I'm going," the man's voice is harsh.

Keith hears a car engine roar. Then a car door slam. "Don't ever get out of the damn car again when I tell you not to."

"Don't be so entitled, Barry. You know, some people aren't so lucky—" The car engine roars again, now moving off into the distance.

In Keith's mind, the engine roar morphs into Candy's venomous voice and her angry face. He sees Harry with a piece of paper in his hand, smiling and pointing to a Massive Records' stamp on it. Then Harry holds a flaming lighter to the document. Lennon cries in the distance, and a dark landscape rushes by in Keith's mind. He hears panting voices as he runs through what feels like briar. Then, abruptly, the ground below him gives way, and Keith is falling, weightless, through empty space. Below him, he sees an ocean of angry faces rising quickly towards him. He braces for impact as he struggles against invisible bonds that restrict his movement.

Keith's body jolts upward in shock, his mouth opens in a silent, strangled scream. It is not a dark night, and there is no blue ocean. He is awake, lying on a filthy Hollywood sidewalk, under the late morning sun, as people walk past him.

He looks at his body to see he is tightly wrapped up

in a faux fur blanket. He slowly untangles himself, and as he does, he realizes there are a pair of khaki pants and a flannel shirt lying beside him.

Picking up the clothes, Keith gets up and starts the new day the same as he ended the old one – walking. When slivers of memories come back to haunt him, he turns his attention elsewhere. Remembering is too painful.

Keith's death was an earth-shaking, life-altering shock for Danny, a supreme cosmic punch to the solar plexus. He was left dazed and confused, unmoored. His anchor to life severed.

But Superfans are a resilient breed, so Danny Wallburger continues to do what he knows best – he evangelizes the creed of Keith: Be Rad.

"Whenever he got onstage, it was like a lightning bolt sent down from the heavens, man."

Broke, unknown, wanna-be rock stars killing themselves isn't big news in L.A. So it is a modest-sized group gathered around Danny. He stands at the Garden entrance, iPhone in hand, playing bits of Keith and Hunger in concert, things that he had recorded himself. The sound files are muddy, but for Danny, they are evidence of the genius of Keith.

All cults start with one, and Keith Unger's begins here with this one obsessive fan. But more are drawn to hear Danny's words, called by the passion of the original.

"When he sang, the truth just came, like, rushing out of his mouth. To, like, see him was to believe him, and he's still here. In the music."

"This is a mission for you, isn't it?" The T.V. news reporter's face is chiseled into a look of compassion and empathy.

"He should have been a star, man," says Danny.

Vondy turns into the camera, looking her viewers in the eyes. "He died in oblivion, but his memory lives on. With this small group of devoted fans, Keith Unger is remembered. This is Vondy Wells reporting."

Skip drops the camera and gives her the thumbs up. Vondy turns to walk to the van.

"You don't think this is a waste of time, boss? I mean, will anybody care about this kid."

Vondy walks to the van and opens the door. She pulls her cigarettes from the side pocket.

"I have a feeling, Crumbs, a gut instinct. This is the story. Katie went with her gut, so did Oprah." And I'm not doing another animal interest story, she thinks to herself. This story has to break big.

She sucks hard on the cigarette as she lights it.

"Hunger. That's what gets you to the top, Crumbs. Hunger. Let's eat."

Harry shifts in his chair. He looks at his watch. Then he looks up at the painting on the wall across from him and behind the secretary's desk.

What the hell is that, he wonders. He tilts his head sideways. It looks like some sort of bird of prey being swallowed whole by a ... a heart? Who thinks this crap up? He shakes his head. Wonder how much it's worth. I should ask.

The secretary rises and walks over to Harry.

"He's ready for you, Mr. Chukstein." She turns and leads Harry to a door next to her desk and opens it for him. Harry saunters in.

It is a large office, whose central feature is a wall that is floor to ceiling window, and features a spectacular view of L.A., from east to west. A large desk sits in front of the window, and in the chair behind it is a middle-aged man, whose sharp-looking trousered legs are propped up on the desk.

The man wears a John Lennon NYC tee shirt, beautifully captured by legendary rock and roll photographer Bob Gruen, marketed by nearly everyone else. A grey button-up shirt hangs loosely over it. His goatee, with its flecks of grey, is meant to convey youth. The dyed comb-over that frames the top of his head is meant to support that illusion. An earpiece rests in his ear.

"Listen, Bono, it's a great idea, great, and you know Brad loves you, baby. I love the theme, the vision thing, the audacity. Your genius is with these kinds of big ideas, spectacles, go-for-it moments."

Brad Rossi motions for Harry to sit in the chair in front of the desk. Harry slides in and immediately sinks to a level that makes him feel like he is a child at an adult table, peering over the top to see the big people.

Bastard. He put this low seat chair here on purpose so he could intimidate people, thinks Harry. I have to get myself one of these.

"I don't question your motives or your artistic vision. I'm just not sure that doing the entire *Unforgettable Fire* album in a Roman amphitheater in Syria will get Assad to stop and reassess his ideology. First off, are there any Roman amphitheaters still standing in Syria? ... No, no, I did not know the Beatles planned something similar, but they're ... No, no, you are absolutely as big as—"

Harry looks at the walls covered with gold records by some of the most prominent artists of the last decade, most of whom Harry doesn't recognize.

"Yes, by all means, discuss it with Larry, and get back to me. We'll do whatever he thinks. Okay, I'll be waiting." Brad hangs up the phone and lifts his hands to the heavens.

"What can I say? Bono, the ideas. The man is always thinking. I don't know how the Edge processes it all."

Harry leans back in the chair, refusing to be intimidated. "He just returns to his drug of choice – tearing up pristine California coastline to build mega-mansion and make more money. Think globally, act selfishly."

Brad laughs, though it's not clear he knows what

he's laughing at. He picks up a baseball that sits on his desk and begins massaging it in his hands.

"So—a very unique situation we find ourselves in."

"Yes, my situation is quite unique."

Brad's smile stays frozen. "This Keith Unger thing is exploding. The track that leaked on the net...was that you? Brilliant! It would be a shame to see all this attention fizzle without fully capitalizing on the potential. Hard getting a record its full exposure without the backing of a label, proper distribution. You know, at World Auto, we tried that with aftermarket parts, mostly for Toyotas, and—"

"That is so true, Brad," Harry interrupts. "In auto parts. And in the old, pre-digital world of the music business. Nowadays, you got the publicity, you get the sales. Maybe you noticed the publicity Keith's getting. Killing it. Free publicity, I might add."

Brad leans back in his chair and looks out the window at the cinematic view of L.A. Tiny cars move along narrow-looking slivers of streets, towering buildings boast dramatic billboards, mountains border the northern end of the picture, while the ocean frames the west. And the sun blesses it all like a benign deity from above. Whoever set designed this place knew what they were doing.

"Don't you just love this town? So big, so alive. It's the Godzilla of towns. I remember the first time I went out of the country. It was a shock to me that everything wasn't the same. The rules here didn't apply everywhere else. It's easy to get lost in L.A., confuse yourself into thinking it's the whole world."

"Let's cut the travel memoir crap, Brad. The reality here is that you had your chance to sign Keith. I sent him to you first as a favor. I believe your response was 'juvenile'."

"Was I wrong?"

"No. But music isn't auto parts, and juvenile's been selling since teenage girls learned how to wet their panties while screaming. You could have been in the driver's seat here, but you're not. I am. I have, under contract, dead or alive, I might add, what is becoming by the day one of the hottest selling artists in the country. Probably the world. I also have a big brown bag loaded with fully fleshed out demos just waiting for systematic release."

Brad turns, his eyebrows edge up.

"Yes, a bag full. So, this thing will be alive for a while. To top it all off, because of the brilliant way the kid went out, he generates some serious and universal sympathy. He's interesting not just to kids and millennials but also to adults, boomers. Senior citizens will be cruising the aisles of Walmart in motorized carts, searching him out. And let me tell you something you may not already know."

Harry leans into Brad. "Those older people, Brad? They still buy their music. Novel concept, isn't it?"

Harry leans back in his chair, having probed and prodded his prey, and made clear that he's the shark in this fish tank.

"So, no, I don't really 'need' you. But having you would be helpful. If you're interested in the deal that I'm willing to offer, we can play Monopoly Music. If not, then I have an appointment at Universal at 2 PM."

8. BALL OF CONFUSION

The pain runs deep in Keith's stomach. Everywhere around him there is food, and all of it is out of his reach because he has no money.

The whole day is spent walking. His only goals are food and a place to sleep. Finally, he sits on the ground to rest.

As he sits there, wrapped in the fuzzy blanket, he notices a little girl staring at him. She is young, maybe four years old, standing with her mother, who is staring intently at her phone. The little girl nibbles on a sandwich in her hand.

Pieces of the sandwich fall to the ground as she chews. Keith drools like a dog over a bone. The little girl holds the bag in her other hand out to Keith. Inside is a plain bagel, and Keith leans in and reaches out his hand.

But the girl's mother abruptly starts walking, pulling the girl with her. The bagel drops to the ground, along with the remainder of her sandwich, and the girl erupts in tears.

"Uh-huh," says her mother into the phone as they walk away.

Keith pounces on the food, quickly gobbling up the remainder of the sandwich, then shoveling the bagel into his mouth, barely breaking it apart.

He rises to his feet. The used chinos and flannel shirt some angel left lying next to him while he slept last night are already dirty. They hang loosely on his thin frame, a couple sizes too large.

As night falls, he finds himself on residential streets. His body is bone-weary, and he is desperate for sleep. In front of a wooden Craftsman house, on the sidewalk, sits an old couch, forlorn and unwanted, left for someone to haul away.

Keith seats himself on the inviting couch and quickly finds a spring lodging itself in his butt. He rolls over, stretching his body out. The sofa is closer to a love seat, and Keith's legs dangle off its edge. Other than that one spring, it feels so soft that his body immediately begins shutting itself down. His mind follows suit as darkness envelops his thoughts. No dreams come, just a blissful floating through emptiness.

But his sleep is interrupted by the sound of two men speaking harshly in a foreign language that has lots of sharp edges. A hand shakes him roughly.

Keith opens his eyes to see two men standing over him in the dark. One hovers above his face, barking words Keith doesn't understand. A bright light shines into his eyes.

The man calls to his partner, and together they pull Keith off the couch and onto the ground. Then they lift the discarded piece of furniture, efficiently loading it onto the back bed of a small Toyota pickup truck. Before Keith fully comprehends what is happening, the two men have driven off.

Keith walks again. As he walks the Hollywood streets, the nightshift has taken over, vampires and night stalkers. Wrapped in his fuzzy blanket, stumbling deliriously, he fits right in. An empty doorway invites him to sit on the step, and his body melts into the concrete. Sleep, oh gentle sleep. He closes his eyes and leans against the doorway and begins to drift off. But a clanging noise rouses him.

Down the street, he sees a group of three teenagers walking towards him, banging a thick metal rod against the buildings as they go. They stop and begin hurling insults at an older, bearded man who is curled up in a doorway. Without warning, the teenagers pounce on the old man, who raises his hands in defense.

Frightened, Keith rises and starts walking. He keeps an eye on the teenagers behind him and a reasonable distance between himself and them. Finally, he sees them turn down a side street.

The days melt one into the next. Little differentiates one from the other. During the day, Keith looks for food, digs through trash cans, occasionally takes rare handouts. Nights, he walks, eyes open, avoiding trouble, sleeping when he feels safe. One night, an exhausted Keith falls asleep on the sidewalk in a doorway with his arm stretched out. When he awakens, he finds three dollar bills in his open palm. He buys a Mars bar.

Soon he has no idea what day it is, and his former life is a distant dream. All he knows now is moving, staying one step ahead of trouble, and searching for food. Sleep deprivation has left him numb, slightly unhinged. He babbles to himself, sees things that aren't always there.

In this state, one night, he finds himself approaching a large structure, a building that looks vaguely familiar. Keith stares with uncertainty at the front of the Garden.

Danny looks at the crowd - it had grown considerably from when he began after Keith's death. The iPhone is now attached to speakers. The pervasiveness of "I Wanna Be Rad" on YouTube and Spotify has had an effect. Keith is a cult star. And here, outside the Garden, Danny feels important again. He has a purpose.

"Do you think he knows about us?"

The girl asking the question looks at Danny expectantly. People crowd around him. Resting on a chair, Danny's speakers play live music of the Hunger. Further out, by the street, a smaller group stands smoking, talking, banished temporarily by Danny's strict no smoking policy.

"I don't know." Danny is confused. "Maybe."

"Do you have any recorded songs? Or is it just the live stuff?" asks a guy who stands next to Danny.

"Yeah, so Keith told me he did some demos. But I don't know who has them."

Keith doesn't see Danny but sees the crowd outside the building. He is curious, so he walks up to the small group smoking beside the tree next to the street. He tries to listen in on their conversation, but he can't hear, so he comes closer.

Tired, he sits down on an empty crate at the foot of the tree. The sound of music wafts through the clear night, and he may be hallucinating, but Keith is sure it sounds familiar.

He stands atop the crate for a better view of the crowd. Leaning against the tree, he puts his arms around it for support. A crowd is dangerous, he thinks, better to keep my distance. He can almost see the speaker. Gee, do I know him, he wonders.

Keith then notices two branches just above him. He grabs the upper limb, slowly lifts himself, and slides into a seated position. Okay, that's better. I can kind of see the speaker now, he thinks.

Then, without warning, he hears a loud and vicious crunch, and the branch he sits on gives way below him. Keith comes crashing down through the dark and lands hard against his side on the solid concrete sidewalk. His knit cap comes flying off his head.

The pain in his hip shoots through his leg. He rolls onto his knees, wanting to stand. It's not easy. Some of the people in the little group near him try to help.

His hair is pushed back, the hat having locked it into place, and now his face is clearly visible. In the dark of night, the streetlamp casts an angelic glow over his pale face. When he looks up at the people aiding him, one girl gasps.

"Oh, my God—" she says, holding her hand to her mouth. "It's him!"

Another girl pushes the dark, fat bangs from her eyes and leans in close to Keith's face. "It is," she whispers. 'It's him. It's really him."

The small group of people stands around Keith and stares at him, stunned. One girl reaches out her hand and touches him. She jerks her hand back quickly when it meets solid flesh. Slowly she reaches out again and probes.

A guy with black hair and silver lightning earrings glittering in each lobe looks at him with wild eyes.

"Keith? Is it you, man?"

Keith looks at him, confused. "Yeah, I think so. How you doing? Do I know you?"

"Holy shit!" whispers the guy. "What ...? I mean, where are you, dude? Like on what plane?"

Keith is unsure what the question means.

"I'm here with you, right in front of you. Use your eyes, man."

The crowd in front of the building is still focused on Danny, oblivious to the scene taking place behind them.

"I don't understand," says the girl who touched Keith first. "How can you be here? You're dead."

"I'm not dead," says Keith. "Maybe I was just gone or something, you know, but I'm here." He holds up two fingers forming a V. "Peace and love, man."

The girl with the fat bangs reaches out her hand and hesitantly touches him again. Firm flesh. Shocked, she stumbles backward, and the guy with lightning earrings catches her. Another girl reaches out to Keith. He takes her hand and holds it in his, not knowing what else to do.

The girl faints, dead away, falling to the ground. No one pays any attention as she hits the concrete hard. Now the whole group is reaching out and seeing, feeling, and touching Keith, prodding him.

"Whoa, not so hard," says Keith, becoming a little concerned as the touching turns more physical. He grabs his cap from the ground and clutches it to his chest.

"It's a miracle," says the first girl to touch him, her words barely audible through her tears.

She turns to the crowd. "It's a miracle!"

"What are you talking about? What's a miracle, I just—" But Keith is drowned out by the growing ecstasy.

"He's alive!" screams another girl. A few of the people standing in front of the building turn their heads in the direction of the calls. Some of them walk over to the little group.

People press in, pulsating around Keith, the individuals morphing into "the crowd." Like bees hopped up on honey in the hive, they buzz and vibrate around Keith, their queen bee.

Keith feels hands reach out and touch his crotch, then another hand goes down inside his pants for a closer inspection. He struggles for air, and his knees being to wobble. Without warning, his legs give way, and he falls, sliding down along the bodies that surround him and onto the ground.

"Where did he go?" cries one girl in the group.

"He disappeared," answers another.

On the ground, Keith is surrounded by legs that are moving in confusion. His hand is stomped on; he is kicked in the stomach. But he sees a light at the end of the tunnel of legs, and he starts to crawl desperately in its direction.

"Keith, come back," squeals one girl, looking to the heavens.

Keith crawls out of the crowd as they argue and wail. Quietly he puts some distance between him and them. He is almost out of sight.

"There he is!"

Eyes wide in fear, he jumps to his feet and begins to run. The pain in his hip disappears as it is flooded by adrenaline. The crowd moves as one behind him in pursuit, and through the streets, they chase.

He turns left at the first intersection he comes to and runs straight into a woman pulling a backpack on wheels. He doesn't stop to look at her or to apologize. He leaps back to his feet and runs for his life.

As he comes to another corner, he turns again but sees that the crowd is still behind him. He is grunting, running erratically, sweat pouring from his scalp, as he makes it around the next corner.

He sees an alleyway between two buildings and quickly turns into it, running to where the alley turns right. There he makes the turn, moving behind another building. He hides in the darkness between the two buildings, a dead end. From the street, he hears ominous bodiless voices.

"Down here," calls one. "He went down here."

"Are you sure?"

Keith hears their steps on the pavement coming his way. He looks around wildly for a way out, like a trapped and terrified animal, only to realize there is no way out. Building walls rise in every direction, except the direction from which he came. Several steps against one building lead to a landing and a door. He runs up and turns the handle on the door. Locked. He runs back down, but he trips and falls against a dumpster as he does.

The voices are closing in, so without thinking, Keith opens the lid of the dumpster, clumsily climbs on top, and falls in. He quietly brings the cover down over him.

He can hear the crowd as it arrives, just as the dumpster lid closes.

"He's not here."

"Are you sure he went this way?"

"There's nowhere to go. He must have gone down the street."

"Go back!"

Keith hears their feet turn and run back from the way they came, hollering his name over and over. He dares not move.

They could have killed me, he thinks. What the hell was that? Why did they attack me? And how do they know who I am? The last question confuses him the most.

Once the voices are far away, he opens the lid of the dumpster a crack and looks. The space is clear. He climbs out.

Looking down at himself, he sees his pants are now dirtier, as is his shirt. Cursing his luck, he starts to stumble out into the alley and make his way back to the street.

As he does, three boys, in their mid-teens, turn into the alley coming his way. As they approach, Keith looks down to make himself less conspicuous.

"Excuse me," he mumbles.

The lead boy stops in front of Keith, blocking his way.

"There's no excuse for you," says the lead boy. His face is gaunt, hair cut short, tattoos across his neck. He puts his nose up to Keith's neck and sniffs like a Doberman.

"We got a bum here, boys," he says to his companions. "Homeless bum."

"Excuse me," Keith repeats as he tries to get by. But the boys block his path in each direction.

"Don't you got no manners? You got to ask real nice, say please."

"Please, can I get by?" asks Keith. He looks from one face to the other around the circle of three before landing back on the first one, who is clearly leading this pack.

"Not nice enough," says the leader.

Without warning, Keith feels an incredible force strike him in the stomach. Air is thrust from his lungs, and the pain is instant, forcing him to bend at the waist. Then another solid force meets his chin driving it upwards, his head hitting the brick wall behind him.

Keith's head bounces off the bricks. He sees a red streak forming an arc in the air in front of him. In slow motion, he realizes it's blood flying from his nose. Another blow hits from the side. It feels as though his head will twist off.

In the eyes of the lead boy is a look of pure malevolence. The other two take their cues from the leader, who begins to chant in a low voice.

"Beat the bum beat the bum beat the bum—"

The boys crowd in on him, all three of them chanting, getting louder. "Beat the bum beat the bum—"

Keith doesn't know where to turn or what to do. And he definitely doesn't know who has taken over his body. Because, suddenly, he rises up to his full height, a crazed look in his eyes, and he begins barking maliciously, spittle flying with his lips.

The barks are entirely manic and out of control. The teenagers are confused for a moment, unsure of what is happening. And Keith seizes that golden moment.

His body, acting on its own, sends his right knee flying upward with great force right between the leader's legs. The softness it finds there gives way, and the leader's knees buckle as he bends at the waist, the breath knocked out of him, face white in pain. The other boys are frozen in shock.

Surprised by his own actions, Keith hesitates for a moment. Then he turns and runs madly through the alley,

"Get him," croaks the leader. Keith can hear footsteps behind him. He looks over his shoulder to see two boys right behind him and gaining. The street is his only hope of salvation.

As he starts to exit the alley, Keith feels a surge of relief. He's going to make it. Then, hope is crushed as a hand grabs his collar, tearing it, throwing him off balance as he goes tumbling to the ground, rolling over himself.

Rising quickly, Keith backpedals onto the sidewalk,

the two boys moving towards him. Then the leader pushes his way between the other two, eyeing Keith menacingly. He limps, one hand holding his crotch, while the other reaches into his pocket and pulls something out. Keith is frozen in fear.

"You're gonna pay for that!"

The leader flips his hand, and with a loud click, the glint of metal appears, shining in the light cast from the streetlamp behind Keith. In his hand, the leader holds a switchblade. He slowly begins moving the blade in the air in front of him in a slicing motion.

"Eye for an eye? You kick me in the balls. I take yours."

The leader expertly carves the air with the blade. He lunges towards Keith, knife held in his fist, thrusting forward.

But before he reaches his prey, an enormous figure obliterates the light from the streetlamp and occupies the space between Keith and the boys.

"Not tonight."

No Name, appearing out of nowhere, towers over the punks, solid, confident, and immovable.

"You wanna beat a bum? I'm a bum, and three on one seems like good odds. For me."

The three boys look up at him. No Name feints a lunge at the leader, who leaps back instinctively. The leader starts to slowly back away, staring at No Name like he's a creature risen from a lagoon.

"Boo!" No Name makes a lunging motion at them.

The lead boy falls back on his heels, then turns and runs, followed closely by his lieutenants.

No Name laughs loud. Then he turns and looks down at Keith. He reaches out his hand.

"You alright, little brother?"

Keith reaches up and takes the hand, and it lifts him up. No Name brushes off Keith's shirt, examining the rips and tears. His hand moves Keith's face around under the streetlight, trying to get a good look.

"Gonna have some bumps tomorrow."

Anger rises up inside of Keith. Embarrassment and helplessness mingle as he turns away, unable to face his rescuer. Tears well up in his eyes, which makes it all even worse. He wipes his eyes with his shirt, then turns back.

"Thank you for—"

But when he turns, No Name is gone. Vanished into thin air again. All Keith can see is the three teenagers just down the street, tucked into a doorway, watching him.

So he rushes down the street in the opposite direction, keeping a wary eye behind him. He reaches the first intersection just in time to see No Name's giant form one block up from him as it takes a right turn. Keith runs up the street, though he doesn't know why except the large black man is familiar. Keith feels inexorably drawn to him.

When Keith first walks up to the crowd at the Garden, Danny is talking to Hunger fans in front of the building. The memory of that night is still fresh and painful inside of him. *Why didn't I know?* He can't help but wonder. Hunger is his life.

But as he talks, something at the back of the crowd catches Danny's eye, and it distracts him. He sees some guy fall out of a tree and onto the sidewalk. Danny wonders if the guy is okay.

Danny keeps talking, but he sees this person stand, and a crowd surrounds him. The guy looks like a bum, or maybe a hippie. Same thing, really. Long matted hair, knit cap, beard, dirty clothes, *that* look. But something about this guy seems familiar. Danny can't put his finger on it, but he looks kind of like ... damn, he looks a lot like Keith.

At first, Danny assumes it's the light or the distance. Or maybe it's the flooding of memories here outside Keith's building. But he finds himself unconsciously walking back through the crowd towards the guy. People follow. Damn it, he really does look like Keith. *I know that face as good as anybody,* he thinks. It's camouflaged by hair and dirt, but that dude could be a Keith impersonator.

Now he is close enough to hear the talking. One guy asks the Keith lookalike where he's been. The lookalike answers.

And that's when Danny knows. It's not what he says, it's how he says it. It's the voice. He's heard that voice so many times. Danny's sense of sound is like a fingerprint detector, and the fingerprint of that voice screams—

"Keith!"

The guy turns in Danny's direction but then drops from sight. Just disappears. That's weird, Danny thinks.

That's when he sees Keith on the ground, just outside the circle of people. Keith gets up and starts to run. The crowd takes off after him. Danny follows behind. When the group turns and runs into an alleyway, Danny hangs back and waits. It's narrow, and he's a little claustrophobic.

The crowd soon comes running back out, looking in all directions, confused. And before Danny can go into the alley and have a look, three other guys walk in before him. They are dodgy-looking malcontents with trouble on their faces. Probably heavy metal fans, thinks Danny.

Moments later, Keith comes running out of the alley, stumbling and falling onto the sidewalk. In hot pursuit are the three teenagers, and they seem ready to pounce. Danny can see the glint of metal reflecting a switchblade in one guy's raised hand.

That's enough for Danny. Keith or no Keith, he isn't going to stand around and watch a gang of three guys beat one homeless dude. He starts to walk towards them but stops when he remembers he never learned how to fight.

Then, out of nowhere, a big black man appears between Keith and the gang of punks. The black man is the size of a mountain, and the punks quickly come to their senses, turn, and run in Danny's direction. They stop in a doorway, watching Keith get up.

"Keith!" Danny calls out. Keith turns in his direction, then turns back around. Danny yells again. Keith starts walking quickly towards the street the black man walked up, occasionally turning to look behind him. Why is he running away from me, wonders Danny?

9. MAD WORLD

Keith has trouble keeping up as the big man moves across one street, then another. He loses sight of No Name at one point, so he stops and spins around, looking for him.

As he turns, something inside a store window catches his eye. He sees a face. It's a dirty, disheveled man with crazed eyes, a face from hell. Keith steps back, frightened. Then he realizes this is no stranger. It's a reflection of himself in the glass. He leans in closer for a better look. Sweat has plastered his hair back across the top of his face, and a beard fills in the rest. It's incredible that anyone could recognize him because Keith barely recognizes himself.

And that's when he sees her.

She is standing on the other side of the glass, next to a table. He recognizes the short bob and lean legs instantly, but he doesn't know why. She holds the coffee pot with such grace. As she moves from the table, it's like she's gliding on a cloud. Angels don't walk, they float. Keith stares at her, mesmerized. Beauty.

And the beast, he thinks, as he catches sight of his reflection again.

Memory claws its way back into his mind, bits and pieces at a time. He shivers at the emotions they bring and pushes them away. He suddenly feels guilty and dirty standing here staring at this girl. But he doesn't know why, and he can't stop looking.

When she turns towards him, it's like turning on a glowing, shimmering light in the deep dark room of his mind. But it also makes him feel naked and exposed, so Keith quickly turns and walks away from her.

Finally, he catches sight of the big man standing next to the Ralphs grocery store in Hollywood. It's like he's waiting. Then No Name turns and walks behind the grocery store. Keith follows.

As he comes behind the Ralph's, Keith sees No Name standing stone still in front of a row of dumpsters. Keith quietly walks up and stops a few feet behind him.

"I know you," he says. But the man continues staring at the dumpsters, his back to Keith.

"Give a man fish, he eats for a day," says No Name. Now he turns to Keith and looks him directly in the eyes. "Teach a man to dumpster dive, he'll eat for the rest of his life. Lessons aplenty here, little brother. Step right up, everyone's a winner, bargains galore within."

No Name indicates the dumpsters with his hand.

"Dumpster diving's a fundamental skill of

homeless living, like somersaults is for a tumbler. Ain't pretty, and it ain't clean, but it's elemental. And it works." No Name winks at Keith

Now the big man steps up to the dumpster nearest to the store.

"I always go for the dumpster closest to the door because I figure most people are even lazier than me. They don't wanna walk further than they have to. So they dump the food in the closest dumpster until it's full." He steps up to the first dumpster. "Now, first thing you gotta do is get your technique down. Get your hands up here on the sides of the dumpster, like this."

No Name puts his hands on the edge of the dumpster and waits. He looks at Keith, who still stands behind him. "We got all night, but we don't have to use it." Keith walks up to the dumpster, eyeing No Name the entire time. Then he places his hands on the edge of the dumpster.

"You gotta get a little jump going to get you over," says No Name. Keith begins jumping in place. But he rises no more than a few inches off the ground. "Ain't no ballerina dance, little brother, even you can jump higher than that."

Keith bounces higher, lifting up from his knees, building momentum, leaning further toward the dumpster with each leap.

"That's right, now tuck your head and go for it!"

With one grand leap, Keith shoots up into the air and begins to tuck his head. But just as he does, something shoots out from inside the dumpster and rises straight into the air until it is face to face with Keith. Screaming at the top of his lungs, Keith falls back from the dumpster.

Looking up from the ground, he sees the 'something' is a man standing in the dumpster. The man wears a worn, dark brown jacket and a grey sweatshirt hoodie underneath it.

With a quick jump and a push of his hands, the stranger's body gracefully swings to the side, like a gymnast, and glides clear of the dumpster. Turning, he retrieves a beautiful, flowery vase with a stopper top and a bulging black bag inside the dumpster. He lays them on the ground next to them.

The man is Asian and wears a broad grin on his face like he's in on a great joke, and he's not telling it to you.

"Anything left in there, Aki?" No Name asks.

"Plenty of fish left in this sea, Ben," Aki answers in a soft, genial tone, then turns to Keith. "Aki Hisakawa, Dumpster Diver's Union, Hollywood Branch." He tilts two fingers to his forehead in a salute.

"If it's a real union, you gotta split the membership dues with us members," says Ben.

"It is a real union – so I'm keeping all the dues for the president!" says Aki. Ben's belly laugh echoes off the walls.

"You got a name, little brother?" he asks

Keith, who begins to answer, then hesitates for a moment.

"Brian," he says. "Brian Jones."

"Any friend of Ben's," Aki's grin broadens. "Sorry if I scared you, but I couldn't resist."

Aki kneels and opens the plastic bag. Inside are loaves of bread and fruit whose only blemishes seem to be a few spoiled spots. There are also slightly withered vegetables inside and a container of milk, and some packaged goods.

"Dinner menu's almost set," Aki says as he turns to climb back in.

"Whoa!" cries Ben, "Brian's gotta get some practice. Let him give it a shot."

Aki steps back. "No problem. But careful where you land. The crushed fruit will kick up your feet and crack your tailbone."

Keith steps back up to the dumpster and begins bouncing in place again. He quickly gains velocity and determination then jumps up into the air arching forward. This time he has plenty of momentum as his head ducks under, and he does a forward flip into the dumpster, making a big crash as he lands.

There is no other sound from the dumpster. Ben and Aki look at each other.

"You okay?" calls Ben. "Brian?"

Still, there is no sound. Then, they hear a soft whimpering, which gradually turns into what sounds like loud sobs.

"Brian, you okay?" Ben calls, his alarm growing as he steps up and looks in. As he does, a vaguely musical sound echoes from inside the dumpster. Keith stands but doesn't appear to be crying at all. Instead, he is laughing – giddily.

"Well, I'll be damned," says Ben in amazement, a broad smile spreading across his face. "Behold salvation!"

In his right hand, Keith holds a cheap, beat-up, ¾ body acoustic guitar. It is definitely much worse for wear. The strings are ragged, the body is dirty and cracked. The tension of the guitar strings is random, and the sound is discordant. But dented, scraped, and grimy, it's a guitar, and it feels so familiar in his hands. Why, he wonders?

Without thinking, Keith's fingers begin to form a chord on the guitar, and he strums again. As that one out of tune chord spills out into the night air, everything comes back to Keith in a symphonic rush, like the end of *A Day in The Life*: the club, the coffee shop, Harry's tub, earth slipping from beneath his feet, bobbing in the water like a fish on a line and finally washing up onto the beach. The visual crescendo peaks in a loud sustained natural E chord.

As the chord's sound diminishes, Keith finds himself again standing in the unflattering light beside the Ralph's trash dumpster.

The streets are littered with the homeless. Tents line the sidewalks, under bridges, some with living room furniture set up around them. In many places, a few people lie on the street in sleeping bags or on the naked ground.

They've been walking a while and Keith doesn't know where they are. He just follows.

Ben and Aki walk in front, effortlessly navigating the minefield of bodies. Keith doesn't know how long they have walked. He is lost in his scrappy dumpster guitar. It seems to connect him to something deep in himself, something primal. And the memory is good.

"Follow me," says Ben.

When Keith looks up, Ben and Aki are gone. He rushes ahead, stopping in front of a large thick hedge along the sidewalk. This section of the street is quiet, and there is no sign of his two new companions. Everything is eerily still. He is alone again, and he doesn't like it.

Suddenly, an alien hand grabs his arm and jerks him violently, throwing him off balance. Keith screams.

Danny follows behind the Keith and the other two men as they walk through Hollywood. It's really rubbing him wrong that Keith is ignoring him. Here he is, the president of Keith's fan club, if there actually were such a club, and he is being totally ignored by that self-same Keith Unger. Why? Danny doesn't understand, and it hurts. It hurts badly and deeply.

Why this whole death charade without telling me, he wonders? What were they doing at that dumpster? And who is this big guy? He looks a little scary. Or maybe ... shit, maybe he's the new superfan?

Danny's paranoia starts to rise, and it tickles a sensitive insecurity nerve that is constantly twitching just below the surface of his skin. Together, the paranoia and insecurity are a toxic mix, clouding Danny's sometimes fragile grasp on reality. Superfans are like that.

He's replacing me. Damn it, that's what this is, curses Danny. The black guy is going to be the new superfan, the new Danny Wallburger. Well, that isn't fair! I spent all that time ... Wait, maybe I'm jumping ahead of myself here. If he only wanted to replace me, why would Keith fake his death? He could just replace me without killing himself.

It's a long walk with many turns. At one point, Danny hears voices behind him, punctuated by harsh laughs. He turns and sees the three malcontent teenagers keeping pace behind him. There is an air of menace about them.

Are they following me? Danny wonders. When he turns back around, Keith and his companions have disappeared. Danny stands in front of a hedge at the sidewalk's edge and looks in every direction. They are nowhere.

The three teenagers are approaching. Danny quickly crosses the street and watches as they continue out of sight. He sits down on the cold sidewalk and tries to understand what is happening. But it's all too much. Something is wrong. Something is very wrong. He grabs his hair and pulls, letting out a scream.

As his scream runs out of air, Keith looks around. What world is this?

Keith stands with his back to the hedges. Ben smiles and lets go of his arm. In front of him are three tents, set up in a semi-circle around a small Coleman cooking stove, an ice chest, and seven camping chairs. There are Christmas lights strung over the tents, and one tree near the Coleman is similarly decorated. An end table between two of the chairs has books on it, a lantern, and a vase with flowers. This small empty area is surrounded by high, thick hedges on all sides.

"Take a seat, Brian." Ben walks towards the chairs. Three of the chairs are occupied by two men and a woman. The woman is pretty, with dark brown hair falling straight to her shoulders and golden-brown skin. She looks to be in her mid-30s. One of the men is middle-aged, a little grey trimming his sideburns, stocky build, curious eyes. The younger one is around Keith's age, slim with wiry hair and dark skin.

Aki sets his bag by the ice chest and opens its contents. He begins taking things out of the bag.

"Hi, I'm Carolyn," The woman says to Keith with a warm smile as she rises from the chair and offers her hand.

"Oh yeah," says Ben. "Guess who's coming to dinner? Everybody, this is Brian. Brian, everybody. That there is Harold." Ben points to the middle-aged man, who rises and approaches with an outstretched hand.

"Harold Wimbler. A pleasure to meet you, Brian."

Carolyn looks at Keith's ripped and dirty shirt, traces of blood on it.

"Oh, you poor thing. What happened to you? Kitch, have you got a tee shirt he can borrow?"

"Wassup, man," says the guy who is Keith's age, as he waves amiably. "Kitch. But you can just call me Kitch." He laughs alone at his own joke.

Rising from his chair, Kitch goes into one tent and returns with a faded brown tee shirt which he hands to Keith. He sits down on a blanket laid out beside the chairs. He offers his chair to Keith with a wave of his hand as he reclines on the blanket.

Keith walks to the chair and slowly sits, holding the tee shirt in his lap. Carolyn joins Aki and helps empty the contents of his bag.

"Veggies! Oh, Enzo and Emmy are going to love these," she laughs. "Brian, are you hungry? We've got some leftovers from dinner." She opens the ice chest and pulls out a Tupperware container. "Chicken sausage?"

"Just feed the boy. He don't talk much," Ben says.

Keith lays his guitar on the ground beside him as Carolyn hands him a paper plate with two charred sausages on it. He doesn't even take the knife and fork she offers, choosing instead to inhale the sausages using only his fingers and teeth.

When he finishes, he looks up to see everyone is watching him. They burst out laughing. Carolyn sits back in her chair.

"Homeless long?" says Kitch with a big laugh.

Keith thinks about the indistinguishable stream of days and nights that have passed by since his fall from the cliff. They are like one long endless day's night.

"I don't know," he answers.

"Long enough to want to forget," shouts Kitch, erupting in laughter again.

"Maybe he's got a lot to forget Like you." Aki taps Kitch on the head

"Oh, that hurts, Aki," says Kitch

"Only if it's true," says Harold, slapping Kitch's shoulder.

The little group begins talking among themselves as if Keith has always been there.

"You play that thing?" asks Kitch, pointing at the guitar.

"Brian's gonna be a rock star. Isn't that right, Brian?" says Ben.

"That's wonderful." Carolyn claps her hands. "Can you play something for us?"

"Yeah, let's hear one of your jams, man." Kitch sits up.

Keith looks at the guitar next to him. "I don't know—"

"Come on, man, don't be all shy," insists Kitch.

"It's not really in shape to play, you know, and I just—"

Ben walks to the guitar lying next to Keith and hands it to him. Keith looks at it for a moment, then slowly tunes the strings as best he can. He fidgets, strumming lightly, hesitantly. His fingers don't move as fast they used to, but gradually Keith builds some courage as a chord progression takes shape.

At first, Keith isn't really sure what he's singing. It seems to come from somewhere, known to him and yet somehow new. He starts to sing uncertainly, the vocal lines like tendrils to a Keith he left on that cliff. By the end, he is wholly lost in his moment of the song.

"Oh baby, I feel so bad, I don't know, but I think you're mad. I can't help feeling sad, but all I want is just to be rad."

As the last chord rings around him, Keith is surprised to find that he has forgotten where he is, transported to another place by the guitar for a few moments. He hadn't realized he missed playing. Maybe because for a while, he had forgotten he could play.

He lifts his head, and he looks around. He's met by a group with eyes focused on the ground. Harold nods his head. Only Kitch and Carolyn look at him.

"Wow. I gotta tell you, man," says Kitch, "that was bad. Like really bad. Horrible ... I mean ... I'm not trying to diss you but I don't feel you, man. It ain't real. The beat's kicking and all, but … what's it about?"

Carolyn looks around the group, then at Keith and his crestfallen expression. "No, it was not bad. It was great, Brian. It has a catchy melody, and I like the way you sing. You've got a great voice."

The silence is heavy on Keith. The old waves of doubt and disillusion begin to creep back in. Now that his memory is expanding, those carry a heavy weight, pulling him down.

"Music," intones Big Ben, "is a balm for the weary soul, a language common to both priest and confessor, the words we speak among ourselves when we speak with our hearts, that elixir we use to uplift and inspire, to acknowledge and empathize."

They all turn to look at Ben, and Ben looks at Keith.

"When you write, what do you think about?"

"I don't know. What's going to rhyme?"

Kitch stifles a laugh.

"To get where you're at, you musta gone through some stuff, right?" says Kitch. "Real pain? Like all of us. You ever try to put that into your songs?"

"I guess. Well, maybe … I think so …"

"You can't *think*, you gotta know, 'cause when you do, you feel it here," Ben taps Keith's chest, "you feel it in the song. And when you feel it in a song, then other people tune in, they relate."

"Ben's right," says Kitch. "Art gotta be real. Your real may not be my real, but I can understand it. See?"

Keith nods his head, but he doesn't understand.

"We all feel pain," explains Aki. "Everybody's pain is different, but in some ways, it's all the same."

"Everybody has a story," says Harold. "Like Aki. He wasn't born on the streets." Harold turns to Aki. "How'd you get here?"

Aki pulls his knit cap lower. "Oh, well, that's a long story. Not that interesting."

"I think it's interesting. Tell the man," says Kitch, motioning to Keith.

Aki avoids eye contact by looking at the ground. But he can tell there's no way out.

"Well, I was living in the Bay Area, where I'm from. I worked planning meetings—corporate meetings at this large facility. The finance part of it is what I did. I like numbers. Ever since I was a kid, digits were my thing. Then my dad got sick."

Aki picks at his hat.

"My parents lived in the same apartment for decades. Since I was a kid. My sister, she moved out a long time ago, went to Boston, got married. My mom, she was a worrier. She worried about my sis a lot."

Aki pulls the vase he carried out of the dumpster when Keith first met him closer to his side.

"I was taking Pops to the doctor, helping at home and all. First, I hired a caregiver, but that was expensive. And I'm Japanese, so, you know, we take care of your own."

Aki's fingers mesh, rub against each other.

"You were working the whole time?" asks Harold.

"Yeah, pretty much. But I couldn't do both. So I quit my job."

"Where did you get money after that?" Carolyn leans forward.

"Well. I had some savings, and we lived off that. But Pops didn't get better, and eventually, he passed."

Aki sits up straighter. Keith's hand slowly goes to his chest, pressing against a soreness there. Everyone is quiet.

"How did your mother take it?" asks Harold.

"She got sick." Aki's face is tight, twitching slightly. "She was married to my Pops since she was 17, over 50 years. When she died, it wasn't some fancy named disease that killed her—it was just an old fashion broken heart."

Carolyn wipes her eyes.

"Didn't your sister help out?" asks Kitch.

Aki laughs. "No, she never came out. I paid for mom's cremation. My sister sued me because she thought I stole my parent's money. The lawyers took the little money I had left in savings. I didn't even have enough to inter mom's ashes with my dad. Then the landlord evicted me."

Keith finds himself nodding, seeing his belongings piled up outside his apartment door.

Aki pulls the floral vase to his chest, holding it with affection. "I moved out onto the streets with nothing but this. It's got my mom's ashes inside." He looks up and smiles. "But I'm not too worried – because we're together, you know? She's watching me. I just want to get her back together with Pops."

Kitch gets up, walks up behind Aki, and wraps his arms around him. Aki absorbs the hug and nods his head.

"At least you've got ashes." Eyes turn to Harold. "I didn't even get a lock of hair or a photo."

Harold looks up with a wry smile. "This is the story of a boy named Harold, slipped and fell down the corporate ladder."

"Tell him your story," says Carolyn.

"Oh, it's an old story. Man meets financial spiral. The economy took a dive, corporate profits plunged, jobs moved overseas. Then they started downsizing management-level jobs. First to go were the people without a connection to the ones doing the downsizing."

Harold shakes his head.

"I don't blame them; white-collar has to pay just like blue-collar. But, I am sorry I was on one of the lower ladder rungs that got cut off. My wife took it worse. She was used to the good life."

Harold chuckles, but it's mirthless.

"She left me for a better position. Married my old boss, took the kids and put a restraining order on me to keep me away from my kids." Harold looks up and smiles. "I think we had a few fights."

Keith remembers Candy and his band members filing out of the coffee shop.

"What happened to your kids?" asks Keith.

Harold inhales. "Haven't seen them in three years. I don't even know if they have my name anymore."

"That's bullshit!" Carolyn's ferocity takes Keith by surprise.

Aki rises and walks over behind Harold. He reaches his arms around him and gives him a solid hug. "Spread the love."

"Not with those skinny arms you won't," cries Harold, as he laughs and pulls Aki's arms tighter around him.

"Different pains, but the same pain," says Kitch, looking at Keith. But Keith's mind is a million miles away and right there at the same time.

If I'd seen Aki coming out of a dumpster two days ago, thinks Keith, I might have been disgusted, avoided contact with him. But now … now he's not someone to be ashamed of, but someone to be proud of.

Aki then tells a story about this one time at work when he lost thousands of dollars, only to find it later in a bookkeeping error. Found it just minutes before he was going to confess the loss to his boss. And it's funny.

Harold laughs the hardest of everyone, tears streaming down his cheeks as he claims it must have been Aki who did the accounting for his divorce. That brings a new explosion of laughter.

Keith notices that as they laugh, the pain stops

belonging to an individual, stops having a singular personality. It becomes a collective thing, shared equally among them all, diminishing its impact. And the laughter rolls like waves of healing through the little group.

He looks at the faces around him. Keith feels like he knows these people, even though he's only just met them.

What world is this?

10. CONNECTION

*D*ownsizing the corporate ladder, pay no mind to the lives that shatter.

Keith wakes up with those words rolling in his head. Everybody bleeds, everybody hurts. Was I paying attention before? Or was I focused on just myself? The morning sun warms him as he gets up and walks through Hollywood.

One more dream in a million pieces.

That was Harold. It's Harold's dream and his pieces, but it feels personal to me too. She's cute.

What? Keith stops.

Brown bob, perky nose, wearing snug jeans, and a tee-shirt with "Today is the day" printed across it, the girl in the window is filling a glass counter with bagels and scones. Keith realizes he's standing in front of the Coffee a Go-Go.

She looks up at Keith and smiles. Keith wants to move, but his feet won't budge. Oh no, she's walking over here, he thinks. She's opening the door. She's—

"Hi! Did you want a scone?"

—talking to me.

The girl looks down both sides of the street.

"C'mon in. The coast is clear." Her smile seems to hold the promise of something fresh and new. Keith has no choice but to follow.

"Simon doesn't like me giving away freebies, but we still have some leftovers from last night." She walks to the counter, picks up a scone from a tray, and puts it on a plate. She hands the plate to Keith. "Coffee?"

"Will you get in trouble?" Keith wouldn't want that.

"It's okay. My dad says we're a community."

I could ride that smile to the moon and back, thinks Keith. But I'd be happy to just scoop a little of it and put it in my pocket, and it could glow, and grow, and wherever I am—

"Cream?" she asks as she holds out a cup of coffee. Keith nods, and she hands him a half and half carton. Keith pours a healthy dose of cream in his coffee.

"My name is Jane."

"B-B-Brian," Keith says, trying to suppress the pang of guilt that quickly rises inside of him.

"You're camping with Ben, right? He comes by here all the time."

Keith nods.

"You can sit." Jane points at a table, and Keith does. She sits down across from him as Keith looks at the scone uncertainly. Jane nudges the plate towards him.

"Go on. I didn't make it." She laughs, and Keith

smiles as he takes a small bite of the scone. "You have a nice smile. You should use it more."

He looks at the table next to the counter, which is covered with books and notepads. He remembers an old question.

"What do you do? Over there?" he asks, pointing at the table. Jane looks over, then exhales and slumps a little.

"Oh, that. It's my schoolwork. I'm studying for a degree in economics. Not that I want to be an economist, I just want to start my own business. I thought economics would be a good thing to study for that. Maybe not. But I started. Guess I have to finish it."

"What kind of business?"

Jane looks around, hand over her mouth as though she's embarrassed.

"Promise you won't laugh?"

Keith nods.

Jane blushes and then whispers to him. "I want to open a coffee shop."

"A coffee shop?"

"I know, just what the world needs, another coffee shop. But I want to open a coffee shop that's different, that has a little hair and nail salon in it, and also sells books. Lots of books. I want it to be a place where people can come and think, and work, remake themselves. You know, rejuvenate?"

Her enthusiasm is infectious. Keith thinks he does know.

"You like to read?" he asks. Keith points at the books on the table, next to the notebook.

"Well, I don't like reading those silly old things. They're really boring. But I love to read. It's maybe my favorite thing to do. Are you a reader?"

Keith considers, for a moment, a question he had never contemplated before. He likes reading *Mojo*, *Uncut*, even *Rolling Stone* when they write about music. And Keith likes reading lyrics from songs. He remembers listening to his dad's old vinyl records, lying on his back, headphones on, and absorbing the sounds, pictures, and words on the covers.

"I like music," he answers. It seems so obvious, but at this moment, it is as if he is discovering it for the first time.

"Oh, yeah - music. I like that too," agrees Jane, though she's not sure why since she really doesn't listen to much music.

He's funny, Jane observes. Not in a typical way, and maybe he doesn't even mean to be, but he is.

She likes funny. He has funny thought patterns, or maybe they just don't follow the usual pathways. She's seen that before with some of the other homeless people she has helped with food at the shop, probably drugs or mental illness. But he is different.

"Do you have a pen?"

"You want to borrow or keep?

"Keep."

Jane likes an honest man. It doesn't seem to be a

common trait. She gets up, goes behind the counter, digs into the drawer beneath the cash register, and pulls out a pen.

"Do you need paper?"

"Yes, please."

He's polite too. Jane tears a few sheets from her notebook and brings the pen and paper to Keith's table. He takes the paper, carefully folds it into quarters, and then puts the folded paper into his shirt pocket. He follows by clipping the pen into the same pocket.

"Thank you. I need to write some things down, to remember. I'm afraid I won't remember if I don't. Does that happen to you?"

"Oh, yeah, all the time. I take notes in class because I never remember what the teacher says. I used to record the lectures, but my dad said if you write things down, it sticks it to your brain better."

Keith looks at his plate, which is now empty but for a few crumbs. He slowly stands next to the table.

"I have to go. I have some work I have to do. Thank you for the scone. And the coffee. And the paper and pen. I'll pay you back."

"Happy to help." Jane rises next to him. She notices he has a distinct odor.

Keith taps the pen and paper in his shirt pocket. "This will really help me." And without another word, he turns and walks out of the coffee shop.

Jane watches him as he exits and turns right out of the door. What an odd boy, she thinks to herself, as she remembers his unusual speech patterns, his kind of cute awkwardness. And that distinct odor. The latter she feels may not be permanent.

Out in the street, Keith feels the warmth of the sun as it washes across his face. At this moment, it feels so good to be alive. He's not sure why, but he enjoys it anyway.

After a few blocks, he comes upon an old Hollywood apartment building located at some minor side street corner. The building is a dirty cream color, with grand flourishes over the doorway arch. Decorative flower urns are resting on either side of the door. The type of personality touches typical of older Hollywood buildings, a Hollywood which is being erased faster than the Arctic ice.

He sees a slanting crack traveling sideways up the four short steps to the entryway, leaving a small crevice, the result of some past earthquake.

Keith follows the crevice and sits down on the top concrete step. From his shirt pocket, he pulls the paper and pen. Without hesitation, he begins to write. It starts slowly, but the pace quickly picks up until the pen is moving furiously. Keith is fully absorbed, bent over, and into his work.

When he finishes, Keith leans back, momentarily spent after this brief eruption of hyperkinetic activity, and looks at the sheet of paper. He's surprised by what he sees.

"This is my shot! People are gonna listen to me now because of that Keith thing."

"Candy, your time is coming. Just be patient. A week ago you didn't even want to be a rock star, now you're on Empty V. We're in talks to get you to—"

Candy flips her hair back and yells into the cell phone. "That piece of shit? Who do you think you're kidding? No one watches that garbage anymore. They're old news."

As she talks, Candy watches the TV closely, with the sound off, as Hunger's guitar player Sly is being interviewed. A large V with a TV screen resting in its crux sits prominently in the screen's lower right corner. She gives Sly the finger.

"My song is almost ready to go."

"You wrote a song?" Harry sounds genuinely surprised. "I'm working on a video for —"

"People will eat that shit up. Get me on *Fox and Friends*. They'll love me over there."

"Who doesn't?" replies Harry.

"Don't patronize me, Harry. I'm going to be a huge star, and you're gonna brag that I—"

"I already do, honey."

The interview with Sly ends, and now Candy

appears on the TV.

"I've gotta go. They're showing my interview again. Get me on the radio, Harry!"

"Enjoy the—" Candy hangs up the phone and turns up the TV volume.

On the screen, the blonde-haired surfing wannabe host of the show is looking at Candy with an overfilled cup of sympathy.

"Yeah, it's been a tough time, Shane," Candy says on the TV. "Keith and me, we were conjoined at the hip. We did everything together, like John and Yoko. We were artistic soul mates, Zionese twins. But music heals."

"Keith's music?"

"Well, yeah, that too. But mostly my music. I've written a couple of songs about Keith, pouring my heart and soul into them, being naked, you know, really emotionally vulnerable." Candy peers up through the curls of her hair. "That's my way of coping. That's me being me."

Shane nods with a pained, constipated look. "Could we hear some of those songs, Candy?"

Candy smiles at him demurely and turns her face sideways, hiding behind one hand.

"Oh, I'm not ready to overexpose myself, Shane. I'm still shy about the songs, and it's really … painful. You know?"

"Did you want sugar or cream, Ms. Wells?" The

handsome, young, black intern holds out a cup as he looks at Vondy from under perfectly groomed eyebrows.

Vondy sits at *Dollars Make Sense's* anchor desk, methodically reviewing her notes.

"No, thank you ... ?"

"Sean."

"No, thank you, Sean. I like it black." She smiles at him.

The intern walks away. Vondy pretends to look at her notes while actually watching the rhythmic swing of his ass.

She shakes her head, ridding it of the magnetic thoughts inside, and looks back at her notes. Okay, what are the pertinent things?

Well, of course, there's the obvious – the new distribution deal between Massive Records and Keith Unger's agents. An electric shock of excitement runs up her spine as she thinks of the latest direction in this continually expanding story. She pinches herself for the hundredth time in the last few days to prove it's real.

The ceiling is moving upwards for me, thinks Vondy. This Keith Unger story keeps growing. Lucky thing he killed himself while I was nearby.

"Miss Wells?"

Vondy looks up.

Standing right in front of her, lips parted in a crisp smile that whispers 'Yes, it's me', is the chiseled Mt. Rushmore visage of the legendary Stuart Carney, financial anchor unparalleled. This is a face anyone who follows the news, or more specifically financial news, has engraved in their head. And he is talking to me – Carlita Garcia of Winston-Salem, North Carolina.

"Please, call me Vondy." She returns the smile. "It's such a pleasure to meet you, Mr. Carney. I'm a big admirer of your work." It's a well-oiled compliment, delivered with a smile of patented sincerity and without an ounce of nervousness. Carney takes it in practiced style.

"Just Stuart is fine. So, I'm just going to ask you a few questions, and you feel free to answer as fully as you care to. If I pull on my right ear, wind your answer to a quick end. If I raise my right eyebrow, extend your answer some more. If I scratch my nose – it itches."

Vondy is caught listening to his rich baritone voice, trying to decide if that's a British accent, a smoothed-out Aussie, or just an American faking it. It takes a moment, but she recognizes the joke and laughs. A pro like Carney knows to put his guests at ease. That's how he gets the great interviews.

The stage manager walks up to Carney. "Ready to go, Mr. Carney."

Carney nods, adjusts himself in his seat, and closes his eyes for a moment. When he opens them, he is focused on the bright, blond sprite seated across the desk from him.

"Are you ready, Vondy?"

She nods.

"Then let's go for a ride."

The stage manager counts in. "4-3-2-1 and ..." He points to Carney.

"Good afternoon, and welcome to *Dollars Make Sense,* where for nearly 30 years we've been breaking down the latest news in finance and money for you, the person who has, or wants, plenty of both. I'm Stuart Carney, and my guest today is Vondy Wells, a reporter for Los Angeles' local morning news show on KNLA. Ms. Wells has earned well-deserved recognition for breaking and diving into the details of the story of Keith Unger. Mr. Unger, a frustrated musician without a penny to his name, took his own life by jumping to his death into the Pacific Ocean. That he did so in the lovely beach community of the wealthy, Malibu, only adds irony to the story."

Carney turns to Vondy and smiles. "Welcome to our show, Vondy."

"A pleasure to be with you, Stuart."

"So, there has been considerable movement with this story, and it continues to startle most observers, like myself. As you have ably reported, Mr. Unger has become an international sensation in a very brief amount of time. Had that happened prior to his demise, it would likely have ensured that Keith Unger would be alive today to enjoy his fame. It is astounding, is it not, that this unknown musician could breach the ramparts of fame and success by merely ending his life?"

"Ironic, to say the least," returns Vondy. "It

certainly has surprised almost everyone and maybe rewritten the rulebook on fame. Though I hope the rest of the rock community won't consider suicide as a good career move."

"Indeed!" replies Carney. "A big step forward today, correct?"

"Yes, a huge step today, Stuart." Vondy sits comfortably, yet with firm posture, her eyes on Carney, without staring. She leans ever so slightly into his body as she speaks.

"Today, in an exclusive, Harry Chukstein, Keith Unger's manager, confirmed to me that he has struck a deal with Massive Records on behalf of Keith Unger and his band Hunger. The deal will garner Chukstein Global worldwide distribution for all of Keith Unger's output, which I understand is sizable, and open up an avenue for any other projects Mr. Chukstein brings to Massive. Unger's music crosses demographic lines due to the circumstances surrounding his death, so it's quite a feather in the cap of Massive. A good deal for both."

"You say the potential output is sizable." Carney shifts in his chair, brings his hands together, elbows on the table. "Can you describe for us what that means?"

"I am told that Keith Unger left behind demo recordings of his songs which are largely complete. How many? I don't know that exact number, but enough that the world will not run out of Keith Unger songs anytime soon."

"Good God, he must have been a very busy young man. Additionally, I believe I read that in the short time since his death, he has breathed life into the former music video channel, the Empty V?"

"Yes, that's probably the biggest surprise of all and one without a clear answer. Empty V has returned some of their music programming. They are featuring this story prominently, and viewers are rewarding them."

"Will wonders never cease. Thank you, Vondy. Excellent reporting. And up next, could the rising waters of climate change mean rising wages for maritime—"

Vondy pinches herself – yes, I really am here, that is really Stuart Carney, and I'm really in the big time. The future looks so bright, she thinks.

Ben and Keith walk briskly around the building and then into the Cedar Sinai Medical Center's emergency room. They wear plastic bags over their bodies, protecting them from the torrential rainstorm they leave behind when they walk through the automatic doors.

"When the rain comes, you gotta hide your head," says Ben, scanning the room. "Ain't no point in getting all wet."

Ben guides them past the crowded ER's front desk

while the person working triage is otherwise occupied. They settle into two of the few remaining chairs at the back, in a corner, out of sight.

Ben places his daypack on the ground, opens it up, and pulls two browning bananas and a couple handfuls of saltines from inside. He offers both to Keith.

"Dinner?" Keith takes a banana and a couple of saltine packets.

"Dry, public," says Ben, "and we got a place to sit. Bed would be better, but for two homeless guys looking to get some shut-eye on a rainy night? Could be a hell of a lot worse."

"We're going to sleep here?"

"Hell yeah. You rather sleep on the bus, holding a book on your chest, so no one thinks you're scamming?" Ben smiles. "Ain't no Hilton on the streets."

Ben sets his banana aside, leans back, and closes his eyes.

Keith lets his weary body sink into the chair. He pulls paper and pen out of his shirt pocket, straightens the wrinkled piece of paper, and reads what he has written so far.

"Don't be sloppy. Respect yourself and your work." Ben holds out a small journal notebook without opening his eyes.

Keith takes the notebook, about the size of his palm, and opens it up.

"More where that came from," mumbles Ben.

Keith takes in the waiting room. Most of the patients here are Hispanic, and they seem to have come in groups covering several generations. So many faces, each telling a different story. An older Hispanic man is seated in a wheelchair, holding his stomach, leaning forward. A younger woman strokes his arm with a concerned look on her face, while three little children are huddled at his feet.

He thinks of Aki and his parents. He had that kind of loyalty and a sense of duty, and where is he now - homeless and penniless, diving into dumpsters to scavenge food.

Keith feels a pain in the pit of his stomach, and he writes that down. The pen scribbles down all the thoughts running through his head - good wishes for the future and sad examinations of his present. Some begin to turn into lyrics.

I'm hanging by a thread, I'm hanging to a dream, that from inside this rotting dumpster, I'll find a way out of here.

Did fate create my destiny, he wonders? Did Aki make his?

"Men aren't prisoners of fate, just prisoners of their minds." Keith turns to the source of the mumbled sound. But Ben is slumped in his chair, head leaned against the wall, tilted to the side.

A jagged, strangled snore escapes Ben's nose and mouth as he turns to the side, and his head falls onto Keith's shoulder. He licks his lips and unconsciously scratches his forehead.

Keith looks around the room. All these people. Waiting, he thinks, waiting for someone above them in rank to call their name, give them their turn. Outside this room, many others are waiting as well - waiting for someone to allow them their space, to unlock their fate—someone to set them free.

Free. Not to live under the control of someone else. To act and be as you truly wish.

I've done a lot of waiting, thinks Keith. I've always done what someone else told me to do. He moves his pen as if to write. But instead of writing, the pen quivers in his hand as his mind struggles. His insides plead with him.

I'm hanging on to a dream, stuck in my own dumpster. I've got to find a way out, thinks Keith. I want to dominate myself. I want to be free!

And that's when he hears it, that voice, clear as a solitary bell ringing in an empty valley. But he knows these words do not come from Ben, the TV, a famous actor, or anyone else. They come from deep inside his own heart. They come with a purpose and in a voice that is older than time.

"Free yourself."

But how?

"It's definitely in the key of G. The same key that Keith

wrote every song in, the only key he ever wrote in, probably the only key he knew. That's how you can tell it's a Keith song - it's in G! Do you need to take a break?"

Sly glares, annoyed, and irritated. His guitar hangs over his shoulder by its strap while his arms are firmly crossed atop his chest.

Candy stands opposite him, looking lost and confused, out of her element. She also wears a guitar. Rami air drums behind them, while Juice sits in a chair, bass in lap, book in hand.

"It's just that I thought it was in another key."

"Yeah, we figured that when you played the F major."

Candy can feel the pressure of everyone looking at her, judging her. Abruptly she unstraps the Telecaster guitar and throws it to the ground. It bounces and falls onto its back, emitting a god-awful noise from the amp.

"Don't be such an asshole, Sly. You're not Mr. Know-It-All-Music. You don't have to play, you know," she screams. "And the rest of you, stop staring at me! I can have you all fired, do you hear me? I can get another band to play. My single is going to be huge, and I can make sure you don't get any of the money!"

"Actually," says Juice, looking up from his book, "you can't. We have a contract. Harry hired us, Harry fires us. And he won't. The single is recorded, ready for release, and we get our share of it. By contract."

Rami, ever kinetic, is tied up in unreleased energy. Air drumming isn't giving him his fix - he needs the real thing.

"Can we just get back to work?" says Rami. "I haven't played Keith's old songs in a while. I'm rusty."

"I don't think three chords and four on the floor is going to be too big a challenge, dude. Except maybe for Candy." Sly looks at her, challenging.

"I'm doing this for you, bozos. I don't need the money - I have a contract with Massive. Okay, key of G. 1-2-3-4—"

The band blasts into "I Wanna Be Rad," sounding as tight as they did at the Killer Klub. Sly walks over to Candy's amp and turns the volume down to 1. Eyes closed, her back to him, she doesn't even notice as she belts out the lyrics. No one could deny that there is a certain empty, dangerous, soulless something to her voice. It screeches at times, but it does so vaguely in key.

And it is once again amazing to see what enormous sins a great band can cover up.

11. GIMME SOME TRUTH

One side of the street is lined with shelters built from plastic, grocery carts, blankets, belongings. There is even a bed mattress standing on its side, functioning as someone's wall. The businesses on this block are almost invisible.

The junction of Hollywood and Sunset Boulevard is a homeless tent city. The rains have gone, and the air is warm and humid. There is a party mood atmosphere.

"I can't run a business with all this trash. It's not fair." Reza Khorasani stands in front of his restaurant, Bruneri's Fine Italian Food, with a hot camera light on his face. Vondy holds a microphone to his mouth. Skip captures the throbbing undercurrent of anger running through this great circus.

A short man with a Dodgers baseball cap, and a thin mustache, leans into the microphone.

"We are not trash!"

"I'm not saying *you're* trash," says the business owner. "It's all this stuff—"

"I know what you're saying!" responds the man, "I try to help you."

"Ha! You offer to help clean up in exchange for food. I do my part, but you start coming into my restaurant, sitting wherever you want, asking customers for money and bread. I say no!"

Vondy turns to the man in the hat and points her microphone at him. "And what is your name?"

The man looks at the camera and smiles wide, exposing more than a few missing teeth. "My name is Martini."

"And what brings you here to this encampment, Mr. Martini?"

"This place close to recycle plant. That is how I make money."

"You recycle?" asks Vondy.

"Yes, recycle! City want to throw me out. But people here," he points at the businesses that line the street behind the encampment, "got to share! Not just they street. Ours too. They make much money, must share!"

The homeless crowd erupts in applause; people slap Martini on the back. He smiles, soaking up the notoriety, flashing two thumbs up. Vondy turns her back to the crowd and looks into the camera.

"And that is the way it is here at the Sunset Junction, Steve. They will begin tearing this encampment down in the morning, so everyone has been told to leave by 8 AM. This is Vondy Wells, reporting live."

Vondy puts down the microphone. Skip quickly starts to wrap the camera in anticipation of going home.

"You didn't get me on the TV," says an old lady, in a knit cap, with a crooked set of teeth. "I want my family to come get me. I lost my medication. I can't do this anymore."

"Stop whining and feeling sorry for yourself." Vondy explodes in a fury. "You're not the only one with problems. A lot of us are finding life isn't all it was cracked up to be!"

Vondy turns on her heels, climbs into the news van, and closes the door, leaving a crowd of stunned people in her wake.

"She's had a rough day, folks," says Skip. "Boss is a little bit nicer than that sometimes."

Further from the crowd, where it's not as congested, sit Keith and Ben and their friends. With Carolyn are her two kids - Enzo and Emmy. Enzo is 6 and wears an Angels baseball hat over his short brown hair. He watches closely as Keith soundlessly strums his guitar. His three-year old sister Emmy, her brown hair in ringlets, sleeps in her mother's arms.

"You like Brian's guitar?" Ben asks Enzo, who shyly retreats behind his mother's arm.

"B, why don't you play a little something for us," asks Kitch. "Get us a mood, man."

Keith slowly starts to find the chords to "I Wanna Be Rad."

"Not that one! No diss, man, but that's kinda tired. You got something else?" asks Kitch.

"I don't ..." says Keith, hesitantly.

Keith looks at the form his fingers have taken on the fretboard. He seamlessly feels his way through a series of chords.

"What's that?" asks Aki

"I just wrote it. I'm not sure if it's any good."

"Play it! We'll be the judge of what's good. What's the worst that could happen?" says Harold.

"We ridicule and humiliate him!" calls out Kitch.

Everyone laughs, except Keith.

Keith's fingers slowly start to move, the chords take their form, and he follows the progression until he falls into its groove. Everyone is looking at him, so he closes his eyes. Slowly the lyrics take form in his mind. Then he starts to sing softly.

"One dream is broken in a million pieces, and it won't come together even just to please us/ Take my job, you took my money too, but you can't take the things that keep me glued."

As he sings, his voice grows stronger. But he doesn't overload it with emotion. The plaintive delivery gives the lyrics all the power they need.

"What's in a name, I never knew, I never thought it'd be such a battle with you/My world is lost far from its stem, is my name the only thing they've taken with them?"

It feels right from the beginning, flowing from his heart to his fingers, from his soul to his mouth.

"So they're downsizing on the corporate ladder, paying no mind to the lives they shatter. I won't spread thin, I'm no looming disaster. because dreams aren't dreams if they don't really matter."

After that, the chorus, and there are two more verses, then one repeats. Keith is caught up in the story he tells.

An abrupt stab across the strings with his pick and this new song ends its first run. There is silence. Keith slowly opens his eyes to see faces lost in thought or looking away. His new music didn't hold them.

But he is surprised to find that it's okay. They don't have to like it. He understands for the first time because *he* likes it. That's all that matters.

The streetlight above shines down on this little group, reflecting off their faces as they sit in the quiet on the ground. It's then that Keith notices the light reflecting off Harold's face, off a tear that slowly drifts down his cheek. He isn't looking away, lost in thought. He is looking away to hide the fact that he is crying.

"Was that me?"

Keith is embarrassed. He nods his head. "Yeah, it started you. Then some of me. Ended up a little ... all of us."

"Thanks, Brian. That ... that really means a lot."

Keith nods. Though he is now okay with liking his song for himself, without anyone else's approval, he finds he likes Harold's tears as well. Both opinions have meaning.

Looking around their little group, Keith sees that Harold isn't the only one with a tear in his eye. The song has affected the others as well—even Enzo, who is incongruously smiling at him.

"That was cool, man."

Keith looks up at the unknown girl who is speaking to him. She has spiky blonde hair.

"You a musician?"

Keith nods.

"You wrote that about him?" asks a man, pointing at Harold.

Keith notices that other people are gathering around them, people he doesn't know. They begin to pepper him with questions. Some ask Harold what the song meant or ask Keith if he can write a song about them.

"I ran away from home when I was 13," says the first girl. "It was a big mistake. I just want to go home."

"I was in Iraq, man, and when I came back—"

"Nobody ever wrote a song about *me*, it would be like I mattered or I was—"

"Brian." Ben interrupts the requests. "You got another song?"

Keith nods. He finds the D minor chord on his guitar, gives it a strum, and instantly sets the mood. Everyone quiets down.

He closes his eyes and softly strums and picks the

strings. It's a slow, steady beat, like rain on the hood of a car, and he plays until he feels the words must come out.

"I'm hanging by a thread, and I'm clinging to a dream," sings Keith, as his fingers move from the D minor to an A minor chord. "That from inside this dumpster is a path out of here."

He moves through the verse, with images of entrapment - trapped not by pain and fear but by the chains of love and loyalty, honor and devotion.

As he goes through the pre-chorus, Keith's pick begins to hit the strings harder, in staccato. It gives the song urgency and drama, lifting the emotion for the major key resolution, and its payoff of familial ties and communal spirit, the reward of giving of yourself in the best cause of all - for the good of another.

"My mother she will always guide me, and my father lifts me up. They ride beside and inside me, one in my heart, one in this flowered cup. Don't need to chase for freedom, for free I'll always be, wrapped in these loving arms, my family, friends, and me."

As he sings, Keith opens his eyes. His audience has grown, and heads nod the beat. Their faces are animated with emotion as rear projectors in their heads play personal movies from each person's past on the inside. They are captive to the story he tells and the message he brings.

Some of the faces look at Keith, some at the ground,

while others stare off into space. But whether their eyes are on him or lost somewhere else, he realizes they are all looking to him. Their faces search for a lifeline, a warm embrace, an empathetic shoulder to lean on. They search for hope, and to his surprise, they seem to find a little of what they seek in his simple song.

But they don't receive it from him. The songs come from someplace else, like little radio waves riding through the dense cosmos until they strike the antenna, which receives and amplifies them. He is only that lucky antenna, resonating invisible good vibrations to all who can hear.

I am the DJ. I am what I play.

He is writing someone else's story in these songs, but it is inescapable that their truth resonates for him as well. Does that make sense? He isn't sure.

What makes sense is when he sees the look on Aki's face as he realizes the song is his story. The eyes are open wide, as recognition ignites, then understanding, and finally—release. Keith can see Aki let go of something buried deep inside him, letting that something go spinning out and away into the universe.

Until now, Aki had covered that something with a smile of indifference and quiet, humble acceptance. Now that it is gone, a hole remains in its place. A hole that Keith somehow understands will be filled with something new, something not yet fully formed, a thing in its infancy. But a thing of beauty.

Music has the power, Keith affirms to himself. And thank God, I've got the music in me.

"Man, that was great!" exclaims Kitch as they walk down the street, unable to contain his excitement. "Great songs, man. I really liked that last one. That's a damn hit!"

"Kitch said a bad word, Mommy!" cries Emmy, who has woken tired and cranky.

"I'm sorry, Emmy, my bad!" He turns to Carolyn, but she silently shakes her head and mouths "don't worry."

"Kitch just made a mistake, honey," she says as she runs her hand across Emmy's head. "What do we do when people make a mistake but apologize?"

"We forgive them!" says Emmy firmly. She turns to Kitch. "I forgive you, Kitch."

"It really was great, Brian." Carolyn adds, "Your songs really ... affected me."

Keith can feel the effect too, but he's not sure what it is. Something has shifted in him.

"Thank you all. You gave me some tough love, and it really helped." Keith smiles. "For the first time, I'm starting to get an idea ... an idea of who I am. Who I really am, I mean."

Ben slaps Keith's shoulder and gives him a knowing smile. "Hold on to that feeling, little brother. You're gonna need it."

"It's a long trek back to Hollywood," says Harold, "and the kids are going to crash pretty quick here,"

"Yeah, let's put a move on it!" shouts Aki. He gives Keith a quick smile.

Keith walks with a new spring in his step. The world really is starting to make sense, he thinks. I'm waking up, coming to my senses. Like I know what's real and what's not. No more surprises, nothing to throw me off my course.

As they pass a trashcan on the side of the street, Keith notices a bright yellow kite sticking out of it. Its tail hangs over the side of the can, dangling to the ground below.

Enzo would love that, thinks Keith. "Enzo, I think—"

But when he looks up, he realizes that he has fallen behind the group. They are half a block ahead of him, at the next corner. So he reaches into the trashcan and pulls the yellow kite out, happy to see it is in perfect condition, hardly a crease on it.

I'll take Enzo out to fly it tomorrow. I loved kites when I was a kid, but dad didn't have ... Wait, what's that?

There is something familiar looking about a piece of paper in the trashcan that catches his eye. He shoves his hand down into the can, excited at what he may find next. But the garbage in the trashcan begins to shift as his hand moves, and the shiny paper slides down further.

Keith chuckles as he continues reaching down,

amused at the new zest he finds in pursuit of a goal. Past the Slurpee cup goes his hand, and underneath a sticky, empty food container. It's tricky.

The trashcan begins to tilt over, on the verge of spilling. Before it falls, Keith snags the paper between his fingers and pulls it from the trash with one swift move. Keith brings the last bit of the paper up with the flourish of a magician.

He laughs at his latest feat. Things really are looking up, he thinks. Even the trash container can't stain me.

He looks at the paper - it's a glossy beer ad with the picture of a bearded man and a beautiful girl on his shoulder. I don't even drink beer, he laughs, wondering what was so familiar about this. He notices some liquid spilling down the page, so he flips it over quickly to drop it back into the trash.

And then he stops laughing.

Keith stares at the picture on the other side, and as he does, the firmness of the ground beneath him, and the certainty of everything around him, disappears in one lightning-fast shift. His world is turned over, and his brain hangs upside down.

Because there, on the glossy paper in his hand, is the cover of the *Rolling Stone*. And under the sensational title, "He's hip. He's hot. He's sexy. And he's dead!" is a full cover, extreme close-up picture of a pouting, clean-shaved Keith Unger.

"You can read up on everything in here. If you read. If not, the pictures are nice."

Harry is slouched into a chair, part of a mock living room TV set. Behind him is a massive picture of Keith wearing a black leather jack and no shirt.

Crojon, the Empty V host, seated next to Harry, holds up a copy of *Rolling Stone* magazine with Keith's face on the cover. Crojon's curly dark hair is cropped short on the sides, rising to a proto-fro on top. His face is young, in its 20's, and its slow ease betrays an adolescence spent in the 420.

Next to him, Harry looks like Father Time. But even in his rumpled, graying state, Harry carries a certain cool which is born of knowing who he is, what he is, and how that fits into the world of things.

"Lots of pictures of Candy Lamour, too. And, they talked to this man right here, Mr. Harry Chukstein, Keith's manager."

Harry solemnly offers a Hindu salutation with clasped hands and a bowing head.

"What it doesn't have is the big news that me and Harry are gonna throw your way, right Harry?"

"You are correct, sir."

"You wanna tell them?"

"Well, Crojon, first of all, it's a pleasure to join you and your minions. The Empty V, Massive Records, and our humble selves at Chukstein Global Domination and Management are happy to announce a day in celebration of the life of our very own Keith Unger. He missed his 27th birthday, but we're going to throw it back at him, and we want you, the world, to join us in this very first Keith Day!"

"At the Killer Klub, where Keith played his last show."

"The same," continues Harry. "We'll have all the usual foolishness, including a performance by Candy Lamour and some celebrity appearances. Come show your Keith love, and enjoy the really gigantic birthday cake."

Harry leans into the camera and winks. "I have it on sources that it'll be spiked."

"And if you're not lucky enough to score one of the very limited number of tickets for the club," says Crojon, "we'll be televising the whole thing live here on the Empty V."

Crojon turns, looking over his shoulder into another camera. "Be there!"

The red light on the camera goes off as they cut to a commercial. Crojon looks to Harry.

"How'd I do? This whole VJ thing is kinda new for me. It's like I'm in a time machine."

"You did fine," says Harry, patting him on the back. "Everything old comes back again. Especially the crap."

Harry's cell phone rings as he walks off the set. He looks at the caller ID, then answers.

"Yes, Brad?"

"Nearly 5 million units of the latest sold in just two weeks! A goddamn EP!"

"I know," says Harry, as he leans on a table and opens a magazine that lays in front of him.

"Jesus." Brad whistles solemnly to himself. "That's more than Taylor Swift. Taylor goddamn Swift! Incredible."

"And he's dead."

"I need more! Much more! We can't let this die now that he's resurrected ... It's a resurrection, right?"

"Why not."

"I need more product. People want more songs!"

Harry nonchalantly flips through the magazine's pages and stops at the photo of a female pop star. Her lips are pouting, breasts pressed together like inflated bread rolls straight out of the oven. The ad reads, 'Babydoll! Get her now'.

"Well, Brad, as the old saying goes, I told you so."

Even over the phone, Harry can see visions of sales charts dancing through Brad's head.

"How about an EP for Christmas? Or some Buddhist shit? The guy's even selling in China! Damn, that internet is everywhere."

"I've got the guys laying down backing tracks to the kid's demos," says Harry as he sets the magazine down. "But it's a pond with a limited number of fish, Brad. You dig? So, we conserve what we have and find creative ways of packaging it."

"Well, think about it."

"Okay. Look, I gotta go, I have a meeting. But don't forget the Candy single. Big push on that. It's good, I'm telling you. She'll stream like crazy."

Harry looks again at the picture of Babydoll, then tears it out and pockets it.

12. I AM THE COSMOS?

Innocent sleep, the sleep which soothes away all worries and puts to rest each day, healing the hurting mind. Keith could get none of that kind of sleep the entire night.

His thoughts were wrestling until dawn, with no conclusive winner. Last night was the stuff of his dreams. The appreciation of the people who'd heard his songs, the deep gratitude in their eyes when they approached him afterward – that should have kept him up in delirious joy.

Instead, it was that magazine cover that kept him awake.

For most of the night, he wasn't even sure it was real. Whenever doubt reached fever pitch, he pulled the glossy paper out from under his shirt and re-examined it.

But each time he looked, there it was – his face looking back at him from the cover of the magazine. He'd sure checked enough times.

I'm a big rock star on the cover of the *Rolling Stone*,

he thinks, battling down the urge to buy five copies, and give one to his mother. She likely already had one anyway or didn't care. I have fans, he thinks, and hits! No matter how hard he tries, he just can't get that reality to sink into his head.

Once the sun is up, he looks around to make sure no one else in the camp is awake. He knows what he has to do. Quietly he climbs out of the sleeping bag.

"Going somewhere?"

Keith turns to see Ben lying on top of his sleeping bag, eyes closed.

"I'm just … going for …"

Keith tries to think of a good lie, but his mind is too confused and tired to assist. He decides to go with the truth, slightly modulated.

"Last night … I just need to be on my own, try to process it all."

"Yeah. Some things take processing."

"Good show, man!"

Keith turns and sees Aki wrapped up in a blanket, looking up at him from the ground with a smile and thumbs up.

With determination, Keith walks through the Hollywood morning, his feet beating the path.

Finally, he comes to a familiar corner. He stops and looks across at the perpendicular street, where he finds what he is looking for: A maroon awning hangs over racks filled with magazines, the words "World News" are emblazoned on it in white.

Keith walks up to the stand, and his eyes quickly scan across to the music section. Then they stop. It is not a dream, or a fantasy, or even a sign that he is losing his mind. Because there on the magazine stand, Keith finds an exact replica of the glossy picture, which is folded up inside his shirt.

Beside the *Rolling Stone* are the British music magazines – *Mojo*, *Uncut*, *Q*, *NME* – all with his picture, in varying sizes, adorning their covers as well. And it's not just the music world that's tuned in to Keith – *People*, *In Touch*, *National Enquirer*.

I'm everywhere, thinks Keith.

Keith's mind is rotating entirely off its axis, spinning like an unhinged top. His hand lifts from his body of its own volition and moves up towards the *Rolling Stone* to grasp it and observe it more intimately. His fingers reach for the magazine, and —

"Hey!"

Keith looks to his left. A tall, burly, solid framed man, whose colossal biceps are armored in tattoo sleeves, stares down at him. The look on his face does not invite confrontation but rather serious discretion.

"You can look, but you better not touch, boy. Unless you got the money to pay for it."

Keith slowly leans back, pulls in the hand which was hovering over the *Rolling Stone*, and pushes it deep into his pants pocket. There he finds his remaining panhandling profits – four dollars and 27 cents in change. The employee continues to stare, as do the other two customers at the stand.

Keith looks at the magazine and tries to imagine a solution to his dilemma, one in which he is reading the magazine, digesting the magic answers within, while avoiding any sort of physical debasement.

Once his options are clear, he turns and starts walking again. He has quite a distance to go.

His feet are numb, and morning has lost its bloom by the time he has the Grove in his sights. Tucked behind the old CBS studios in Hollywood, the Grove occupies land once inhabited by a dairy farm. The vast warren of stores and restaurants inside are styled to look like a town. It is no longer inhabited by cows, but the owners still suck plenty of milk out of it. Nowadays, the milk is green.

Keith walks through the streets of this fake city until he stands in front of the three-story bookstore, a remnant of a dying breed and a vanishing culture. He hurries through the doors and rushes across the ground floor, walking right up to the newsstand.

Shoppers make way for him and his scent as he scans the magazine rack. His efforts are quickly rewarded because there, prominently displayed, is the *Rolling Stone* with him on the cover.

Slowly, Keith reaches out his hand and picks up the

magazine, handling it like a spiritual relic. He takes its measure by sight, feels its weight in his hands, affirming its realness. Its glossy pages part like a paper sea. They open agreeably to another photo of Keith, in black and white, accompanied by words that mark the beginning of his serialized story.

Keith holds the magazine open before his face as he turns and walks like a man possessed to the escalator. He rides to the top floor, where the café resides. En route, he absorbs the details of his death, learns new facts about his childhood as he navigates his way to a seat in the cafe, all without looking up.

Along the way, he is oblivious to the faces that turn in his direction as he passes them. His intense gaze, along with his degraded outward appearance, gives him a slightly deranged and, at least, potentially dangerous look, which causes those he passes to give him a wide berth. He doesn't acknowledge their existence.

The baristas take note of him with some concern. People at the tables near his get up and find more distant places to sit.

Keith has eyes for only his own face and the largely fictionalized story that accompanies it. He doesn't even the cafe manager at the cash register checking him out.

Gently turning the magazine pages, fearful of folding them, Keith begins the slow process of piecing together answers to some of the questions raging inside his head. But it's all too much to comprehend, too overwhelming. It feels as though his head will explode.

"Did you want anything to drink?"

Keith looks up to see the cafe manager above him. Keith's bearded face, wild hair falling all over it, and his crazy piercing eyes spook the manager to his core. He is already a slight guy, who looks as if he could be blown over with a hairdryer, and the sight of this mentally crumbling homeless man causes him to roll back on his heels.

"Why?" asks Keith, staring at the manager blankly, with eyes whose story is open to interpretation.

"Nothing. No reason," says the manager, choosing to read a horror novel in those eyes. "Just checking. Enjoy your magazine." And he walks briskly back to the cafe bar, where the barista asks what happened.

"He's cool. I got it all sorted."

Faces are looking at Keith from the other tables. They turn away when he looks in their direction. He hears someone whisper, 'needs a bath', so Keith sniffs under his arms. Smells normal.

Keith looks back at the magazine with a clear understanding that he must have it. In the upper right-hand corner, the price reads $8.99. He reaches into his pockets and pulls out the change he found there earlier. Counting tax, he estimates that he needs five more dollars.

Seated two tables behind him is a man in his early

20s, dressed in exercise shorts and a tee shirt. The man sits alone, reading a book, laughing, and enjoying an M&M cookie with great relish. Dollar bills and change sit on the table, right in front of him.

Keith rises from his chair and stumbles over to the man's table. Tired from his long walk, he decides to sit down opposite the startled man. He looks him directly in the eyes.

"I need money."

The man stops chewing. He quietly lays his hand over the money on the table and slowly begins pulling it towards him.

"I don't have any money."

Keith looks down at the hand moving away from him and hears the sound of metal sliding across the table. Small pieces of a ten and a one-dollar bill stick out from under the man's hand, and they hold Keith's attention.

"I just need five dollars."

The young man quickly slides the money across the remaining distance to his body, off the table, and then pockets it. He rises quickly.

"Sorry. Don't have any."

With that, the young man quickly turns and hurries away, stopping once near the escalator to look back at the cookie he left lying on the table in front of Keith. He considers for a moment but decides against it and then begins descending the escalator.

That didn't go well, thinks Keith, as he takes a bite

of the M&M cookie. Maybe I shouldn't sit. It might be impolite. He turns and looks at two girls in their teens, who are seated two tables away. He gets up to walk to them, but with his first step, his pant leg gets caught on the chair, and he stumbles, falling in the direction of the girls. He catches himself at the last moment, with his hands on the edge of their table. His body is hunched over, and his face hovers right between the girls.

One girl, whose dark brown bangs accentuate her sharp-ridged Gallic nose, quickly pushes herself back from the table. She looks incredulously at the spit's worth of her double-double chocolatey chip frappuccino, made with whole milk and whipped cream, that has spilled onto the table.

"You moron! Do you have any idea how hard it is to get those idiots to make this thing the way I like it?" She looks at Keith with frightening venom. "This was the third one, and they finally got it right. Now you better get your ass over there and buy me another one, right now! You hear me?"

Keith is frightened. "I don't have any money."

"Now, doesn't that just figure. So who's going to pay for it? Huh?"

The other girl holds her nose in disgust.

"Gross! You stink! Take a bath, freak."

The two girls get up and walk to the cafe bar to summon the manager.

"I want another double-double chocolatey chip

frappuccino, with whole milk and whipped cream. For free," says the girl from Gaul, with a healthy dose of gall. "That homeless freak you let in here spilled mine. Now make me a new one! And get my friend one too, just for the inconvenience."

The manager apologizes profusely and says he will take care of Keith as soon as he makes sure their drinks are done to perfection, knowing full well he has no intention of doing anything about Keith.

"Young man."

Keith turns. He sees an older woman with dark skin and grey hair, wearing an Indian sari with a knit jacket over the top. She is seated at a table against the wooden rail that separates the cafe from the rest of bookstore. Her brown eyes are soft and wide, cheekbones ride high, and her dimples border a gentle smile. She curls her finger slowly, indicating for Keith to come and sit in the chair opposite her.

He walks over but keeps his distance so as not to alarm her. She smiles angelically at him and motions to the chair. Keith sits.

"Do you need money?" she asks in a whisper as she leans towards him.

"Yes, ma'am. I need five dollars to buy this magazine."

The lady squints at the magazine without recognizing Keith and nods her head. "It's a lovely magazine."

She pulls her purse strap off the chair back, places the purse on the table, and opens it. From inside, she takes a black plastic pocketbook and slides out a green bill. She softly uncurls Keith's clenched fingers, places the bill into his palm, and closes his fingers around it.

"I'm happy you read. Reading will open a new world for you, and you will see yourself in a different light, as a greater person."

She lifts herself up, puts her purse strap across her shoulder, and pats Keith's hand.

"Good luck, young man, Be brave."

The lady turns and walks slowly out of the cafe, leaving Keith stunned in silence. He opens his hand to see a twenty-dollar bill resting comfortably inside his palm.

Cover of the *Rolling Stone*, and twenty dollars, he thinks. Things are definitely looking up.

13. FAME

Scott: This is "Weekend Edition" from *NPR News*, and I'm Scott Simon. It is perhaps the most significant popular culture event in recent memory. You need not be an aficionado of the once-popular form of music known as rock and roll to appreciate the extraordinary set of events that have unfolded since the untimely death of one young man nearly a month ago.

We are, of course, talking about Keith Unger, the young musician from the Los Angeles area who abruptly ended his life on a lonely stretch of the Pacific Coast Highway north of Los Angeles, in the beach community of Malibu.

But that story in itself, while tragic, would have slipped past our attention without much notice were it not for what followed. Because in the weeks since his death, Mr. Unger, and his music, have stormed the gates of the public consciousness and the registers of commerce. So much so that his music has now become instantly ubiquitous.

Among the many unknowns in this story, one critical question remains: Is the music of Keith Unger any good? Has Mr. Unger's success been a product of his tragic story, or is it based on something more genuine, perhaps talent? Joining me today are two respected music journalists ideally suited for this completely subjective examination.

A contributing editor to Rolling Stone for over 30 years, Anthony DeCurtis is also the author of numerous books, perhaps most pertinent today being *Present Tense: Rock and Roll and Culture*. Welcome, Anthony.

Anthony: It's a pleasure, Scott.

Scott: Anthony joins us from New York. And with us from my hometown of Chicago is Greg Kot, music critic for the *Chicago Tribune* since 1990, where he has reported on all aspects of music from its social and political impact, to the often Byzantine flavor of its business dealings. Welcome to our show, Greg.

Greg: Great to be here, Scott.

Scott: Gentlemen, here we have a strange set of circumstances. We have a young man, a musician, whose utter lack of success causes him to take his own life. Subsequently, the fame that had eluded him is suddenly his, but he is unable to enjoy it. Ironic?

Anthony: Ironic, yes. Keith Unger also happened to die on his 27th birthday. That is the age that some people have called the Death Club of rock and roll.

Scott: Because so many musicians died at that age?

Anthony: Yes, a very long list – Amy Winehouse, Robert Johnson, Kurt Cobain, Janis Joplin, Jimi Hendrix, and more. In general, death has a habit of stalking rock musicians, regardless of age, but 27 seems to hold particular interest for the Grim Reaper.

Scott: Does Keith Unger register in the future in the same way as the artists you mention? It is understood, of course, that you do not have a crystal ball.

Anthony (laughs): If only! You know, it is remarkable, in this music economy, for any artist to sell this many records – I think his first EP is approaching or has surpassed 5 million copies sold. That is a lot of CDs bought in a time when no one buys them. It's hard to predict the future, but it seems inevitable this will be a story that will be remembered going forward. If for nothing other than the surprise of it – no one saw this coming.

Scott: Greg? Do you have your crystal ball with you?

Greg: Anthony has mine. We should tell anyone listening that if you're looking for answers – we don't have them.

Scott: Do you have any answers on his music, the quality? Is the music of Keith Unger worthy of the attention it is receiving?

Greg: Well, a lot of music that is unworthy of attention sure gets a lot of it, so that's probably not the paradigm to view this through. I like to say that music is our most immediate art form. Music is us talking to ourselves, and from that perspective, there's quite a conversation going on. You can't ignore the fact that some nerve has been touched because people are really responding to it – the music and the story. And maybe they inform each other.

Scott: So, can we separate his music from the manner of his death? Can we ascertain its quality? Anthony?

Anthony: I don't think that's a straightforward question. It clearly has meant something to the people who listen to it, as Greg said. Something in these songs is resonating. They are also responding very much to his death. I think the idea of an artist who takes his own life has a certain unfortunate romance to it. The lonely artist carrying his banner into the economic battlefield, doomed from the start ... it's a romantic, appealing figure. I mean, you know, he clearly meant something as an artist. Just exactly what he meant may take the fullness of time to resolve.

Scott: Greg, I've scanned some of the lyrics, certainly the first single – "I Wanna Be Rad" – there is a stunning lack of depth there. Am I wrong?

Greg: You definitely won't be the first one to say that, Scott. That's been the biggest complaint of those criticizing his work. Others would argue that some of the most impactful music of the last half-century hasn't had any of the lyrical depth of a Shakespeare sonnet. But if you hold Keith Unger's work up against, say, "Eleanor Rigby," "Waterloo Sunset," anything by Dylan - it is clearly lacking. And its musical structure isn't–much removed from three chords - which in rock and roll is actually high praise.

Scott: And yet this deceased young artist is selling better than the top acts of the day.

Greg: It's incredible, really. The minders of Keith's music have been pretty shrewd in their strategy - I don't know if it's Massive, his label, or Harry Chukstein, his manager. They've also attached a couple of songs to commercials, which has helped to proliferate them internationally.

Scott: Anthony, Keith's girlfriend, Candy Lamour, has released a song, a very catchy song, which has garnered considerable attention, and I believe it is selling almost as well as Unger's music.

Anthony: Yes, the song is a tribute to Keith called "I'll Remember You." It's just starting its sales route, but it's quite a good song, better than the Keith Unger material. So while the sales can in part be attributed to the Unger story, it certainly stands on its own merits.

Scott: There are rumors, I understand, that she did not write this song. The rumors are that it was, in fact, written by Keith Unger. Any thoughts?

Anthony: I think that rumor may be sexist. Judging by this one song, it does seem she is capable of writing quite a good song. Until we have some more definitive proof, I would be inclined to accept her word on its authorship.

Scott: Let me bring into our conversation another colleague from my hometown of Chicago, Chris

Morris. Chris is a long-time writer for *Billboard*, author of several books. A former Cub fan, he now roots for his current hometown team, the Dodgers. Welcome, Chris.

Chris: Great to be with you, Scott. But to clarify, I still root for the Cubs. I'm just a little gun shy after having my heart broken for so many years.

Scott: Point taken. So let me ask–you - the music of Keith Unger - good or not good?

Chris: Scott, I come here not to defend Keith Unger, but to bury him. Frankly, to my ears, his music is crap. There is nothing in it to sustain any kind of durable interest. It's shallow, and the single is absolutely silly. I'll gladly go where my esteemed colleagues feared to tread.

Scott: Well, you certainly cut through the fog there. No durable interest? Are we sure we can gauge the totality of his legacy just yet?

Chris: Great bands are inventive, creative, and courageous. Keith Unger is none of those. He is repetitive, redundant, and boring. Now, there may be more material that we haven't heard that's better, he may be like Jimi Hendrix and have an endless half-life of archived material, but at least Jimi was famous when he died at 27. Unger had to die to achieve fame.

Scott: It sounds like you think the evidence for a verdict has already been presented?

Chris: Well, certainly based upon the evidence that has been presented, he is guilty of crimes against art.

I don't think they have anything to change that perception.

Scott: What say you, Greg - is there more fuel in the Unger tank, or is it empty?

Greg: Well, that's the million-dollar question. They've been really cagey about slow releasing the material. Which is really smart, I think. So, there's no way of knowing what's to come. We'll have to wait and see.

Scott: Anthony?

Anthony: It seems hard to imagine a strategy that would prioritize the worst material to be released first, as Chris said. In these events, it's generally the scraps that are left on the table. But we just don't know.

Scott: And that seems to be an excellent spot to end this segment, wondering what will be next in the unexpected odyssey of Keith Unger. I want to thank all three of you for your time and insight.

14. BOY WITH A PROBLEM

Keith doesn't feel well. He stands in the middle of the sidewalk, uncertain where to go or what to do. The last part isn't unusual. Candy or Harry usually told him what to do.

So, what should I do?

"Hi, there!"

Keith turns to see Jane smiling and waving. Unwittingly he has stopped directly in front of the Coffee a Go-Go.

"I didn't know we had a real rock star in our midst. Why didn't you say something?"

Keith is stunned.

"You know?"

"It's the talk of the street!"

"Well, I didn't ... I didn't know either. I just found out yesterday. Crazy, huh?"

"It sure is! Some people might not have guessed, but I knew something special was lurking under that hair."

Keith's hand moves self-consciously to his beard.

"When did you find out?"

"This morning. Ben told me."

Keith's jaw drops. "Ben knows?"

"Well, of course, silly. He was there. He told me all about it this morning. I have my sources on the street," she laughs. "Brian Rock! He said people loved your songs. I didn't know you play music. It must be exciting having all those people listening to what you created."

Keith exhales as he realizes Jane is talking about the songs he played at Sunset Junction.

Jane turns and looks at the T.V. "Just don't end up like that poor guy."

On the screen is the same face that graces the cover of millions of copies of *Rolling Stone*. The rock-style hair and the baby-smooth skin of his face accentuate the pouting of his lips, giving him the look of a male model.

"Sad," says Jane, as she goes behind the counter. "Why would you give up your whole life? Your only life. It's a gift."

"Maybe his dreams were out of reach, and he couldn't go on."

"Most dreams don't happen like you think they will. Poor thing must have been a really lost soul."

"I was."

"What?" she turns back to Keith.

Keith recovers quickly. "Yeah, he must have been."

"There are lifesavers for lost souls. You just have to

find the lifesaver meant for you." Jane looks into Keith's face and smiles.

"What are you up to today? Finding new places to play your songs?"

Keith laughs. "I think this act may be a limited edition."

"Oh, don't say that. If it's your dream - make it happen! My dad says that hard work always wins. You have to face the obstructions head-on. When in doubt, go to the source of the problem, and face it down."

Source of the problem, thinks Keith. Face it down? Of course! That's what the moment calls for - action!

The woozy feeling in his head is replaced by clarity. And determination. He's made his decision.

"I'm sorry, I have to go. I just remembered something I have to do."

And without another word, Keith turns and walks away, leaving Jane a little baffled.

What a funny boy, thinks Jane, as she watches him walk briskly westwards down the street, hands clenched into fists.

Across the street, another pair of hands holds a phone. On the phone's screen are pictures of Keith and Jane. The photographer smiles before following Keith's path, keeping a safe distance between them.

I've got you now, thinks the head behind the hands.

"It's an incredible story about the theft of water from the central valley of our state, on a scale we could not imagine." Vondy delivers her words with the assured confidence and gravity of a veteran reporter at the top of her game.

"Information I've uncovered implicates not only the commissioner and the governor, but numerous corporate interests as well."

"That is so fascinating."

Ellen DeGeneres sits cross-legged in her chair, leaning forward, completely engrossed.

"I hope that doesn't mean my Jacuzzi is going to get shut off!"

Funky music kicks in, and Ellen is up and out of her chair, swinging her hips in time to the beat with enough comedic aplomb to have the audience shaking their booties and laughing with her.

The music stops, and Ellen slips back down into her seat. She pulls on the collar of her sweater, worn on top of a shirt, whose tails hang over her khakis.

"So, this Keith thing ... it's really getting crazy, right? We have a clip we can show."

The video clip Ellen plays shows young Keith fans gathered outside his apartment. One girl explains: "He said he was here with us. Always." A girl with fat bangs cries as she remembers seeing Keith: "He said use your eyes, and you can see." A young man with glasses smiles broadly: "He's not dead, man." A broader shot of a large crowd of Keith fans appears, and they chant: "Keith lives! Keith lives!"

The clip ends, and Ellen looks over at Vondy, who sits uncomfortably next to her.

"Can you tell us anything new," asks Ellen, leaning in conspiratorially. "Just between you and me – what's going on with that girlfriend of his, Candy? She may not be sweet, but she sure can stick to a story like super glue."

The audience crackles with laughter. Vondy's smile hides deep annoyance.

"And is he really back from the dead? This resurrection thing is so ... Biblical. I hope he doesn't smell like a mummy!"

Ellen makes a face like she's just done something bad, and the audience rewards her with howls.

"Well, it seems a little farfetched, but as you can see, many people believe it," explains Vondy, shifting forward in her seat. "If I could just add that Mono Lake is now nearly dry, and parts of the Central Valley are actually sinking as water is depleted from deep inside the earth. L.A. will run out of water much sooner than anticipated."

"Not before Keith runs out of hit songs!" Music again starts up, and Ellen is out of her chair. She makes a couple of moves, then sits down. "That Candy's got a single coming out. Have you heard it?"

Ellen looks at Vondy, whose face is frozen in place, caught in a Keith maze with no exit.

Crojon looks into the camera. He is seated on a soft red couch in what appears to be a small living room. The wall behind him is covered in photos and posters: White Album era Beatles against a white background; Kendrick Lamar with his arms held up high, bathed in bright blue stage light; Jack White leaning on a maroon 1961 National Reso-Phonic guitar; the vastness of Beyoncé's back end.

"With a lot of great moments in rock and roll, you don't even know they're coming until they're gone." Crojon is appropriately pensive for the gravity of the moment. "But not tonight. For the first time anywhere, the debut of the new video from Candy Lamour, a song she wrote in tribute to her man, Keith Unger. Backing her is Keith's band, the Hunger. It's heavy, y'all."

Crojon bows his head briefly, out of respect for the memory of Keith, and to check his script. The Empty V logo spreads across the screen and Crojon's face.

"People, it's the new queen of rock, Candy Lamour!"

Crojon and the logo fade, replaced by a picture of Keith, with his birth and death years in text. This is then replaced by a new image: a rough and distressed-looking drawing of a red heart. It is battered and bruised, with an arrow sticking through it. Then the heart image comes to life and begins beating.

The sound of rushing wind comes in, rising in volume. It is accompanied by random distorted guitar notes, and finally, a big guitar chord strummed straight through. As the resonating, reverb-drenched chord washes over everything, a soft staccato-picked guitar power chord creeps in.

The heart image on screen morphs into a human head. The head is bent forward, a mass of tangled, gnarled blonde hair. It slowly lifts to reveal Candy, with her now trademark gash of bright red lipstick strategically smeared from one corner of her mouth to the other. She wears heavy dark eyeliner, also lightly smeared, blending into her dark eye shadow.

"Time will go away and finally disappear," Candy sings directly into the camera, without blinking. "And all that's left behind is one lonely tear. I don't have a crystal ball, just a crystal maze, built on a memory that time won't erase."

The screen widens to show Sly, Rami, Juice, and a New Guy who mans a keyboard.

Candy stands center screen in second-hand store dress, a light breeze blowing through it. Her thin legs extend below the ragged hemline of her dress, and her feet are strapped into high-heeled shoes that make her look like she's standing on her toes. Already a tall girl, Candy towers like Gulliver above her Lilliputian band. The sense of danger is palpable when she hits the pre-chorus with a snarl.

"So take these words, and hold them close, cause this I swear ..."

The power of the band is undeniable as they come

crashing into their instruments on the downstroke for the big chorus hook. And you can hate her all you want, but Candy is an undeniable, natural-born star.

"I'll remember you, I'll remember you. I'll remember whispers in the night, and yeah, I'll remember you. I'll remember you."

Spare and straightforward, the song is an irresistible slice of power pop pie. Its juicy, empty-calorie chorus circles around and around like a hungry Great White Shark. It tears away pieces of your brain as it burrows itself deep inside that special place reserved for the sounds and refrains that will echo and repeat in your head on an endless loop, regardless of your commands to the contrary.

And as millions of air guitars swing in empty space, in bedrooms and living rooms, in cars and bars, all across the country, there is inside the minds of kids throughout America a new revolution brewing, its power as old as Chuck Berry and Jerry Lee Lewis, and its new anthem screams from their collective lips at full throttle: "I'll remember you, yeah I'll remember you."

The power of a big, fat pop song is undeniable, and it's not going away. Not now, not ever.

15. LEARNING THE GAME

Keith presses down firmly on the buzzer. His body is alive with the electricity of anticipation. Source of the problem, face it down, he repeats to himself.

This is where it all started. Face it, erase it. He presses the buzzer again.

Finally, the door opens.

"Alright, alright already. Just put the pizza on the counter."

Harry turns and walks back into the apartment without even looking up. Dressed in only a long tail shirt, boxer shorts, and black socks, Harry rummages through the pockets of his slacks, which lie draped over the chair at the counter. He pulls out a wallet, then fingers through the bills.

"You're late, so don't even complain about the tip! I can't afford to pay for—"

Harry turns, holding out a five-dollar bill, and for the first time, he looks at Keith's face. Somehow, through the matted hair, the growing beard, and the ratty, dirty clothes, Harry Chukstein actually recognizes Keith as Keith. Instantly.

"Holy shit," he whispers.

Harry's face is frozen in disbelief, eyes dropping in concert with the left side of his lip, hand suspended in mid-air, five-dollar bill dangling from it. He leans back against the counter for support.

"I hope this isn't some kind of Christmas Carol thing, 'cause I'm Jewish."

Then he abruptly turns on his heels, rushes into the living room, and pulls a bottle of Grey Goose vodka from the little built-in bar. He quickly pours himself a half glass of liquor. He looks over at Keith, then impulsively pours more vodka.

With one lift of the hand and a long gulping swallow, he empties the contents into his throat. Keith is still there. Harry pours another glass and walks to the couch. But he reconsiders, turns back to the bar, where he picks up the Grey Goose bottle and carries it to the couch with him.

"Do you disappear with the second glass? Or the third?"

"Hi, Harry." Keith raises his hand and gives Harry a little wave.

Harry swallows the remainder of the second glass, holds his hand over his chest for a moment, then pours another.

"Ghost of the past or the present? Must be past. Okay, you got my attention. I don't need any time trips or psychedelic effects. I've done plenty of acid. Just tell me what I need to change, and I'll change it now. Because this shit is freaking me out."

"It's me, Harry. I'm not a ghost."

Keith offers up his arm as proof. Harry reaches out his hand, and with great trepidation, touches Keith's arm like it's a dead rat. He recoils at the touch. Rather than calm him, the firmness of Keith's arm panics him even more.

"Oh my God, you're undead. It's *True Blood* in real life."

Harry quickly pours more vodka into the glass, then downs it.

"Harry! I'm not dead." Keith grabs Harry's drink and quickly takes a gulp. He instantly starts to cough the liquor up.

"See? I'm human, I'm alive," he chokes out.

"How in the hell is this possible? You jumped off a damn cliff. Into the ocean. And now you show up on my door, without any seaweed, and you say you're alive? No. People don't survive that. So you better explain it."

Harry sits down on the couch.

"I can't explain," says Keith, standing in front of his former manager. "I don't remember what happened. All I remember is falling, then crawling up on the beach in Santa Monica. Nothing in between. It's a mystery to me, too."

"You floated around the ocean this whole time?"

Harry asks incredulously.

"No, I didn't wash up today. It was the day I fell in. I washed up on the beach that day, but I ... I just wasn't right, in the head, you know? So I've been living on the streets ever since, sleeping in a park, panhandling for, I don't know, a long time. But I'm not dead!"

Harry nods as he slurps more vodka.

"So, if that's true," he says suspiciously, "and I'm not saying it is, why now? Why wait five weeks? Done enjoying your vacation on the Skid Row Riviera?"

Keith begins to sit on the couch.

"NO!"

Harry leaps up and grabs Keith before he makes contact with the couch's fabric. He runs to the kitchen, grabs a towel, and covers one section of the sofa. He then guides Keith down onto the towel.

"Because of *this*." Keith pulls the folded *Rolling Stone* magazine from inside his pants and opens it in front of Harry.

"I saw this last night, and it - it freaked me out."

"Yeah, I get the whole freaking out thing," says Harry. He reaches out quickly and pinches Keith's arm.

"Ouch! Dammit, Harry, that hurts!"

Harry's eyes widen, his mouth opens as if to speak, but no words come out.

"It's me! I swear it's me. I'm alive. Jeez. I'm as freaked out as you are. Don't do this to me, Harry."

"It really is you." Harry slumps back onto the couch.

"Yes, it's me. And I'm famous! I can't believe it!

How did you do it? How did you get the story to blow up like that?"

Harry's ego trumps his shock.

"Well, it wasn't easy. It took a lot of my time and talent, I might add, with no help from you. Well, you did make the demos. And you died, that helped. But selling a dead artist is no walk in the park, man, let me tell you. But I did it."

"You did!"

"You're the biggest goddamn star going right now. You're outselling everybody. You outsold Taylor Swift's new—"

"Taylor Swift??"

"Hell, yeah," says Harry with a laugh. "I told you I was good. We're selling everything, records, streams, tee shirts. The bad news is we're running out of songs. When they're gone—"

"I'll write more,"

"—we're gonna be shit up the creek because if you don't have any new product—"

Harry stops. His eyes narrow as he leans into Keith.

"Wait? What did you just say?"

"I'll write more."

"You'll write more. Hold on, you could write more. You could even record them!"

Harry's eyes now open wide. Any doubts he had about Keith's current form evaporate as quickly as the new money-making ideas begin forming dollar signs in his head.

"I've got tons of new material. I wrote a lot the last couple of weeks, good stuff, my best. You just have to book some studio time."

"Yeah, we'll ... No, no, I can set you up to record here, with your computer." Harry's mind is fully engaged. He stands and begins moving around as he thinks. "I'll have to come up with a new story, maybe how you came to me in a dream with more demos or—"

"Why a new story? Tell the truth, I'm alive. That's a great story. Right?"

"Well, yeah, it's a good story, but ... you know, I mean, right now we have a sure thing. People are into Dead Keith. That's a big part of the appeal. You're dead."

"I've been living on the streets for a long time, Harry," says Keith. "And I'm tired of it. I want my life back."

"Of course you do." Harry puts his finger to Keith's lips to stop him from speaking. "But if you show up alive now, it'll kill the story, the money dries up. Your suicide is the goose that laid the golden egg. You're worth more dead now than you are alive."

"I won't be part of some scam about me being resurrected, Harry!" Keith is firm on this.

"Scam? What scam? We're selling hope. We're giving the people what they want. That's not a scam."

"It's not?"

"No, it's perfect! Give them what they want. We get what we deserve."

Keith looks dubious.

"We just need to get some more songs out, amp up the sales. Then we find you in some shit-stained, flea-bitten tent, covered in blankets. And we still have the Keith Day coming up, and ..."

"Keith Day?"

"Oh yeah," Harry smiles with pride, "a little something I cooked up. It's a worldwide celebration of your 27th birthday - the club's newest member. You know, all the dead guys. I'll introduce some new songs then, perfect marketing platform!"

"Perfect time to announce I'm alive?"

"Yeah, yeah, that too." Harry's feet pace a path around the condo. "I have to get your gear."

"I can sleep in your spare room."

"No! You can't sleep here. Reporters are snooping around here all the time."

"What's the difference if I'm recording here or sleeping here?"

"Stop confusing things! Can't you see I'm creating a plan?" Harry goes to an Indian teak end table against the wall under the intercom. He opens the drawer and digs through the mess inside. "There!" He pulls out two loose keys.

"This is for the back entrance, through the garage. And this one is for my door."

Harry ties the keys together with a paper clip, then hands them to Keith.

"I'll have your stuff over here tomorrow. You can

start working then. I can stay in Brad's beach house at Broad Beach up in Malibu."

"And on Keith Day, you announce I'm alive?" Keith presses him.

"Yeah ... what? Oh, yeah, whatever."

"No! On Keith Day, I get to be alive again, right Harry?"

"Okay, okay."

Harry reaches into his pocket, pulls out two $20 bills, and hands them magnanimously to Keith.

"There'll be plenty more where this came from, pal." Harry rubs his hands together in anticipation. "It's just the beginning."

"When I touched Keith, I was healed."

Vondy nods her head. "Is that so?"

"Before that night, my face was, like, covered in zits and stuff. Acne, you know? And since then - nothing. I've been cleansed."

Vondy's red lips part slightly in an expression of amazement. She notes the moon craters that push against the surface of the teenage girl's thick white pancake make-up.

The girl holds her fingers up in a peace sign and looks into the camera. "Keith lives!"

Vondy turns back into the camera. "So you can see Jenny, the Keith Nation takes this resurrection pretty seriously."

Jenny Chen, the Morning Show anchor, is watching Vondy's image on a large screen behind her as Vondy delivers a live report.

"That is wild. Have there been other people 'healed' by Keith?" asks Jenny.

"Yes, there have," replies Vondy. "One girl claims she had insomnia. Now she sleeps all the time. She fell asleep while I was interviewing her. And one young man told me before Keith touched him, he could not drink coffee without a lot of cream. He only drinks it black now."

"I couldn't do that," says Jenny. "Could you do that?" She turns to her co-host Brett who is seated next to her.

"No way," he shakes his head, traumatized by the thought.

"Okay, thanks, Vondy! Keith Day is only a few days away. We'll see you there!" Jenny's face scrunches into a super cute smile.

On the screen, people crowd in on Vondy, raised fingers in the peace signs, as they begin to chant: "Keith lives! Keith lives! Keith lives!"

In the studio, Jenny is shaking her head as they cut from the live feed with Vondy.

"Wow. Just wow. Right, Joe?" She turns to her other co-host, who shakes his blonde hair.

"Yeah, wow. Big wow!"

Vondy waits in the passenger seat as Skip finishes packing his camera gear.

"Where next, boss?" he says as he plops into the driver's seat.

"Can't be hell because I'm already there," growls Vondy, with an expression of abject misery on her face. "Let's get something to eat."

"In-N-Out?" asks Skip.

Vondy picks up the Washington Post lying on the dash. It's her favorite daily reading. But it's bittersweet because it also reminds her of the stories she could be covering. If she had a real news job.

As she scans the front page, Vondy's eye hits on a drawing right in the middle of the page. Someone has drawn a clock face with a black sharpie. An arrow extends from the clock, pointing right, indicating the page should be turned.

"Did you do this?" Vondy says, holding the paper up for Skip to see.

He glances at it. "Not me, boss. I'd never touch your Post."

Vondy furiously follows the direction of randomly placed arrows, cursing the entire way, until they stop on her favorite page - the horoscope. There, in the middle of the page, blotting out her own Leo sign, and scrawled with the same black Sharpie, is a tantalizing message:

"I know the truth about Keith. 990-757-7625."

"Wow," says Enzo, taking in the scene.

Keith, Ben, Kitch, Harold, Carolyn, and her kids, are seated in a temple. It is an ornate and beautiful space. The pews lead up on both sides of a center aisle to an altar at the front. The screens above the altar, as well as the tables and chairs and almost everything else, are carved from wood and covered in gold flake.

"You disappear for weeks, then you show up again, out of nowhere, and troop us all downtown – what up, dude?" Kitch has his eyes fixed on Aki, who stands before the group in the aisle.

"You did not explain to your friends, Akihiro?"

A man in black Buddhist robes, decorated with intricate, white circular designs, stands behind them. Aki introduces Bishop Horyu Abukara. The Bishop solemnly bows his balding, grey head. His demeanor is one of modesty and calm.

"The Bishop has been attached to this temple for over 30 years," explains Aki. "He was my dad's best friend since they were kids in Osaka."

"Hiro, very naughty boy," the Bishop says sternly, then laughs. "I joke, he was a lovely boy, like Akihiro." He smiles warmly at Aki and puts his arm over the younger man's shoulder. "You have told your friends the meaning of your name?" he asks.

"No, I haven't," blushes Aki.

"Bright prince!" exclaims the Bishop.

"Little darker in the dumpster," laughs Kitch.

"Yeah, I've given that pastime up," smiles Aki.

"And to answer the question – I didn't disappear. I got a job."

A moment of stunned silence is followed by a million questions.

"It's a simple job," says Aki. "I'm doing some accounting work in the Valley. I ran into an old co-worker who I'd helped out of a jam once, and he hooked me up. I've been sleeping on his couch. Now—" He turns to the urn behind him. "Well, I saved enough money to get my mom and dad back together."

"Your gonna have a funeral?" asks Harold.

"Aki already have a funeral for mother," explains the Bishop. "We perform memorial service only for her and father. Their ashes will be combined, together for eternity."

The friends look to Aki, who only nods, his taut face restraining his emotions.

"Aw, that is so beautiful, Aki," whispers Carolyn.

A large gong rings through the temple announcing the ceremony's start, and the Bishop begins chanting. The sound of his voice rings through the hall. Incense is lit and offered. It's all a mystery to the circle of friends, but it feels like a fitting way to reach someone in the void that lies beyond death.

Once the service is completed, the Bishop carefully places the urn containing the ashes of both of Aki's parents in a special place on the altar.

Afterward, the group finds their way to a small tea shop in Japantown and sits outside at a table. Everyone wants to know about Aki's makeover.

"It's because of Brian," he says.

Keith is surprised. "Me? What did I do?"

"Your song," says Aki. "That song you wrote about me. It made me think a lot. And the more I thought, the more I saw myself differently. It really stuck inside me. So when I ran into my friend, and he made the job offer, well, I knew. Sometimes one path ends, and another begins. You just have to be ready. I was ready."

Keith is moved by Aki's words, touched that his song has had such an impact. And he's a little bit proud of himself as well.

He watches Enzo and Emmy play a game of tag along the sidewalk. Carolyn sits next to him. She is quiet, her thoughts elsewhere.

"They're so good," Keith says, nodding at the children.

"Oh, yeah. Kids are resilient. They don't let things bog them down. Not like we do." Carolyn shakes her mood off with a laugh. "They just take what is and move on. I guess they haven't learned any better yet."

Keith's hand is in his pocket. He feels the still crisp $20 bills Harry gave him. He pulls one out, looks at it, and then holds it out to Carolyn.

"Maybe Enzo and Emmy would like a movie. Or a museum."

Carolyn hesitates. "Wow, that's a lot of money. I couldn't—"

"Go on. I won't have as much fun with it as they will," Keith says, smiling. He sets the bill on Carolyn's lap, then quickly walks away.

The minor seventh chord wafts over the ledge, between the rails, and drifts down into the hills. Soul searching and humbling, the beautiful chord penetrates deep, working its way into empty pockets of the hills and those within its player.

Keith looks out over the vast, endless sprawl of Los Angeles, poured out like concrete across the landscape below his feet. With its haze of pollutants, the air is like dirty water in a cluttered fishbowl. So many people, so many stories. As he plays, Keith thinks about the events of the day, about Aki and his parents, Carolyn and her kids. Both have their history.

Seated here on a low, white brick wall at the Griffith Observatory, guitar in his hands, pen and tiny notebook lying next to him, Keith tries to make sense of history.

"Like a landslide falling on my head, I couldn't see through the iron and the twisted lead," he sings, the words coming out of the chords, given form by his thoughts. He nods his head, pleased with the words he's found. But where does it go from there?

Candy had been everything for him. Now he hardly

ever thought of her. He did think about his mother. Lennon he thought about a lot, and each time the pain hit him hard. It was a pain of hunger and loss – hunger for things that matter the most, lost in a shattered looking-glass past.

I had to lose what really mattered, to find my soul beating but battered. Healing doesn't come from jars of ointment, it comes from touch and love that's potent.

He quickly picks up the pen and scribbles the words in a rush, just as they come to him. He reads them as another image appears.

So bring on the big parades, and fly the banners high.

It is already inside him, waiting to take form. Once the last drops have spilled out onto the pages, he closes the notebook, puts it into his pocket, and slings the guitar over his shoulder, across his back.

The afternoon sun is sinking as Keith begins walking in its direction. He takes a bus through tourist meccas and shopping streets, past working girls and Harley riders. He decamps and walks until he finds himself in a gilded neighborhood with large stone houses and fortress walls. His steps finally lead him to that one familiar house, which is not his home.

Keith looks at the house as the sun goes down. The lights in front automatically come to life. He walks up to the tall cypress trees along the house's right side, finds the well-worn space between trees four and five, and the low part of the wall that has served so often as an escape but now paves his way for entry. He jumps over the wall, hits the ground, and walks to the rear of the house.

There he finds his way along the back wall to the one room with a light on. The den, he remembers. He approaches the window slowly, making no sound, avoiding the spots that turn on the exterior lights. He kneels down at the window and rests his chin on the pane.

Somehow Keith knew where he'd find him.

All around Keith, it is dark. On the couch, with her back to him, is a woman bathed in the light of a TV.

A head pops up from a prone position on the couch and turns in the direction of the window. Lennon drops down off the couch and walks over to the window.

Keith presses his face against the glass pane. His breath creates a fog around his nose and mouth. Lennon jumps up, his paws on the windowsill, and looks out through the glass. His tail wags furiously as he sniffs the window. The dog licks the glass, his groaning and squealing getting louder. Keith presses his cheek against the window, silently taking kisses through the glass, reveling in them.

The woman finally hears the commotion at the window and turns in their direction.

"What's the matter, Lennon? Is something out there?"

Rising from the couch, she slowly walks to the window, where Lennon is howling in joy. She puts her head next to his. He excitedly licks her face, then looks back outside.

"What's out there that's got you so excited? A cat?" She peers out the window, past the last smears of Keith's nose and mouth on the other side of the pane.

"I don't see anything."

For a long while, she stays with Lennon, looking out the window into the dark, as the unseen Keith climbs the wall, moves between the trees, steps onto the street, and starts to walk back towards his new world and his other life.

Shrinking into the long gray overcoat he found on a bus stop bench, Keith slowly walks up to the side of Harry's building. He quietly slips through the door leading into the garage, then takes the elevator up.

Harry's apartment is empty. Keith finds a little table set up facing a wall. His computer, headphones, and the little box that translates signals from his guitar into his laptop are on the table. Next to the desk are a Silvertone bass, a portable keyboard, his black Strat, and the Orange amp. A microphone on a mic stand sits to the other side.

Keith quickly settles in, puts the headphones on, and begins searching through pre-set drum patterns and loops on the drum machine. Hearing and feeling the rhythm is a familiar sensation. It helps focus him.

Strumming the chords of "Downsizing on the

Corporate Ladder," Keith listens for a beat to make the right pairing. Once found, it's like a seat belt clicking into place. Keith Unger is back in business.

The following two days take the same pattern: He wakes late in the morning, walks to Coffee a Go-Go, and gets a coffee and a scone. The best part is the surprise on Jane's face when he pays cash. Then he goes to Harry's flat to work.

The work is good. In fact, it's very good. In two days, Keith has completed seven entirely professional sounding demos, recorded and ready to go. They include all the songs he has written for his homeless friends.

What drives him is the knowledge that on Keith Day, he will be liberated. That thought is never far from his consciousness, and it colors everything. There is so much he wants to do and one wrong he desperately wants to the right.

Keith knows the songs are good, better than the drivel he'd written before. In fact, he is embarrassed by the music that made him famous. He wants to show people who he really is – an artist with something to say. He can already hear the loud acclaim from fans and critics.

"What is this crap?"

Harry barely makes it through the second chorus of "Corporate Ladder" before rising.

"Miserable tale of pathetic losers who quit on the

world because they got some little setback? Who do you think is going to listen to this depressing shit?"

"Well, there are a lot of people who—"

"No one!" Harry interrupts.

"These are people on the margins of society, who—"

"Hey, I vote Democrat, straight down the line, in every election. I give plenty of money to help these losers. But people don't listen to music to get depressed."

"This is me, Harry," objects Keith. "This is what I feel, what I'm experiencing."

Harry takes a deep breath and tries a different tack. "Look, we need these songs for tomorrow. We need a couple of songs to reveal, and they have to sound like your old stuff. After that, you can—"

"No!" Keith slams his first hard into the wall in front of him. He screams. The pain causes him to spin around and bounce in place.

"It's not going to work," he says through the pain.

"Really?" says Harry. "How are you so sure? How about some Pop-Tarts? That always starts my creative engines."

Harry starts walking towards the kitchen.

"Harry! Do you hear me?" Keith's voice rises with frustration. "I don't work like that anymore. I have to write about something real, something I feel, not something fake. Like Lennon, not McCartney."

Harry spins around and stares at Keith. His face instantly turns deadly serious as he fixes Keith with a disapproving glare.

"Is that so? Because you know McCartney was the real innovator, the real avant-gardist. McCartney loves a challenge, lives for experimenting. He could write a song on a matchbox. So maybe you're not McCartney, 'cause that's real talent! And don't diss Paul McCartney or John Lennon in my house. Ever."

Keith is caught off guard. He slowly turns and walks back to the recording table, where he sits and stares at the computer screen.

"I'm sorry. I didn't mean that. I love McCartney, too."

"Damn right! You should pray to him like a patron saint."

Keith nods. On some level, he does understand that the songs may not be commercial. "I don't want to sell out, Harry, I'm done ... "

"Sell out? Who's talking about selling out?" Harry sits down, and nods his head. "You got new songs? Great. But you have to remember – the dollar comes first. It's the tree; everything else is just a branch. Fertilize the tree."

"But Harry," protests Keith, "I have to be true to my—"

"You like your picture on the cover of magazines? Sure you do. It's nice – lots of people looking at it, especially girls. You need people to listen when you release these new songs. Big picture." Harry forms a frame with his hands. "We can put out your protest songs—"

"They're not protest songs—"

"Whatever. Folk songs, yip yap songs We are at a very delicate moment here. Okay? Write one true sentence, one true and *simple* sentence that is not depressing, and go from there. Just not this true. Or this depressing." Harry points at the computer.

Keith is confused. He's not quite sure what's expected of him or how to deliver it.

"Okay. Now back to work. Let's get some mindless, simple pop songs going."

"Simple songs," says Keith.

"And mindless. With a beat."

It really seems like a pretty straightforward thing: Write simple songs. His old songs were based on a hooky melody, a driving beat, and simple lyrics. That was a much easier formula than the more complex melodies and lyrics he's been writing lately. One is 2+2, the other a complex algebraic equation. So what's the problem with writing simple songs?

The problem, Keith finds, is that one is math and the other is art. And the math isn't adding up. Turns out simple songs can be harder to write than complex ones.

Even if his old songs were not complicated, they were still a cousin of art. Maybe a distant cousin, but still in the family tree. And the trick of creating art is a lot like catching lightning in a bottle - you have to avoid getting blown up. This assignment seems to be exploding all over the place. And he's only got until tomorrow.

But after some time, he comes to a new realization: maybe writing simple songs actually is a lot like doing math.

Keith never studied or understood songwriting - or math for that matter. It was something he just did. When song ideas came to him, he just wrote them down.

But now, he pays attention to songs he likes. Which songs begin with a chorus or an instrumental hook? Which start on the root chord, or something more adventurous, like a diminished 7th? If the opening is x, what is the most exciting y?

Harry's massive collection of old CDs becomes Keith's research library. He notes the structure of different songs, and the mystery of creation begins to make more sense to him. The secret door is less mysterious now that he has a key.

He applies the same work to his own songs, and the work starts to pay off. Soon, he has a new batch of songs that sound much more like his old songs, but they aren't the same. They're better.

16. SHE'S GOT SPIES

Vondy rolls down the window and blows smoke out of her mouth. She scans the parking garage, noting that it is not nearly as nice or new as the one a couple blocks away at Hollywood Highland.

She keeps telling herself she is done with this idiotic story, that she is moving on to a new life, a new vista. But then, like Al Pacino in Godfather III, it sucks her back in. Her transport out of morning news obscurity has officially become her personal ball and chain.

A figure is coming out of the stairwell doors. Vondy sits up and pays attention. It's a man, and he's wearing a sports coat, tie, and dress slacks. Could that be him? The man keeps walking, carrying a briefcase close to his legs, without looking up from the ground. Not him.

Her Prius is purring so softly that only the lights on the dash remind her it's still running. She hits the off button.

Wish I could hit an off button on Keith Unger, she thinks. How did I ever get tangled up in this loser's dead-end life? Then she remembers, ruefully, that she chose the story.

Vondy wasn't surprised when she got the note written in her *Washington Post*. Even though it did make reading the article on China's rapidly expanding Pacific fleet a few degrees more difficult. Nothing about this story surprised her anymore. But that weirdo who answered at the inscribed phone number - what a crackpot.

Still, he did seem to know some specific details that were not public knowledge. But did he know that Keith Unger was resurrected?

Just then, Vondy sees a shadowy figure hiding behind one of the garage pylons. It is hard to see who it is. It appears to be a male, wearing a trench coat, a dirty white Sufi headdress, and oversized sunglasses. The figure emerges slightly from behind the pylon and motions for her to come closer.

Vondy climbs out of her car and walks carefully towards him. When she gets within twenty feet, he raises his hand for her to stop.

"Good afternoon, Ms. Wells." His voice is higher and more unsteady than it was on the phone.

"Hello, Mister ...?"

"You can call me the Voice," he answers.

"Like the TV show? Is that still on the air?"

"Yes. I mean, no, it's off the air. Those bastards,

they don't know a thing about programming." The Voice is agitated. He takes a deep breath. "And no, I'm not from the show. You can just call me the Voice. It's like an alias."

"Okay, Voice," says Vondy in a calm tone. "So, you say you have information on Keith Unger?"

"I have information that will blow this story sky-high, little lady."

I wish I could get a better look at him, thinks Vondy. Hidden as he is, next to the pylon, his face mostly obscured by shadow, the only thing that stands out is the white tee shirt under his trench coat. The Sufi headdress is unraveling, falling into his face and part of the way down his back. But that voice is familiar.

"You're a Keith fan."

"What makes you say that?" he replies, clearly startled.

Vondy points at his chest. The Voice looks down at his "Feed the Hunger" tee shirt and smiles.

"Wow, that's really smart. No wonder you're famous." He realizes he has dropped his mysterious persona, so he quickly regains it. "I have information."

"I'm all ears." Vondy folds her arms and stands patiently in front of him.

"Keith Unger ... is alive!"

He says this as if it's the big reveal on a daytime soap opera, full of drama. But his revelation hangs in the air between them like a stuffed piñata.

"So they say."

"Someone told you?" the Voice says, surprised.

"Haven't you been watching the news?"

"Not that. I don't mean he's come back from the dead." The Voice leans in for maximum effect. "I mean, he was never dead in the first place! The whole thing is a hoax. They faked it, and left really devoted, loyal, long-suffering fans, who had committed everything to him, sacrificed their time and lives for him, just left them out in the dark!"

Vondy's interest is now piqued. The resurrection stories are clearly crazy, she thinks, but it is obvious that something happened. Why else would so many people have the same story?

"What do you know?"

"I saw him with my own two eyes. He was walking down the street. Well, he was running first, but then walking. With his accomplice."

"His accomplice?"

"Yeah, this really gigantic black guy."

"Where did you see him?"

"In Hollywood."

"And why did they fake his death?"

"Well ..." The Voice knots his fingers up and unconsciously starts pulling on them. "I'm still working on that. I don't want to say until I can confirm it. Oh, you have to promise not to reveal me as your source."

"I don't even know who you are."

The sound of Abba singing, "Dancing Queen, young

and sweet, only seventeen," suddenly rings and echoes through the garage.

The Voice fumbles in his pockets and pulls out a mobile phone, answering just as the second round of Abba is beginning.

"Yeah, mom ... I know, I said I wasn't going to be home ... mom, I'm kinda busy, I'll be home in a little ... I don't know ... I know you do ... Yes, I can ... I can so say it ..."

The Voice turns his back to Vondy, then mumbles in a low voice, "I love you. Goodbye."

He hangs up the phone and turns back around to Vondy, embarrassed.

"Where was I? Oh, yeah, I'll have the info by Keith Day. Okay, I'll see you then."

The Voice turns to leave.

"Whoa, hold on a minute here." Vondy pulls his shoulder and turns him around. "You tell me you have crazy info, you want me to put my reputation on the line for you, but I have to wait to get that information. Uh-uh, I need some sort of proof."

"Like what?"

"Something tangible, something that gives me some confidence in you."

"That's not possible."

"Okay, fine." Vondy turns and starts to leave

"Wait! I'll have proof for you. Tomorrow."

Vondy scribbles her cell number onto a card, turns, and hands it to him.

"Call me!"

The Voice takes the card, stares at it. Then he looks up at Vondy.

"Okay. Nice meeting you. I thought you were great on Fox & Friends, by the way. Though I hate Fox. Fascists!"

"Don't I know you?" Vondy tries looking at him closely. The light is terrible in the garage.

The Voice turns and walks away quickly, making sure to stay in the shadow of the pylons.

"John Lennon was right," he calls out over his shoulder.

When he reaches the end of the pylon's shadow, the Voice stops and hesitates while seeking another shadow to follow, then jumps to it. He continues like this until he slowly disappears from view.

Vondy watches and wonders out loud again. "How the hell did I—oh, yeah."

Jane is so wholly absorbed in her task that she doesn't even notice the new customer. She jumps when his hand touches her shoulder.

"Sorry," says Keith sheepishly. "I didn't mean to scare you." He sits next to her.

"Oh, no, it's okay." Jane catches her breath. She points to her books on the table. "I'm done! Well, not yet - I have final exams this week. Then I'm done!"

"Congratulations!" Keith reaches in to give her a

hug, and she responds. But they both feel a little awkward once they start the hug. Since they've committed, they follow through with it. But they stay engaged in the hug for an eternal second or two longer than they should.

"I'm sure you'll do great," says Keith, a little embarrassed after they separate.

"Thank you."

An image on the TV catches her eye. It shows a big crowd gathered outside of Keith's old apartment building, The Garden. Jane frowns.

"I don't even listen to that kind of music, and I still feel sorry for him."

Keith looks up at the TV screen, then at Jane. "You feel sorry for him?"

"No, not sorry. Maybe guilty. He was here that night, and ... oh, it's just my weakness. I want to save the world - one coffee at a time. Did you want a scone?"

"No, thank you." Keith rises. "I've got work to do. Us homeless people are always busy."

"You know, you don't have to stay homeless. Not judging, just saying."

"I know, find another path." Keith smiles. "I'm working on it."

"Good!"

Keith hesitates, then he reaches in and hugs her again. This time with more feeling and less awkwardness. They look at each other, tacitly acknowledging both the ground shifting beneath them and their uncertainty over how to navigate that shift.

The store phone rings. Startled, Jane jumps to answer it. Her mood shifts dramatically. When she hangs up, she grabs Keith by the arm and leads him through the back of the shop.

"My boss is a block away. He's furious at me because Kitch was in here the other day. Simon thinks I'm giving away food to the homeless." She smiles. "Which I am."

Keith turns to say something, but before he can, Jane kisses him quickly, then pushes him out the back door.

Once he's out, Jane leans against the closed door and sighs. Then she rushes back to the store.

On the other side of that door, Keith unconsciously brings his hand to his lips as he turns and begins walking. He's walking on air now and whistling a new tune.

A caterpillar must shed its skin to evolve, so it can release the hidden butterfly within. Sometimes it's the same for dead rock stars in Hollywood.

Danny stands across the street from the coffee shop. He's been waiting there since he saw Keith walk in. He watches the shop nervously, concerned.

It's been nearly an hour. What could he be doing in there? What part does the coffee shop play in this whole scheme?

One man comes and goes from the shop. It isn't Keith. Then a couple, who he didn't see enter, exit. Finally, an older man dressed in hipster threads goes in. He doesn't leave either. Danny decides that to get to the bottom of it, he needs to have a closer look. He walks across the street.

Peering through the shop window, blocking the sun's glare with his hand, Danny sees no one inside other than the waitress. She is sitting at a table, writing in a notebook. He goes to the door and enters as Jane looks up at him.

"Hi! Sit anywhere you like."

A man suddenly appears at a door behind the counter. He is the older faux hipster Danny saw enter earlier. The man is balding, in his late 40's, shirttails hanging out over the top of his jeans, expensive sneakers on his feet.

The man holds a handful of receipts and eyes Danny suspiciously. A couple of receipts slip from his hands, and Danny bends to pick them up.

"What do you want?" the man asks.

A trick question, thinks Danny. Be careful how you answer.

"Coffee?"

"You have money?" the man asks, grabbing the papers out of Danny's hand.

He's testing me. Act normal. Watch your step, Wallburger.

"Yes, sir. I have on my person five dollars,

American. I do not believe in handouts or freebies. Every person should be responsible for themselves."

The man looks at him hard for a moment, then slowly begins to nod.

"Good. Keep it that way."

The man turns to Jane.

"Remember what I said - no loitering, no feeding bums. Don't waste my money!"

Some kind of code, thinks Danny.

The man turns and walks out of the shop.

I passed the test, sighs Danny. That was close but necessary. Because I was testing him too, developing my own theory.

Danny looks around the shop, confirming again that it's empty. One employee, a white girl. Not even a Mexican dishwasher or cook. Where could Keith be, he wonders? He hasn't exited, so he must be in here somewhere.

"Can I use your restroom?" asks Danny, looking towards the door behind the counter.

Jane looks at this odd guy, long, curly blonde hair and black-framed glasses. He makes her uncomfortable with his nervous, jittery hands and those furtive, restless eyes.

"I'm sorry, the bathroom is for employees only."

Ah-ha, 'employees', Danny nods to himself. That must be what they call themselves. She's hiding something. Who's back there? Is it Keith?

Danny thinks on his feet. He needs to know for

sure. It's time to act fast, do the unexpected. Without warning, but with great speed, he darts towards the backroom door. Before Jane can stop him, he is through it.

"Hey! What are you doing?" Jane screams in alarm.

Danny looks around the back room fast, taking it all in. There is a lot of stuff, but no Keith. It's all orderly and neat, he thinks, just as I expected. There are three doors, two on one side and one at the back. He opens one side door - it's a storage room, not enough space for a person to enter into, let alone hide. He opens the other door - an empty bathroom.

Oh, my God, he thinks, is it possible? This is bigger than I thought.

"Get out! Do you hear me? I called the police. They'll be here any second."

Jane stands in front of him, holding a baseball bat at the end of her thin arms. She is nervous, but she isn't showing it.

I can't let them catch me, thinks Danny. I have to tell the reporter lady before it's too late. I'm the last hope. He eyes Jane, who's holding the bat and blocking the doorway.

Only one way out. She's just a girl, for Pete's sake. What can she do?

Without warning, Danny rushes at Jane as she backs towards the doorway. She squeals, but she doesn't collapse. Instead, Jane twists her body to the side and winds up the bat. When she swings, it's with all her might, and it's no *girl* swing. It's a solid, Little League swing that lands hard on Danny's arm as he runs past her.

Danny doesn't stop. He spins around and keeps running, barreling right out through the door and into the street. He turns and screams at her through the door. "I know! I know!" And he keeps running.

Jane falls back against the door. Her breathing is hard, and her mind is racing. When she lifts her hands, she can see that they are shaking. What the hell was that all about?

Out on the street, Danny runs, turns a corner, and runs to the next corner, where he turns again. He looks over his shoulder and sees no one is coming, so he slows down and tries to look inconspicuous.

He massages his arm, which is already starting to throb. Damn, they're strong—even the little ones.

Now it's all starting to make sense. How could he have missed it? The obsession with money, self-reliance, a small group of fellow travelers, interchangeable people, white and bland. Well, there was that black man.

The more he thinks, the more trouble he senses. The secret back 'room' in the coffee shop, where they meet, a place no one can hear them or know their names. The room Keith enters, but doesn't leave, because—

Danny runs into a solid wall that knocks him off his

feet. He looks up from the sidewalk to see that the wall is a person. He jumps up.

"Hey, watch where you're—"

But he quickly realizes the person is very tall and very intimidating.

"Even his superfan, whom he trusted and drank coffee with, has lifted his heel against him." Ben looks down on Danny soberly, his eyes piercing him to the core.

Danny slowly rises, inching backward as he does, cowering under Ben's shadow.

"He betrayed his fans, man. That's not cool! He lied. He lied to me!"

"Woe on you, Danny Wallburger." Ben raises his hand, and Danny closes his eyes, expecting to be struck. When the blow doesn't come, he opens his eyes to find the black man has disappeared.

17. THE MONEYGOROUND

"It is a stunning scene, not to mention quite a shock to residents of this Hollywood neighborhood."

Vondy turns to look at the crowd behind her gathered in front of The Garden. It resembles a fat, disorganized conga line comprised mainly of young people.

A short, older man walks out through the front doors of the Garden and raises his hands for quiet. It is Mr. Krajchik.

"We have the building owner getting ready to speak, Chris. Let's hear what he has to say." Vondy turns with her microphone towards Krajchik, who once again raises his hands. The crowd quiets.

"Thank you. We start in few minute. My son Igor," Krajchik gestures to a young man who stands to his left. This young man appears to be around 18 years old, has short-cropped blonde hair, and wears gold aviator sunglasses and a dour expression.

"Only four peoples in one time. Please not to touch.

We have tee shirt for sale."

Igor holds up a tee shirt with Keith's pouting picture on it and text that reads: *Living like Keith.*

"You wait, we make ticket for you. Thank you."

Mr. Krajchik turns and walks into the building while Igor stands, enjoying the attention. Krajchik reaches through the door, grabs Igor by the collar, and pulls him into the building.

"So there you have it, Chris and Alicia," says Vondy, as she turns back into the camera. "The first tours of Keith Unger's former apartment. Couple that with the news today that the Killer Klub will be offering daytime tours, and it's clear that the business of Keith Unger continues to grow."

"Any other tours coming up, Vondy?"

Alicia Villanueva, a co-host on the *Morning Show* in L.A., is seated in her chair on the show's set, looking into the camera while feigning interest. She is pretty, with smooth tan skin and blond highlight streaks through straight brown hair.

"Well, anything is possible, Alicia," says Vondy. "Keith Unger, and his brief life, are generating interest on the level of music titans like Jim Morrison and Taylor Swift. We'll just have to stay tuned."

"Thank you, Vondy," says Alicia with a smile. "You've owned this story since the beginning."

But in her mind, Vondy hears Alicia say different words. "Thanks a lot, loser. Keep running around in your broken-ass van while I enjoy the luxury of the studio, like the superior talent I am. Where the hell is makeup?"

Vondy is furious, and when the light on Skip's camera goes out, she spits violently onto the sidewalk.

"Puta!"

Leaning against the van, Vondy pulls out a cigarette and lights it. She slips on her sunglasses as one of the Keith fans approaches. He too wears sunglasses, and a baseball cap pulled down tight over his brow, crazy hair spilling out the sides.

"Reporter lady," he says. Vondy turns her back to him, hoping he'll sink back into the sidewalk.

"It's me, reporter lady!"

I know that voice, Vondy thinks. She turns.

"Voice?" Vondy quickly remembers her surroundings and begins to whisper. "What are you doing here?"

"I was following Keith."

"He's here?" asks Vondy, quickly scanning the sidewalk.

"No, I lost him. I don't know where he went." Danny leans into her, looking spooked. "But that black guy is here."

"I need proof, Voice, or we're going no further," says Vondy.

Danny smiles and holds up his phone. Vondy grabs it out of his hands.

Vondy looks at the picture on the screen. She spreads her fingers on the phone's screen, and as the photo enlarges, so do her eyes. The image is a little fuzzy, the light is dim, and a beard covers a large part of the man's face. But side by side with an old picture of him, those eyes, that nose, that face – Keith will be recognizable.

Vondy's excitement grows as she flips through the pictures.

"Yes, yes, yes! These are good, very good." She slaps Danny on the shoulder. "Email them to me. I'll have my cameraman print them. But use my private email – Vondy the anchor girl at Gmail dot com."

"Vondy the anchor girl," says Danny, tapping away on his phone. "Okay, sent."

Vondy's mind is working furiously. A conspiracy. Explosive. Real news, not celebrity death crap. This is a scam of the highest order, possibly initiated by individuals linked to a powerful corporation, set on defrauding millions of dollars from consumers.

Delicious. But when to reveal?

"This is gonna ruin that Keith Day thing," Danny smirks.

Keith Day? Of course! Perfect, Vondy thinks. I can just see the coverage. I'll be everywhere again, but this time with real news. That anchor is mine! Actually, I don't even know if I want the anchor anymore. Times are changing. I might want my own cable show.

She turns to Danny smiling.

"So who's the girl?" Vondy looks at him, waiting.

"I can't tell you now. A few more details to work out."

"Damn it! You know I'm putting myself on a limb for this?" Vondy collects herself. He's been dependable so far. "Okay, don't let me down. And I'll keep my promise – you'll only be known by your alias."

"No!" exclaims Danny. "I don't want to keep it a secret!"

"I thought—"

"Everyone will hate the superfan when the truth comes out. They'll think I'm part of the scam. I want to be remembered as the guy who told the truth. You and me, truth-tellers."

"Whatever," Vondy shrugs.

"You can interview me at Keith Day. Call me the Voice, but use my real name too. You want to rehearse?"

"No. Just find me at the event. I'll leave you tickets—"

"I have a ticket. From the band."

"From the band? You get around Voice. Okay. Then just find my cameraman Skip. He always knows where I am. Oh, and Voice—"

"Yeah?"

"Ditch the shirt."

Danny looks down at his "Feed the Hunger" tee shirt.

"Well, fine then Bernie, maybe it is his building, and maybe he does have every right to give tours of it if he wants to. But I'm watching him on T.V. right now, and he's selling tee shirts with a picture of Keith Unger on them, and he doesn't have permission from me to do that! And since I control all revenues accrued from the use of the likeness of said Keith Unger, I'm telling him to stop now!"

Harry pulls the phone from his mouth and yells into it like he has a bad connection with Estonia.

"Or I want my damn money!"

Phone back to his mouth, Harry now quietly and calmly answers his lawyer on the other end.

"Thank you. That would be lovely. Ta-ta."

Harry hangs up the phone and places it on the nightstand. He switches channels on the T.V., looking for a new perspective.

The bedroom of Candy's new apartment has that "just moved in" look. There is little furniture other than the bed and no wall decorations of any sort. Several unopened boxes are scattered around the room. Harry's clothes lie across the back of a stuffed chair, and his briefcase is on the floor next to it. Candy's clothes are everywhere.

"Damn leeches sucking my blood! Don't mess with Harry Chukstein!"

The bed rustles as the body next to him rises. Harry gives the naked ass now in front of him a good swat.

"Ow! Cut it out, Harry, that hurt!"

Candy turns and gives him the finger. He takes the opportunity to admire her long, lean body, smooth legs going on for what seems like miles.

"Can't you get a seek and resist or something, stop

the tours?" she says as she hops off the bed and goes into the toilet.

"Why would I do that? It's free publicity! I just want my cut."

Harry can hear the long stream of Candy's pee.

"How much did you drink last night?"

"More than you. Shit, I'm out of toilet paper."

"Important thing to remember when you move into a new apartment. By the way, I like it."

"Hell of a lot better than that dump in Hollywood. Goddamn, homeless freaks kept me up all night."

Candy comes back into the room, grabs some underwear off the floor, and wipes her crotch. She stretches, lazily reaching to the ceiling. Morning light slips through the crack in the window shade, falling on her body. She climbs back onto the bed and then on top of Harry, covering his body lengthwise with hers.

"Be careful. This is like flipping the 'on' switch," Harry purrs.

Candy starts to move lightly, up and down his body, kissing him around his ears.

"Ignition has begun. Houston, I believe we have lift off," Harry mumbles, then he flips Candy over. She giggles.

"When are you going to ignite me, Harry?"

"I don't remember any complaints last night."

"I mean my career, I need another song. One hit doesn't make a career."

"We'll get to it," moans Harry, who is now getting to it in his own way. "You'll get tons of new exposure at the Keith Day tomorrow. In the meantime, I've got to work the Keith angle."

Candy pushes Harry off of her and springs up in the bed.

"Keith, Keith, Keith! I'm tired of that asshole. He's dead. Get over it, world. I gave you a great song, a big hit, and now I want another. If you can't get it for me, I'll find someone who will."

Candy rolls her legs over the side of the bed, her back to Harry. Unseen by him, her face shows no anger, only mathematical calculation.

"Well, that's not exactly true. Is it?" Harry's voice is calm and relaxed.

"What do you mean?" Candy says warily.

Harry rises from the bed and walks to his black briefcase, which sits next to the chair.

"I mean, you didn't exactly 'give' me a song. You sort of borrowed it. Didn't you? From Keith?"

"Are you calling me a liar?" Candy explodes, jumping off the bed. She takes two large steps towards Harry, but Harry doesn't shrink.

"Yes, I am. Not that I care. Lying for profit is good business."

"Don't throw that internet BS at me. Trolls are just jealous of a woman doing what they can't. They don't have any proof for their stupid lies!"

"Yeah, but I do." Harry holds up a computer hard

drive.

Candy looks at it suspiciously, uncertain.

"What's that?"

"Well, as guardian of Keith Unger's recorded output, I've gone through every song demo he left behind to document what I can sell. And it's kind of funny – while digging around, I found a demo for a song called "I Remember You," written by Keith, all instruments by Keith, and dated four months ago, by Keith. Same song you rode to number 2."

"Maybe he stole it from me," Candy replies with feigned conviction.

"He might have," nods Harry. "But then why would he include a spoken word intro explaining he wrote it for you and that he was giving it to you. But then, you already knew that. Didn't you?"

Candy fumes. "So?"

"So nothing. The kid never copyrighted it, but it was a stupid thing to do on your part. What happens when he finds out?"

"Ha!" laughs Candy. "How? Big ears tracking me from the other side of the grave?" She flaps her hands behind her ears and makes spooky movie sounds. "I don't think so."

"Never underestimate the impossible. It happens. And it doesn't matter, because I know. You'll get another hit as soon as I'm ready. Right now, I stoke Keith's flame. If it goes out, so does your little one."

Candy gets back on the bed, on her hands and

knees, and crawls over to Harry.

"Don't worry, Harry, I know how to be a good girl," she says as she starts kissing Harry around the ears and down the neck. "I can be very, very good."

Candy continues kissing her way across Harry's chest.

"Well, don't be too good."

"Don't worry," answers Candy, as she kisses him down the line of chest hair. "It's all an act anyway."

Explain, briefly, the difference between a sharp and a fuzzy discontinuity design.

Jane tries to reign in the swirling thoughts inside her head as she reads the words to herself.

Yes, she thinks, sharp and fuzzy, lots of discontinuity, little design. It's crazy. I love looking at his face. It's dirty most of the time, and his hair is a mess, but it's a kind face with compassion. He's smart. I can see that, and he's trustworthy.

She focuses again on the pre-test in front of her, struggling to keep her mind on her studying.

Explain, briefly, the difference between a sharp and a fuzzy discontinuity design.

Trustworthy, that's the sharp. Trust is the key component, the razor's edge on which everything else is cut.

The fuzzy is how do you possibly date a guy with no money and no job, she wonders, someone who lives somewhere out in the open, on the street?

Oh no, this is all wrong, she thinks. I need to think clearly, slow it down. Just focus on the individual thoughts.

The difference. Between a sharp. And a fuzzy. Discontinuity design. In a sharp RDD, crossing the threshold determines receipt of the treatment deterministically. In a fuzzy, crossing the threshold affects the probability of receiving the treatment, but not deterministically

"Whew. I really need to get a grip. Even the easy questions are causing me trouble."

Her eyes gaze down the list of possible questions for her Econometrics final exam. Each question has multiple parts, reading like a foreign language to the uninitiated. And she's only on the first one.

Jane puts her pencil down, goes behind the counter, and makes another cup of coffee. Maybe cup number three will do the trick, she thinks, keeping from herself what she knows to be true – the coffee is just another means of avoiding doing what she doesn't want to do: study.

What she wants to do is think about Brian and that hug he gave her. The hug she can still feel lingering around her arms. In her mind, she can see the look of surprise in his eyes when he held her. And she can still feel the warm tickling feeling that startled her as it moved from deep inside her stomach, rising up through her body and into her head, where it left her feeling lightheaded and dizzy.

"Ahh."

Her sigh startles her because it's unexpected. She sits back down at the table, takes a gulp of coffee, scrunches her eyes, and tries to force them to focus on the paper on the table.

Do you expect the true causal effect of interest to be positive, negative, or about zero?

It must be positive, she thinks, because it makes me feel so good. I've had so many letdowns with guys. They never turn out to be what they seem to be at first. Kind and considerate, polite and caring, until you get to know them, and then they're not!

Well, maybe it's not fair to judge all men on the few I've dated, she thinks. She had only dated two guys for any extended length of time. But experience, no matter how limited, is hard proof to shake. Even if it is a small sample study.

No, the most reasonable answer is negative, though, in reality, anything goes. I'll have to justify that on the exam, Jane decides. But it won't be difficult.

What is difficult is trusting. She understands that's where the real game is, and the points scored in that game aren't on a scoreboard. They're etched forever in your heart, like watermarks on the buildings of a riverside village, showing how high the last flood climbed. And how close you came to drowning.

I feel flooded, she thinks, by emotions, thoughts,

impulses. But not by choices. There are only two of those – yes or no.

Jane can tell he feels the same way. She could tell at that moment, in that embrace. It seemed as though the universe moved, like in a book, and a whole new reality opened up. It wasn't just so for me, she affirms to herself, but for him too. So is it yes? Or is it no? And what will those two futures hold? Oh, I'll have to come back to that question. She shakes her head.

Describe briefly the ideal randomized experiment that you would like to run in order to answer the question of interest.

A kiss, she thinks. Yes, definitely a kiss.

"No, no, not a kiss. An experiment!" Jane clasps her hands together. Oh, please, God, she prays, help me get myself together. I have an exam to take.

"So what is it?"

"I can't tell you."

"You can't tell me?"

"No."

"You're serious?"

"Dead serious."

Bill Dailey looks at Vondy, unsure what to make of this. She is more than a good piece of ass, he thinks. She's an almost decent reporter. Hell, she may actually be a good reporter, not that she's going to get paid like one. Can't deny her that Keith Unger story, and look at how that turned out. It's one of the biggest stories of the year, and that counts for something. Yes, she may be a good reporter.

He owed her at least the benefit of the doubt. But as the *Morning Show's* news producer, it was also his job to vet the stories. And this one is already in free fall from the top the looney tunes falls, thinks Bill.

"So, let me get this straight, just so we're sure we are on the same page." Bill walks to his desk, where he feels his power the most.

"This kid, the musician, who couldn't get a pot to piss in, killed himself because his whole life was one big dead end. Now dead, he becomes the biggest thing this side of *Dancing With the Stars*. Then, without warning, he resurrects himself, or some people believe he has. That much we've mostly confirmed, thanks to your reporting. But now you're telling me that, in actual fact, he did not miraculously resurrect himself, like his bat shit crazy fans insist he did, because he never died in the first place? So the whole premise of your story and reporting was wrong, to begin with?"

"That's not going to matter when I report the new evidence," says Vondy, standing in front of Bill's desk. "I'm showing journalistic integrity here by pursuing—"

"No, no, I'm not blaming you," says Bill. "I just want to make sure that I've got the story straight."

Bill settles into the chair behind the desk.

"So, going back ... This kid did not actually die in the first place, and you, the KNLA *Morning Show* reporter, have the story and the proof. But I, producer of said *Morning Show,* have to just trust you, and our program's reputation, on the details, because you won't let me see or hear said proof until you reveal it all live on T.V. this afternoon. Is that about right?"

"Pretty much."

"Well, isn't that just about the most ridiculous pile of horseshit I ever did step into? And I grew up in Montana."

"I forgot to add that I have an interview with *Fox & Friends* set for right after the Keith Day show, and I could just reveal the info there, for their viewers, their ratings, if you'd rather—"

What a bitch. Sleep with a reporter once, or a few dozen times, and they think you owe them. Though she was a hell of a good tumble, Bill remembers.

"No, I'd not rather. What the hell, Vondy? Are you blackmailing me? Like we haven't done everything for you here?"

"Except give me an anchor."

"Well, damn it, you know I can't do that. Alicia's screwing Jack Riley, and the station manager is up the food chain from *Morning Show* producer. I don't have that kind of power."

"Then maybe I should do Jack Riley."

Damn, she's hot when she's angry, thinks Bill. Must be those spicy Mexican jalapeños. I can't take my eyes off her breasts. And that ass. Wish she'd turn around so I could—

"Don't objectify me, Bill."

"What?"

"You're objectifying me. I can tell by how you're looking at me like I'm a piece of meat. I'm a reporter, and a damn good one, so stop looking at me like I'm rump steak. Now, do you want the story, or should I give it to Fox?"

Bill Dailey knows his blood pressure is bubbling up because his ears are tingling. He searches his pockets for the heart pills. Damn it. I must have left them in the car.

"Alright, alright," he says, the slow, low ringing in his ears rising as he gets up out of the chair. "You can do it. Though I don't know why you have to keep it all a big secret. But if this is some bullshit story, you're back on human interest for the mid-day show, you got me?"

"I got you," Vondy smiles, and I'd be happy to tell you what the whole story is, except I don't have a clue myself. She steps over and squeezes Bill's mouth with her hand, scrunching his lips, and gives him a juicy wet kiss, while her other hand grabs his ass firmly and squeezes hard.

"Oh, Bill, you really need to tone this up." Vondy turns and walks out.

Bill watches Vondy's ass as it swings up and down, back and forth, like firm tapioca bouncing on a bungee cord. Those heart pills, he thinks, where the hell are they?

Vondy walks out the door and into the hallway,

feeling triumphant. What a waste of time that low ladder Daily. He can't do squat for me, she thinks. Yes, he helped get me the *Morning Show*, but he's totally outlived his usefulness.

Her purse vibrates. She pulls her phone out and sees that she has a text message. It's The Voice. He wants her to call. Immediately.

"Reporter lady?" answers the now familiar voice on the other end of the phone line.

"What's so important?" demands Vondy.

"I got it figured out. I know why they faked Keith's death, the resurrection, everything."

Vondy looks at her reflection in the glass window of one of the offices. She pulls some lipstick from her purse and begins applying it.

"And ...?"

"And what?

What a dolt. She puts the lipstick away and tosses her hair. Keep it neat, but just enough unkempt to look slept in.

"What's the conspiracy? Isn't that why you called me?"

Vondy makes sure her blouse is opened up enough to give her cleavage ample counter space. She pulls her breasts up in the tight, low-cut bra.

"Oh, yeah, conspiracy. So, I have it figured out."

A woman in the office, sitting at a desk facing the window, pops Vondy the bird. Vondy returns the greeting in kind. She starts to walk down the hallway a little unevenly in her high heels.

"Yes, I figured that much out. So, what is the conspiracy, Voice? Why did they do it?"

"I can't tell you."

"What do you mean you can't tell me."

"I mean, I can tell you, but I have to wait until later at the club. I'm sure these phones are tapped. I just know it. They can do anything."

"Who can do anything?"

"I can't tell you."

Vondy stops at an open office door. She leans back against the wall adjacent to the door and hikes up her skirt a little, exposing more flesh. She looks down at her tanned and toned legs, all the way to the gold ankle bracelet around the bottom of her left leg, above her high heels. Damn, they look good, she thinks.

"Okay. You find me at the club. But be ready to go live with this info. Oh, and what is your real name? You never told me."

"Danny. Danny Wallburger."

"Danny ... Wallburger?" she repeats, the syllables crashing off her lips like waves on rocks. Oh yeah, I know that name. "Stick with the Voice, kid."

Vondy turns off the phone and puts it back into her purse. The nerve, withholding information from me. Maybe I won't put him on T.V. after all. No, he's my corroboration. I have to use him.

Smoothing out her blouse and skirt, she turns and steps into the office doorway. She places her right elbow and forearm against the door frame and leans on it, causing her skirt to hike up a little higher, underwear tantalizingly out of sight.

A heavy-set man, bald, with small horn-rimmed glasses and a twitchy upper lip, is seated at his office desk. He lifts his eyes from the papers he's pouring over, and sees Vondy, stretched provocatively up his door frame. His jaw slowly drops while his eyes zero in.

"Jack Riley. I need to talk to you."

18. CANDY SAYS

As he enters Harry's building, Keith can't help but feel like he is on spring break. The sun is warm, and it's a perfect day in L.A. Whatever frustrations and fears he had have now drifted away on a gentle breeze. Freedom, he thinks, is hours away. His life is coming back to him today. Keith Day. Then he can make things right, explain to Jane. That's the most important thing.

Across the street, Danny watches. His feelings of betrayal are intense. They eat away at his stomach, feasting on all the good memories and converting them into false dreams of bitterness and resentment.

But Keith is floating in a world of his own and cannot see the shadow of doom that is closing in on him, just twenty feet away, as he enters Harry's building.

Once inside Harry's apartment, Keith sits down at his recording desk and begins to work. He quickly finds a suitable drum loop for the current project, something stolen from a hip hop song, which in turn was borrowed from a rapper's song, who lifted it from an old James Brown song, who ... Actually, J.B. invented it.

Using the guitar, Keith lays down a chunky rhythm to hold a place over the beat. Next, he records a guide vocal and adds another guitar part in a different voicing. On top of that, he introduces the lead guitar.

Now he pulls out his little Silverstone bass, its compact size perfect for a guitarist turned bass player. He uses his pick to find the right groove, underscoring the vocal while moving in and out of the guitar part and still filling in the bottom end. Juice could play rings around him, but what Keith does play is simple, direct, and right for the song.

He needs some color in the upper register, so he finds some melodic lines on the keyboard to accent the grit he's already laid down. After that, he re-records the vocals, leaving them a little rough because it suits the lyric.

With the song complete, Keith listens to the whole mix together. He smiles. It fits what Harry wants, and without sacrificing any art. It references death and rebirth, though, in the song, it's a rebirth of the mind. It is genuine and sincere because it comes from his own experiences.

I lived a life so empty and vain. I had to leave it behind so I could come back again.

Start with one true sentence. Keith smiles at the thought of Harry's suggestion leading him down a new road of discovery and creation. Who'd have thought that Harry Chukstein would be a catalyst for real art when he was usually just an engine of crass commerce?

The complicated melody line ascends before stumbling for a couple of notes in a short descent, followed by the inevitable, powerful, chromatic rise - rebirth. He is filled with a warm glow, recognizing the thing of beauty that has come from him. Or rather through him, for he is only the conduit. A conduit for sale, he laughs.

Keith rises and walks to the window and looks out its large frame at the West Hollywood buildings surrounding him. How many other songwriters are out there, looking at the same view, finding their muse in this city of empty dreams?

Not many. Who could afford the rent?

It's only when he hears the door open that he remembers Harry has workers coming over, and he is supposed to be out of the apartment by early afternoon. Keith panics and turns to rush to the bedroom. But something stops him.

Some wordless, non-rational part of him knows what's next before the snarled and tangled web of blonde hair spins in through the air. But the shock is no less disturbing because of the knowing.

"Candy–"

It is all Keith can manage to utter. He slinks back against the wall, wrapping his arms around his body, hiding his nakedness, even though he's fully clothed.

Candy glances over at him, barely taking notice.

"Oh, hi Keith," she says nonchalantly, dropping her bag on the kitchen counter and going to the refrigerator.

Candy pulls a beer out of the fridge, and a bottle opener from deep inside the counter drawer, then she pops the top off the bottle and takes a big swig. Opening the freezer, she takes out some ice cubes, lifts her dress, and drops the ice into the front of her panties.

"So, you're alive?"

Gliding over to the chair opposite the couch, Candy plops down. She pulls up her dress and spreads her legs wide to air them out.

"Damn is it hot out there, or what?" she says, taking another big gulp of beer. "Wonder if it's gonna cool down before the show?"

Keith looks at her, uncertain of what to say. Candy looks at him curiously and waves her hand in front of his face.

"Earth to Keith! Earth to Keith! You are alive, aren't you?" She leans over and prods the flesh of his arm with her finger.

Candy laughs as she rises from the chair and walks out of the living room towards the bedroom.

"That was some pretty funny shit," she says over her shoulder as she walks into the bedroom. "That chick poking you when you resurrected, or whatever that was. It would have been better if you really were dead, though. You know, for sales and stuff? Whatever, Harry'll find some way to make money off of it."

Candy pokes her head back out into the hallway. "He's good at that shit. Not as good at other stuff." Then she disappears again.

Getting up off the couch, Keith follows her into the bedroom.

"Did you see what he did with my song?" says Candy, kicking off her shoes. "Number 2! Some song of yours kept it from the top, which pissed me off."

Candy lifts her dress over her head so that she is naked except for panties. Letting the dress fall to the floor, she opens the walk-in closet door. As she takes off her panties, remnants of ice cubes tumble to the ground. She grabs a rolled-up pair of underwear from the floor and brings them to her nose. After taking a sniff, she puts them on.

"I got Rami writing one for me now. Can you believe that idiot can write?" Candy looks through the dresses hanging in her closet. "I didn't think he could spell. Or stand still long enough. Not as good as you, though."

She pulls two dresses from the closet. One is a reddish color, the other a pale, antique color scheme with flower designs.

"If you were a fan boy, which would make you want me more?"

Keith is overwhelmed and unable to process the

onslaught of information coming his way.

"Are you and Harry—" There is a long pause as Candy waits for him to finish.

"Hello! Yeah, stupid." Candy laughs as she sloppily hangs up the paler dress.

She picks up the beer bottle and takes another big gulp. "I'll go with the red one. Guys are like bulls anyway."

"How ... long?" Keith manages to say.

"Long time. It wasn't because of grief or anything, don't flatter yourself. Way before that. Girl's gotta cover her bases, right?" She pulls the dress over her head. "I mean, let's face it, you weren't going anywhere. Dying was the best thing that ever happened to you."

Candy digs through a pile of shoes on the closet floor until she finds a pair of leather platform shoes. She takes them out to the living room. Keith follows.

"You were cheating?"

"You need me to spell it out for you? You're always so slow picking up on things."

Candy sits down on the couch and buckles the boot straps around her ankles.

"Why Harry?"

As if on cue, the door opens, and Harry walks into the apartment. He sees Keith. Then Candy. Harry stops in his tracks, trying to decide whether he can slow motion his way back out the way he came in without being noticed. No chance. But being Harry, he improvises with the flair of a jazz musician.

"Candy! What are you doing here?" he asks, in a voice that carries a little less than zero credibility.

"He knows," Candy says cooly, pulling a small mirror and some lipstick from her purse. She begins to paint in red.

"Didn't I tell you to be out of here before afternoon?" Harry demands of Keith, shifting to a new key.

"Because you had workers coming over. You didn't say the worker was my girlfriend."

"EX-girlfriend," interjects Candy.

"Yeah, well, she is a worker. She works for me."

"I don't work for you, sweetie," says Candy. "You work for me."

Closing up her purse, Candy stands. "That's the part you neglected to remember, dead boy. The manager works for you."

Keith's lips are sputtering, but no words are coming out.

"I'd love to stay and chat, and you know, compare sizes with you both," Candy says as she turns to face them. "But I have a hit record to play live on T.V. So, gotta go."

"What hit record?"

"Oh, didn't Harry tell you? 'I'll Remember You', the song I wrote in tribute to you, is the hottest single out there right now."

"That's not your song. I wrote that." Keith looks at Harry incredulously.

"A 'massive hit,' says Billboard." Candy smiles deliciously.

"A hit I wrote!" screams Keith, shaking in anger. "You're making money off this record too, Harry?"

"And he's going to keep making money off of it."

"Now, Candy, it's not right to discuss business in front of —"

"Not when I tell everyone I wrote it," threatens Keith. "I have proof - my demo. Everyone's going to know the truth, that you're just a big thief!"

"Oh, no," Candy feigns horror. "Now you're really hitting where it hurts. Well, then everyone's gonna know that you're a scam artist. Because I'll let them know you and Harry hatched this whole faked death thing so you could make money off of your poor fans."

"You wouldn't dare," Keith says without conviction.

"Don't mess with me, loser." Candy turns and walks to the door. But as she opens it, she slowly turns back to Keith, wearing a Cheshire smile.

"Come to think of it, I might need a few more songs from you, with a Candy Lamour co-writing credit. I'm not completely happy with what Rami is doing. But I like what you do. So start working on it. Now."

Candy then struts out the door, letting it close behind her. She leaves Keith in the aftermath of shocked silence.

"She can't do that!" Keith says, then turns to Harry. "Can she?"

"I think she could."

"I'm telling anyway. I'd rather have custody of my songs."

"Whoa, now, let's not rush into a bad decision." Harry jumps in front of him. "Let's look at the facts here, and the facts say she has the upper hand on us. And by us, I mean you, because I'm just the manager, and everyone knows managers are lying scumbags who will steal and cheat from their own mother. But you, you're a rock star. You have trusting fans."

"I didn't do anything to—"

"But the fans don't know that. And if the fans turn on you, it could get ugly. Really ugly."

"Dammit!" Keith feels like he's on quicksand - the more he moves, the more he sinks. "Jesus, Harry, why did I listen to you in the first place?"

"Because I'm your manager."

Harry gently pushes him down onto the couch. Then he sits down next to Keith, his arm slipping around him like a father snake.

"This doesn't have to be so bad. We can make it work for us. You've got great new songs, right? Fine. You record those. But you have older ones that are dated. You've outgrown them. Why not have Candy sell them? You still make a ton of money. The resurrection story is hot. Sales are through the roof. Brad and Massive are all in. Candy's just another revenue stream."

"I'm done with that resurrection thing. And I'm not writing any songs for Candy!"

"Fine." Harry pats his back. "We'll do it your way. We just don't reveal you're alive. At least not yet."

"No, not again, Harry!" Keith rises, pushing Harry's arm off of him. "You promised after I wrote those new songs—"

"That's before you met up with Candy. I told you not to be here today."

Keith turns and looks at him incredulously. "So it's my fault that you're having an affair with my girlfriend?"

"Another technicality. Don't turn this around and make me the bad guy. You're getting bogged down in details. Look at the big picture. You stay dead a while longer, and we can milk this for all its worth. Once you come out, you're radioactive. You get that? No one will buy your records. No. One."

Keith can see his whole career, if you could call it that, going up in smoke.

"You know how to spin this, Harry." Keith tries appealing to Harry's ego. "We'll tell the truth, that once I found out about my celebrity, we got scared and—"

"There's no spinning this, man. People will be pissed. And I'm sorry, but your songs just aren't good enough to take a front door battering like that. If they're going to be mad anyway, let's make sure we get as much cash as we can!"

"No." Keith erupts, his face is red, and his spine stiffens. "I'm done hiding, Harry. Every time I'm supposed to come back to life, you kill me again."

Harry rises and picks up his keys from the counter.

"I don't have time for this right now. I have to go back out there and work my ass off making money for you, and—"

"It's not all about money, Harry!"

"Oh, isn't it?" says Harry, as he steps up to Keith. "If it isn't about money, then why couldn't you pay your rent? Or your food bills? And if it isn't about money, why did you decide to jump off that cliff?"

"That's was different."

"Really? Because it looks exactly the same to me. Don't be a hypocrite. Money's money, buddy, it keeps the world humming. When you got it, life's great. Without it, you got nothing. Period. You should know that – you've been living it."

Keith crosses his arms. He won't even look at Harry.

"You just stay here like a good little rock star until I get back," says Harry. "I'll talk to Brad, and we'll figure this out. But stay here!"

"I do what I want from now on, Harry."

"No," says Harry firmly. "You do what I say."

Harry walks out the door, leaving Keith fuming, the blood pounding through his veins and into his head. It feels like his whole being is trying to escape from inside him. He has to move, try to shake this feeling.

Before he knows it, Keith finds himself on the street, in front of Harry's apartment, where the air gives him new energy and a new idea. He turns and starts to walk. Keith knows his destination - it's the one place sure to offer compassion and comfort. He's so absorbed that he doesn't notice that Ben follows behind him.

Walking helps fill his head with all the things he'll say, so it seems he's there before he's formulated a plan. Just ahead of him is the Coffee a Go-Go. And with movie-like timing, the door opens, and Jane steps out. The excitement rushes through Keith like electricity. He raises his hand and opens his mouth to call for her. But everything stops.

A man follows Jane out of the shop. He is around Keith's age, but he's not like Keith. This man is handsome, well-dressed and well-groomed, hair combed back, face clean-shaven. And he wears stylish footwear. Keith notices the streetlight reflecting off the shiny leather shoes like they have magic dust on them.

Jane's head tilts back, laughing over something the man says as she turns to lock the coffee shop door. She turns in Keith's direction, and he ducks into a doorway. Jane waves. But not to Keith, whom she can't see. Ben smiles and waves back at her.

The man puts his arm around Jane as they walk away. They step up to a late model Porsche, and the man opens the passenger side door for her. She climbs in. It feels like slow motion to Keith. Then he goes around to the driver's side, hops in, and they drive off.

Keith stands and stares as taillights slowly fade away. He continues staring after the car is gone. Finally, he slowly turns and begins to walk. Ben falls in line beside him.

"Wanna talk?" asks Ben, and Keith shakes his head. Ben nods but follows a few steps behind.

When he gets to Harry's building, Keith walks through the garage and enters. Ben stays on the street watching.

Harry's apartment is empty, and all the lights are on. Keith keeps moving, pacing, trying to shake the vision of Jane and the other man from his hard-wired thoughts. He remembers the man's groomed hair and shiny leather shoes, and at the same time, he happens to look up into the mirror.

What he sees is not an appealing sight: a ragged character from a modern-day Dickens story, bearded and bedraggled. Horrified, he turns sharply from the mirror.

Instinctively he flips on the T.V. His anger and insecurity fuel nervous energy in him that keeps him pacing the room. Unable to calm himself, he begins opening drawers, looking for something, not knowing what.

He walks to the bar and opens the cabinet. Inside

he finds a multitude of liquor bottles. He takes one out. Jim Beam. Opening it, he smells its contents. The smell makes him gag. But nonetheless, he grimaces, holds the bottle to his lips, and tilts his head back, taking a big swig. His face scrunches up as the liquid burns its way down his throat into his stomach.

It hurts so bad. But the pain of the drink seems to take away some of the toxic pain of betrayal. So he takes another swig.

This one hurts kind of good, he thinks, looking at the bottle in his hand as he moves from the bar.

He steps in front of the T.V. and opens the top drawer beneath it. Inside is a pile of restaurant menus, topped by two flashlights, several lighters, a pair of knotted-up lime green female underwear. And a small, well-used pot pipe.

Keith takes out the pipe and looks inside. It is loaded with partially burned marijuana. He assumes it's marijuana because he's likely the only rock star in L.A. who has never actually touched the stuff. Until now. He picks up the lighter, clicks it, puts the pipe to his lips, and lights the bowl.

Within moments his chest explodes, and he's coughing from deep inside his lungs. Smoke pours out of his mouth and nose. Once he catches his breath, he starts to notice a ripple of warmth, a tingling sensation, moving from his head down to his feet. It feels good.

Keith closes the drawer and picks up the bottle of

Jim Beam. He takes another swig. As he does, the image on the T.V. catches his eye.

It is a young boy, maybe 6-years old, standing on a beach with his feet in the water, smiling happily. A beautiful woman with dark hair, dressed in a revealing bikini that flatters her toned body, kneels next to him. She holds him lightly at the waist and smiles adoringly. Stretching away from the boy is the dark shadow of the person taking the photo, a man, tall and lean.

Keith sits down on the floor, Jim Beam in one hand, pipe and lighter in the other, transfixed by this image of himself as a kid, with his mother and the shadowy figure of his father. The vision fades, and another appears. This one is of a smiling, young Keith seated on the lap of a man whose face is not visible. Something knots in his stomach, so Keith lights the pipe again.

That image morphs into yet another. Keith is ten. He stares at the camera, eyes sullen and cagey, face tight, holding back a torrent of emotion. His mother stands behind him. It's a photo he has seen a hundred times. But for the first time, he sees the pain and concern, love and compassion, on his mother's face.

He turns the volume up.

"The trauma of dealing with the loss of his father brings fear and isolation, two emotions that fuel the desperately positive music he will make in the future. Maybe he can erase all the negative he finds in the world around him and replace it with something better in his songs."

Crojon's narration is overwrought. But coupled with these images, it mesmerizes Keith. He watches as his life rolls past, like an x-ray, one long visual eulogy.

Keith sees himself grow physically, though his clothing style and hair change little. Candy enters the picture, her blonde Medusa hair in place. His external image begins to change under Candy's firm hand. But the lost boy inside remains, and as he sits in front of the T.V. drinking from the Jim Beam bottle, Keith can see it all.

"It's no surprise that Keith became obsessed with the 27 Club. It's the age all his heroes died. The age his biggest hero was taken from him - his father. He was sure it would be his destiny too. Like father, like son."

Keith's body is warm, and his mind is muddled, clouded by J.B. and weed. His emotions rise quickly to the surface. Tears streak down his cheeks as he sees the happy and the sad as one interchangeable emotion with two sides. He takes a big hit off the pint-sized pipe. The coughing fit works as a harsh chaser.

Finally, Vondy Wells tells the story of Keith's death. One of the officers who arrived on the scene describes the lonely dog tied to the pole, the suicide note, the long drop from the cliff at Deep Canyon. And Keith relives it all in his now altered state.

Harry explains the plans he had for Keith and the tragedy of hearing of his death. He hides his face behind shadows created by the lights, covering his simulated crying. Keith pops Harry the bird.

The documentary ends with Candy's video version of *I Remember You.*

"Thief! You thief!" Keith screams at the T.V. in a fury. He stumbles to his feet. "Go find your own talent!"

The song ends, and the image fades into an outdoor shot of a large crowd in Hollywood. Crojon appears on the T.V. screen, holding a mic and standing inside the Killer Klub.

"Limited tickets here at the club," says Crojon, turning to show the club filling up inside. "But you lucky people at home got a hell of a show coming your way here on the V. Candy Lamour's playing, Bono giving a memorial talk about Keith, plus we'll be topping it all off with Keith's mom who's gonna unveil a huge Keith birthday cake."

Crojon steps off his platform and walks down into the crowd.

"We got coverage from everywhere. I'm going to switch it over to my girl Molly Lips outside the club with a special guest. Whassup girl?"

Molly Lips appears onscreen. Her bright, scarecrow yellow hair is streaked with purple. She stands with a smiling Vondy, who is dressed casually in a designer Sex Pistol tee shirt, and expensive jeans, purchased with rips included.

"Thanks, Cro. I'm here with the woman who started

it all, KNLA reporter and girl power role model, Vondy Wells! Crazy how this all took off, right?"

"Yes," Vondy nods vigorously, "very crazy. But it goes to show you the power of a good story."

"You know, since Keith 'revealed' himself to his fans, it seems like it's all just gone to a whole 'nother place. Dontcha think? I mean, this resurrection thing is insane."

"Well, we don't know what exactly is behind this latest episode yet. I will have an important announcement tonight regarding the truth behind Keith Unger's death, and—"

"Look, it's Candy Lamour!"

Candy walks in behind them, surrounded by security, as fans reach out, trying to grab a piece of her. Many girl fans sport red gash lipstick, with smears at the lips' edge, just like their idol Candy.

"Candy! Candy!" calls Molly. Candy walks over to the mic.

"Candy Lamour, everyone, Keith's girlfriend, and now a star on her own. Congratulations on your new single, Candy. 'I Remember You,' still rockin' number two, and it's awesome."

"I know, I know," says Candy coyly, waving to some fans off-screen. "I just can't believe it. I'm so blessed and lucky. I owe it all to these wonderful people." She turns to the crowd around her, which erupts with screams. She blows them kisses.

"So much still coming out about the Keith story,

and Vondy is breaking some big news tonight. Still won't give us a preview?"

Vondy smiles and shakes her head. "Sorry, Molly, everyone finds out at the same time. But I'll tell you this - it's explosive."

"I'll bet it is," says Molly, turning back to Candy. "So this resurrection story, is that freaking you out? Does it make it hard for your grieving?"

Candy's eyes go downcast as she effectively pantomimes sadness.

"Yeah, it's very hard, Molly. I mean, it was hard enough dealing with Keith dying like he did, torn from me without warning. I still remember when Harry told me he was dead, I just couldn't believe it."

Candy lifts her head and looks pointedly into the camera. "I knew it was true because they'd never lie about his death. I mean, that would be so horrible and unforgivable, right? The lowest of the low. The fans have been so loyal and trusting. They would be so mad. So I don't know what to think about the insurrection."

"Resurrection," corrects Vondy.

"Yeah, that too."

"Me neither," says Molly Lips, shaking her head. "Can you tell us if you have anything else in the works, a new single maybe?"

"Well, I can't talk about it too much, but I'm working on some new material," Candy says excitedly, seamlessly switching moods. "I'm so lucky to have worked with

Keith's band, you know, but I think I'll need to branch out on my own. More news to come!"

"Well, we'll be looking forward to it. Vondy, any questions for Candy?"

"Just one," says Vondy. "Who did your hair? It's magnificent."

"Oh, this old thing?" says Candy, shaking her hair back.

"Girl's gotta have her hair right," says Molly, as Vondy and Candy whisper to each other behind her. "Gonna send it back to you, Crojon, for more on Keith Day."

"Thanks, Molly," says Crojon from his location in the club. "Not long until we kick things into gear. Still have Mashup Max from WROK out there. Max, you got some fans for us?"

Mashup Max, the aging disc jockey, aged 38, is standing outside the club with two much younger girls in their mid-teens, wearing 'Feed the Hunger' tee shirts and ripped jeans. One girl has a nose ring. The second girl nervously twists her brown hair in two of her right-hand fingers.

"Carrie, right?" Mashup Max asks the nose ring girl. "And Maria?" he turns to the girl with the brown hair. "So, you think he's more than a rock star. He's some kind of supernatural being?"

"Oh, yeah," Carrie and Marie respond in harmony.

Back at Harry's condo, Keith turns off the T.V. and fumes. This is ridiculous, he thinks. How dare Harry tell me what I can and can't do. Hell, it's my party. I can go if I want to!

Who's going to know? asks a small voice inside his head. It's not like anyone will recognize you. Harry just wants to keep all the glory for himself. He's going to be in the club, at the show, and where will you be? Nowhere. Like always.

Keith stops pacing, looks in the little teak mirror on the wall.

"Yeah, why can't I go?" he asks himself out loud.

When no answer comes, his decision is made.

Keith walks into Harry's bathroom, which has been remodeled since his last visited. From a drawer, he pulls a shaving razor, then quickly lathers his face with soap. The blade is brutal as it charges through the dense forest of his beard, stinging as it rips the hair from his face, leaving a highway of cuts in its wake.

He then moves to Harry's room and into his walk-in closet. There he finds a long, dark, lightweight jacket. He slips his arms into the sleeves. It hangs to his knees. Then he takes Harry's new Cubs cap off the shelf and shoves it over the greasy hair atop his head.

Walking out of the closet, Keith looks up into the mirror over the bed. The jacket, fitted for Harry's larger frame, swallows him whole, making him almost invisible inside it. The hat shades his eyes. It's simple, but the disguise is complete.

Keith grabs a pair of oversized sunglasses with black frames and puts them over his eyes. No one will recognize me now, he thinks, as he walks out the door and steps out into the unknown.

19. SAY GOODBYE TO HOLLYWOOD

"**G**et your locks of Keith's hair! 100% proven locks of Keith Unger's hair."

The sidewalk that fronts the Killer Klub resembles a carnival or a Medieval fair. People sell all things Keith: picks, tee shirts, caps, Keith's spit, slivers of the branch of the tree he fell from in his resurrection. One girl in a tie-dyed chef's hat is selling cookies shaped in Keith's profile. Spiked, of course.

Only Harry, mid-interview with Molly Lips, seems offended.

"This is outrageous! And illegal!" Harry looks around at the crowd that is paying him no mind. "All items bearing Keith Unger's likeness are licensed material. If you buy or sell any of this stuff, fake or not, you're trafficking in illegal merchandise. You're stealing money from a deceased artist! Have you no respect for the dead?"

"So they're not really locks of his hair?" asks Molly.

"Of course not." Harry looks at her incredulously as Molly furtively slips a small plastic baggie with a lock of hair in it out of her pocket and lets it fall to the ground.

"It's all bogus, and these ... Hey, watch where you're walking, buddy!"

Harry gives a little shove to a man in a dark jacket, who brushes up against him.

"These sellers are infringing on a copyright. That's a criminal offense."

Keith looks back at Harry, whom he's just bumped into. If Harry doesn't recognize me, then the disguise is working.

He pulls the baseball cap a little lower as he wanders through the crowd. He's taking it all in with something less than joy. When he first became aware of it, his posthumous fame was a balm for his insecurities and bruised ego. Now it all seems ridiculous and offensive.

A big screen installed over the entrance to the club streams a live feed from inside. The crowd has grown, and the Killer Klub is filled to capacity. The excitement is palpable, even from the soundless screen.

That's where I need to be, thinks Keith. He watches the entrance as people go in, assessing the situation.

A group of seven walks up, and one man hands the bouncer their tickets. The bouncer waves the group in. The bouncer is talking to his co-worker.

"Nothing's gonna happen," says the bouncer. "These deadbeats got no clue about music. Back in the day—"

The bouncer stops one man who is dressed all in

black. He taps the breast of the man's coat. He hits something solid.

"I'm sorry, sir, no outside drinks allowed."

The man pulls a silver flask from inside his jacket. "And what do you expect me to do with it?"

"That's your decision, sir," the bouncer replies politely.

The man grumbles as he pours the liquid at the bouncer's feet.

"Enjoy the show, sir."

Another large group of people approaches. A tall woman with a red nose and redder cheeks extends a wad of tickets to the bouncer.

"For me, and all my friends!" she calls out, sweeping her arm to indicate her entourage. Her friends laugh loudly.

"Some of us are just here for the tickets, Helen," responds one of her friends. The group breaks into laughter. Keith steps in with them, just one of the gang.

The bouncer takes the tickets from the woman, then motions them to enter. Keith keeps his head down.

"They were giants in those days, man," says the bouncer. "The music had balls. Limp Bizkit, Creed, the Cruzados, they were the real deal. This shit is for pussies."

Keith walks through the entrance. But as he does, the bouncer grabs him firmly by the jacket collar and spins him around.

"No entry without a ticket, sir." The bouncer gives Keith a gentle push to send him on his way.

Keith walks away, dejected. He looks for another wrinkle in security, but it soon becomes clear that it will take some sort of miracle to get inside the club.

"Going in?"

Keith turns to his left and sees Big Ben standing beside him, staring straight ahead.

"I don't have a ticket, Ben."

"That all? Little thing like no ticket gonna stop a resurrected man like you?"

"Happy Birthday, little brother."

Ben opens Keith's palm and puts something in his hand. When Keith looks down, he finds that it's a ticket to the Keith Day event.

"How did you—" Keith looks up to find that Ben is gone. He quickly scans the crowd, but Ben is nowhere, vanished.

Keith strides up to the club door and hands the bouncer his ticket with a proud, challenging look. The bouncer gives the ticket a slight tear, then motions Keith in without looking up at him.

"Enjoy the show, sir. I saw Vanilla Ice at—"

The club is crowded. Hipsters dressed for a night out mingle with regular fans. Two cameramen whirl through the audience, recording it all.

The stage is empty, and the loudspeakers begin to play "I Wanna Be Rad." Keith remembers playing that song right here, at the Killer Klub. It's an odd deja vu feeling.

In fact, the entire scene feels alien, as if he's fallen into someone else's adolescent dream. He is an interloper in his own story.

Standing near Keith, Vondy looks over her notes. The ideal time to break the story is right after the birthday cake, she thinks. Story-wise that makes the most sense - top of the arc. When people are riding the highest high, you hit them with a body blow. That way, the story has the most impact and takes over from the original narrative.

I'll be the story then, she smiles to herself.

"I'm gonna get a soda. You want anything?"

Skip stands expectantly, his always disheveled hair offset by a tropical shirt.

"Hurry. I'm going to do a live shot after Bono."

"Okay, boss," says Skip as he walks off to the bar.

What am I doing here? This isn't my scene at all.

Jane shifts in her shoes, on the other side of the stage from Vondy, and looks around at the crowd. I bet I don't know a single person here. And that last band, the Keith boy's girlfriend - she was just awful! The song was catchy, and the musicians seemed very talented, but that girl—yuck. Jane remembers that night at the coffee shop, and her opinion of Candy hasn't been improved by a hit single.

Jane hadn't intended to come to the show. But her friend Gary had tickets, and well, why not? But it's such a sad tale. She can't imagine hitting such a rock bottom, to have so little love for yourself, that you throw your most precious gift from a cliff. For a career in music? There were so many other worthy ways to spend one's life, she affirms. Play music because you love it, do something else to make your living.

She vaguely remembers Keith from that night. But she is no fan girl. It was something else about his pictures that got her attention. Something about him, something familiar, in his eyes. Jane couldn't put her finger on it, but somehow, she felt like she knew him.

She smiles as Gary brings their beers. Gary thinks Keith was cute, but then Gary's gay.

Onstage, Crojon walks out and approaches the mic stand at center stage.

"Yo, yo, back again, people. Hope you all are feelin' this dope show?" The crowd roars its approval.

"Just getting better from here. I'm gonna bring out a real live star, now, a man who knows popes and presidents, McCartney and Springsteen. He don't need no introduction. You know him from the Rock 'n Roll Hall of Fame, and as a saint to poor Africans - shout out to my brothers and sisters on the Soul Continent! And you also know him as the lead singer of one of the biggest bands in rock history. People, bring the noise for Mr. Bono!"

Bono enters from stage left wearing black jeans and

a black jacket over a "Feed the Hunger" tee shirt. The crowd erupts into boisterous applause. Bono acknowledges their adoration by waving his hands high over his head, lips parted in a wide grin. He looks like a rich housefly behind his gold wraparound sunglasses.

"Thank you. And thank you, Cro, my brother," he says, as he applauds Crojon, who is leaving the stage. Keith is stunned to see one of his idols only twenty feet away.

"You might think," Bono begins, slowly, "why is Bono here? Did he know Keith? Or is he here because he's Irish, and everyone knows he loves to talk."

The crowd laughs. Keith wears a shit-eating grin of stunned joy.

"Yes, I love to talk. And no, I did not know Keith. But I knew him if you know what I mean." The crowd shouts its support.

"Yeah, man, we all knew Keith. Right? I mean, Keith is a very unusual rock star, isn't he? He didn't make it like most rock stars do. He got rich and famous, but he never got to enjoy all that success. And that doesn't seem fair."

Heads shake in the crowd, and some girls wipe tears from their eyes.

"But then, no drug busts, either. And no golfing or waving a silly flag onstage. No beanies on his head, no bad hair period. I mean, even I know the 80s are over."

Some laughs crackle through the crowd as Bono

benignly smiles down on them.

"He never wore a dress in a video, though Candy looked good in hers, didn't she?" Bono bows to Candy, who stands at the side of the stage.

Keith curses under his breath. Then he notices a familiar figure standing towards the side of the stage, a little closer to the front than he is, her brown hair reflecting light in the dimmed club. Jane watches intently, listening to every word. Keith has a hard time shifting his attention back to Bono.

"Rock stars are supposed to make soap operas of their lives. Keith didn't. He made his an art piece. Yes, I'm Irish, and we like to talk." The crowd applauds more loudly as Bono grins. "Did I say that? But we also like to drink." Now they are applauding even more loudly, clinking their bottles add to the noise.

"So let us raise a toast to this man, to this artist—this saving angel who is watching over us and protecting the sanctity of our artistic souls. No, we'll never see him or his like again, never have him here again to talk to us, tell us what we need to know, or how to think. But he's already told us everything we need to know in his songs, his beautiful, precious songs."

Jane wipes a tear from her eye, though she's not exactly sure why. The speech doesn't affect her, so maybe it's just the sadness of the story.

Keith, who had been caught up in the Irish rocker's speech, is distracted by her gesture. She's crying, he thinks. For me.

Bono raises his glass. "Here's to you, Keith Unger. You didn't live long, and you didn't die happy, but you've rated a mansion in heaven for the afterlife. Cheers!"

Hundreds of glasses and bottles rise high above the heads of the crowd as Bono raises his glass to them. The sound of full-throated screams and hearty toasts fills the air as Bono takes a big gulp of his drink. He then salutes the crowd as he walks offstage.

It starts as a couple of voices, but the calls quickly build until nearly the entire club is chanting.

"Keith lives! Keith lives! Keith lives!"

Keith's ego can barely resist reveling in the adulation directed at him. He is human, after all.

But another side of him is revolted by the cheers from people who don't even know him. They only imagine they do. It feels phony, artificial, and he feels trapped in its plasticity. While being dead is no longer tenable, being alive to this scene is increasingly painful.

It is as though alien forces drove him off that cliff in Malibu. Now that he's grown and gained perspective, his father's death seems increasingly pointless and hurtful to those he left behind. Selfish, in fact. Like Keith's death. Fame was no affirmation of art or its value. It was a completely separate commodity. And now that he so desperately wants to be alive, 27 seems like such a young age to die.

Brian, Jimi, Janis, Kurt, Chris, Amy - all of them left

great art behind when they exited this earthly plane. But what did they leave undone? What colossal leaps of creative consciousness could they have made? As he thinks of the enormous strides his own art has made in the short time since his death, that thought becomes overwhelming.

I love you, dad, but I wish you'd loved me more. It was a grind with mom sometimes. She didn't understand me, tried to control me. But at least she stuck around. She understood you better than I did. She wanted to save me from your fate.

The loudspeakers erupt, coming to life with a jolt to the opening chords of Keith's new song, "Back Again." Keith is caught off guard.

"I lived a life, so empty and vain, I had to leave it behind so I could come back again."

As it plays, a more profound truth begins to reveal itself to him, one he hadn't fully realized when he wrote those words. Because only now is it becoming clear what he has really left behind, and just what coming back would mean for him.

Vondy is looking up at the stage as she calculates the best position from which to deliver her career-altering live-shot, when her phone rings.

"Yes, Bill."

"Everything good? For the story?"

"All set. Just wait until you hear it."

"Good. I'm counting on you."

Vondy scans the crowd, desperately looking for any sign of the Voice. Her nervousness increases by the minute. Her career is hanging like a thread from his coat. But none of that fear enters her voice.

"And you know you can."

"When this is done," says Bill, his voice lowering, "maybe you can come over and give me one of those special massages."

"Sounds great," she replies. "I've got to go."

Skip stands next to her, sucking on his soda. Vondy looks at the stage and decides to stand near it.

"This is where I'll stand. You stand there, so you have me on an angle frame right, birthday cake upper left. Got it, Crumbs?"

"Got it, boss."

Vondy scans the crowd and tries to contain her panic. Without the Voice, she is screwed. There will be nothing to report. She's going to have to think fast on her feet.

A hand on her shoulder startles her. Vondy jumps back, bumping into a girl standing behind her, spilling the girl's drink.

"Watch it, bitch!"

"She didn't mean it, boss," says Skip. He then turns to the girl with the drink splotched shirt and whispers importantly, "She's with the news."

Vondy turns to see a dark figure dressed in a black leather jacket, black jeans, a white tee shirt, and a salt and pepper jockey hat pulled down tight over his head.

"Where the hell have you been?"

"How are you, reporter lady?" Danny smiles. "I was here. You like the outfit? I thought it'd look good on TV. Should I wear sunglasses?" He pulls out a pair of aviator glasses.

"Yeah, whatever. Do you have the info? Because we go live right after they sing Happy Birthday."

"Oh, yeah, I am so ready!" says Danny.

Vondy leans into him, checking to make sure no one else can hear.

"So spill it.

"What?"

"You said you know why they staged Unger's death, the whole story?"

"Okay. So, this is so good. So, Keith, the black guy, the girl ..."

Danny leans in conspiratorially.

"They're aliens. All of them!"

Danny smiles as he misunderstands the gobsmacked look on Vondy's face.

"Mind-blowing, right? The coffee shop is like where they teleport to and from their ship. There's a portal, or a black hole or something, in the back room. Keith's their instrument to brainwash America with."

"What?"

"Yeah. It's the beat, the beat in the music, see? It hypnotizes everyone! That's how they put their alien message into everybody's heads, and—"

"Are you serious? You expect me to go live on the air to the whole world and say that Keith Unger is an alien and he faked his death as part of a plot for alien world domination?"

"You think there's more to it?"

"Oh, my God, you're nuts. *Pendejo*! I'm going to be the laughingstock of the news business."

Panic is in a bull market for Vondy right now.

"You don't think he's an alien?" asks Danny. "I know what you mean. I had trouble with it too, but I thought my original idea might sound too far-fetched."

Danny motors through, leaning into Vondy.

"Okay, we're still going with the whole brainwashing scenario here, so stay with me because they're - Republicans!"

Danny waits for a response from Vondy. When none comes, he assumes he should continue.

"Get it? They have this obsession with profits, personal responsibility. You should hear the guy who runs the coffee shop. He's like a regular capitalist. They're all white. Well, except that black guy. I haven't figured that out yet. But, the resurrection is like a signal to the religious—"

Vondy puts her hand over Danny's mouth.

"Go!" She points in the direction of the exit.

"But, I've got more, and—"

"Go!! Before I hit you! Do you understand? GO!"

"Does that mean I'm not going to be on TV?"

Vondy lunges at him, but Skip steps between them.

"I guess not. Cool. It's a lot to take in and all. But you should think about—"

Skip gives Danny a little shove that propels his slight frame deep into the crowd.

"It's true," calls out Danny. "Keith is alive! I know the truth! Well, I don't know all of it. But I know some of the truth. He's alive! John Lennon was right!"

Skip turns to Vondy, who is frantically searching through her pockets.

"You okay, boss?"

"Where did I put them. Oh, shit, I am so screwed!"

"You looking for these?"

Skip holds up four pictures of Keith on the streets of Los Angeles taken by Danny.

"Yes! Okay, okay, good, now think, think. What am I going to do? Bill Daily, big story. Come up with something. Something good. Oh, no, I'm so ruined!"

Skip puts his arm around her and talks gently, as he would to a baby.

"It's going to be okay, boss. You have the pictures, right? So you have proof that Keith is alive. Well, that's a huge story! When we break for the live shot, we just show the pictures."

"Right, proof, we have proof," Vondy nods her head, grasping for this lifeline. But panic spews from her again. "What am I going to say? There's no story. Then what?" She looks pleading at Skip.

"You just show them pictures, tell them he's alive.

It's a teaser. You can make something up later when you have time to think about it. Like we always do."

Vondy begins to calm down. A small smile brightens the corners of her darkened face. "It's just the news, you're right, Skip, you're right. It's just the news. I can make something up later, something good."

The storm has passed, and Vondy is regaining control of herself. There are decisions to be made, orders to be given.

"Okay, slight change of plan, but it's all good. He's alive, and I have pictures. I won't give an explanation. I'll just show proof. Mystery. Yes, it'll add suspense to the whole thing … Skip?"

"Yes, boss?"

"I'm going to do a live cut in after the birthday song, okay?"

"Will do."

Jane sways silently to the music, lost in her own thoughts. It makes her look fragile, which she is not. Jane knows who she is.

She is strong and brave, and all-girl, thinks Keith. But who am I? An imposter. Then and now.

I had to leave it behind.

Fame turned out to be a trap with no escape hatch, a cage holding him in, when what he desperately wants now is to break free, to bust out of his own skin.

Metamorphosis.

The music fades, and Keith watches Crojon reappear onstage. Crew members carry a large cake out. Crojon has them tilt the cake so it is visible to the crowd.

"Isn't that pretty?" he asks, expecting the reply he gets.

The chocolate cake is a 3-D representation of Keith's face. Atop the cake is a pastry black Stratocaster that rises like a skyscraper perpendicular to the cake. Candles in the shape of microphone stands run along the entire edge. An Orange amp sits next to the Strat.

"It's time to wish the birthday boy a Happy Birthday, and you can't do that without a cake, right? Chocolate chip rum pudding, people. Keith's favorite!"

I hate chocolate chip, thinks Keith, who also happens to be a teetotaller.

"Let's bring our people back, what you say? Bono? Candy?"

Bono and Candy come out. Bono grabs Candy's hand and lifts it up in the air. The crowd erupts in thunderous applause. Harry follows them, along with the Hunger band.

"Harry Chukstein, Keith's manager, and the guys from Hunger. Is that it? Are we missing anyone?"

Crojon looks out at the crowd, holding his ear open as if waiting for a clue.

"Ain't no birthday party without the birthday boy's

mama! For the first time in public since Keith's death, I wanna hear a big Empty V welcome for Keith's mom, Mrs. Joyce Riffinian! Whoop whoop! Let's hear it, people!"

From the side of the stage, Keith's mother appears. She smiles nervously at the crowd and stiffly waves her hand. With her other hand, she holds a leash attached to the collar around Lennon's neck. The dog struggles at the leash and barks at the crowd.

"And Keith's dog - Lennon!"

Bono walks over to Joyce, chivalrously offers his arm, and accompanies her to a spot beside the cake. Lennon looks up at Bono and sniffs his pant leg. Bono reaches down with his spare hand to pet Lennon, but the dog ducks and barks at him.

The crowd applauds wildly for Lennon. Joyce leans over and looks closely at the cake.

"Thanks for being with us, Mrs. Keith. Did you want to say anything?" Crojon holds the mic out to Joyce.

"That doesn't look a thing like Keith." The audience howls in laughter.

Keith can't help but smile at the sight of Lennon. Every time Lennon barks, the smile gets bigger.

"Anything else you'd like to say on your son's birthday, Mrs. Keith?"

"Well, it's not his birthday..." The crowd quiets. Joyce looks at them. "He was a good boy. I didn't tell him that enough. I should have. I should have done a lot of things that I didn't. But ... he didn't have a father. Well, a stepfather, but...That's not the same, I guess, so he just ... I miss him."

Keith feels something in his throat, caught there and not moving. Lennon barks loudly, pulling on his leash.

Jane wipes another tear from her eye, standing in front of the stage.

"Hush, Lennon. Quiet boy," says Joyce, as she gently pets Lennon. "He's not used to this many people."

"That's okay," says Crojon. "What you say we all sing a Happy Birthday to Keith? Everybody ready? Okay, 1-2-3 ... Happy Birthday to you—"

The entire club joins in singing to the poor, dead musician, gone but not forgotten.

But I am forgotten, thinks Keith. I'm just a plastic shell they fill with their own dreams and needs. The old Keith is gone. I have to claim the new me. I have to kill Keith, or I really will die, he thinks.

Keith is dead. Long live Keith.

The crowd finishes the song while Crojon readies the knife to cut the cake. Lennon is barking and looking straight in Keith's direction. He pulls at the leash, trying to get free. Joyce struggles to hold on to him, her small hands clinging tightly to the leash.

"Lennon, calm down, boy." She looks at Crojon. "I don't know what's gotten into him."

Lennon tries to run from the stage. He rises up on his back paws, pulling against the leash.

He sees me, thinks Keith.

The group stands around the cake, posing for pictures. It's a Dutch masters' tableau with Bono next to the cake's right side, opposite Joyce, Crojon between them. Harry, Candy, and the band stand behind the cake.

"Lennon, please calm down!" But the dog is more than Joyce can handle.

"Start me up." Vondy urgently motions for Skip to start filming.

Skip quickly turns the camera on, says something into the headset, and nods to Vondy. He points the camera at her and gives her a thumbs up.

"Hello, everyone, this is Vondy Wells reporting to you from the Keith Unger birthday celebration. I am cutting in because of important breaking news that has been brought to my attention. This news is so devastating, so shocking, that I felt it was critical to bring it to you immediately."

"Maybe he just wants a bit of that cake," says Bono from the stage. "It's rum, right?" The audience laughs along with him. Bono leaves his spot and moves towards Joyce and Lennon.

"Let me give you a hand," he says. "I know a thing or two about Lennons."

Vondy looks seriously into the camera.

"My source, a close confidant of Keith Unger, has brought me irrefutable proof that Keith is in fact ..."

At that moment, Lennon suddenly spins around

behind Joyce to get away from Bono. Joyce tries to turn with him, but her legs become entangled in the leash. Lennon barks wildly, and as Bono reaches down to grasp the leash, a frightened Lennon bites Bono's hand. Bono screams and falls backward. Joyce loses hold of the leash, which unravels from her legs, spinning her around. Lennon leaps up, hitting the cake from underneath and sending it flying forward.

Bono bends at his knee and catches the falling Joyce as the cake flips forward. It falls in what feels like slow motion, coming down in a big splash on top of Bono, exploding over his head, with pieces flying everywhere.

Bono's chocolate pudding-covered face makes him look like a black minstrel, his clothes are covered in brown chocolate cake and white frosting.

Another piece of the cake flies through the air and hits Crojon. His face is now covered in white frosting, with bits of chocolate sticking to his hair.

Joyce's face remains clean but frozen in terror as her hands cover her mouth.

Lennon bounds from the stage and runs through the crowd, which parts before him. He runs straight to Keith.

Skip spins as Lennon runs past him. His years as a cameraman have taught him to instinctually follow the story first, and right now, Lennon is the story. Vondy's face registers the short distance between shock and anger.

As Lennon reaches Keith, he sniffs his feet and then

barks, leaping into the air, resting his paws on Keith's chest.

"No, Lennon, down," Keith whispers to his buddy as he tries to sink into his overcoat. But Lennon persists. When Keith gently pushes him down, Lennon takes the long black jacket into his teeth and pulls at it.

"Lennon, stop it!" Keith pulls the coat back, but Lennon has his teeth firmly dug into it. "Lennon, stop!" The dog looks up at him and lets go of the coat.

Everything stops. The room around Keith, and all the people in it, are frozen in time. At the center of that frozen world are Keith and Lennon, with all eyes on them. And there is one thought in Keith's head that sits atop a mountain of other thoughts: The old Keith must die, so I can live again.

"Sit, Lennon."

Lennon sits down in front of him. Keith turns to face the stage and slowly slips his arms from the long jacket, letting it fall to the ground. He removes the baseball cap and drops it as well. Keith then takes off the sunglasses, holding them in his hand.

He can feel the stunned silence that now surrounds him as he lifts up his head and reveals himself to the crowd.

Keith is dead. Long live Keith.

Lennon leaps up again onto Keith's chest, overjoyed, and begins slathering him with furious kisses. Keith can't help but laugh.

"Keith? Oh, my God, it's my boy!"

Keith looks up to see his mother looking down at him from the stage, tears in her eyes. Then he looks around him.

"Keith lives?" one shaky voice calls out.

The audience is confused, and the only sound is the excited panting of Lennon. Every face in the club registers shock, mouths agape, eyes wide open in disbelief. Every face that is except for one - Harry's face is buried in his hands.

Bono sits on the ground, covered in chocolate pudding. He wipes a bit from his cheek, then tastes it. His face brightens in delight.

"Rum? Rum! More rum, more rum!"

Keith catches sight of Jane, who is as stunned as the rest of the crowd.

"Keith?" she says to herself as if trying to understand a foreign language. But slowly, understanding comes, and more than one truth is revealed to her. Keith stands silently, not knowing what to say, except -

"Jane?"

She looks at him and slowly shakes her head as tears well up in her eyes. Then she turns and dashes from the club.

"Jane!"

The sound of his voice echoes in his mind, like a call into an empty cave, flying in and then rebounding back to him.

Vondy looks deflated, limply holding her mic,

while Skip's camera is trained on Keith.

"Keith Unger is alive," she says blandly and without interest. "Whoop dee doo."

People begin to crowd around Keith, tentatively at first, then more confidently. They touch him gently with their fingers, then press harder, probing his body, and finding the flesh real. Slowly it dawns on the crowd that this is no resurrection. Keith Unger is indeed alive.

The stunned silence begins to erode as voices rise and questions are called out. Resentment builds and begins to find its primitive expression.

For Keith, everything moves as if in a dream. There is only one sound in his mind and in his ears - the reverberating echo of his own voice.

"Jane!"

His mother rushes down the stairs and across the club. She pushes through the crowd and throws her arms around her son, crying for joy. She kisses his cheeks, confessing her sorrows and sins, pleading for forgiveness over and over, through the chest rocking sobs.

"I'm so sorry."

The crowd moves away from Keith. He is an island now, alone with his mother, in the middle of a sea of people. There is anger, and there is disgust. The sense of betrayal is palpable.

Harry also comes down the stairs from the stage and walks towards Keith through the crowd. He enters the empty circle around Keith, and as he reaches him, he says in a low voice:

"Say goodbye to Hollywood, kid. They used to love you, but it's all over now."

And Harry walks past him too.

20. YESTERDAY'S PAPERS

The drop from the pinnacle heights of superstardom to the utter depths of revilement is a sharp and long one. It's a free fall more significant than a jump to earth from outer space and much more treacherous. Especially if you forgot to pack a parachute.

For Keith, the fall is a blur. The crowd's shift from shock to anger to rejection all seem like different parts of the same wave - the rise, the curl, and the crash over the falls.

He remembers the blond woman reporter trying to get an interview with him for TV. Keith doesn't remember what he said to her or if she said anything to him, but he knows he didn't give her an interview. He's glad about that. She was very pushy.

His mom led him out of the club, got him into her car, even put the seatbelt over him. Keith didn't seem capable of doing anything for himself in those minutes after his second fall. Lennon kept on slobbering in his ear with wet kisses from the back seat for the entire ride home.

The drive to his mother's house did not take long, or maybe it took forever. The TV room, where he'd seen his mother and Lennon, sitting together in their mourning on the couch, became his new cave as he slowly rewound the coil that had spun out after the Killer Klub.

In the beginning, he mostly watched TV with Lennon. There were plenty of news stories about him as they replayed his denouement - the falling cake, the reunion with Lennon - endlessly. The blond reporter said that the death and its aftermath had been planned. She didn't have any proof or explanation as to why, but she did have pictures.

She interviewed his friends - Aki, Kitch, Carolyn, Harold. They all seemed reluctant to put a bad word to Keith's name. Protecting him. Even his old band members were reserved.

After a couple of weeks, the blond reporter's reports started to diminish. When he did see her now, she was doing stories on turtles getting married or a ghost town with real ghosts. Once there was a story about a bar that had a swinging door that only opened one way.

Whatever, thought Keith, better than reporting on me.

Brad Rossi was on TV firmly denying that Massive had any prior knowledge that the story of Keith's death had been false.

Harry, for his part, denied that the fake death was in any way a planned con. He even tried defending Keith in his own way. He said Keith wasn't smart enough to think up a plan like that, and he, Harry Chukstein, wasn't stupid enough to try one.

But Keith couldn't stay confined indoors. He was used to walking the streets of the city. So soon, he started walking again.

First, he only walked at night, when Keith Unger could go unrecognized. He walked across Hollywood, around his old neighborhood, past the club, and his apartment building. Locations in the movie of Keith Unger's life. He often walked by the Coffee a Go-Go, but he never found there what he was looking for.

It was more challenging walking in public during the daytime. People stared at him wherever he went; some cursed at him, some wanted an autograph. Many just laughed. But most were angry and not only told him so but showed him as well.

The attention was too much. Keith couldn't find a private place, except in his mother's house. Everywhere he went, there were prying eyes, people with cameras, cell phones. The online celebrity sites stalked him because people were hungry for news about him, which translated into a large bounty for Keith Unger's pictures. The people want to know.

He was their hero, their savior, and he'd been proven to be human, with faults and weaknesses, clothed in actual flesh, and that was too painful for the rock god's disciples to bear. People couldn't take responsibility for seeing what they wanted to see in him, so instead, they made him to blame for not being what they expected to see.

But slowly, interest in Keith began to wane, and in a few weeks, the looks were much less common. By the time a month had passed, he could walk the streets of Los Angeles with nary a nod directed at him. The masses had moved on to the next hero, the next villain, the latest drug-addled model, the most current anger-spewing actor. And if not, then they just kept their noses in their cell phones. Sooner than he expected, Keith was just another face in the crowd.

Inside him, though, the change was more remarkable. Taking control of his life, stripping off his jacket and cap, standing emotionally naked in the middle of the club, had been like a new birth, a declaration of independence. This rolling stone had shed its moss.

Rather than being devastated by his fall from grace, he felt a growing power as a result of it. He'd lost a lot, but he'd gained things that were infinitely more important. They just needed time to bloom. But it was harder for them to bloom without the sun, in the shadow of his loss.

It took him a while to find the courage, but Keith finally stepped inside the Coffee a Go-Go. Jane wasn't there. The new guy working the counter is the perfect face of modern slacker lethargy, barely able to acknowledge him, let alone give him any information. Though in reality, he didn't have any information to share. Jane had quit the coffee shop the day after Keith Day, and no, he doesn't know where she was now.

Keith had sort of expected that, but it was nonetheless a painful bit of rope to chew on.

At home, his mother didn't say a lot. She made him food, washed his clothes, offered to take him wherever he needed to go. She didn't ask questions. Mostly she just seemed penitent. And happy. Very happy to have him back. With his stepfather in Europe, Asia, or someplace, on business, she was alone. And even though Keith wasn't the best company right now, she didn't seem to mind.

Finally, he worked up the courage one day to go to the homeless camp. He didn't know how he'd be received. They had all been honest with him about their pains and their foibles, and he had betrayed that trust, lied about himself.

When he got there, he was surprised by how vacant it was. There were only one tent and two chairs.

"Brian?"

Keith turns to see Kitch walking towards him. Once he realizes it is indeed the Brian he once knew, Kitch smiles broadly and wraps his arms around Keith in a warm embrace.

"Man, I wasn't sure that was you. You look different. You know the—"

"The new clothes?" said Keith, embarrassed.

"No, man," laughs Kitch. "It's the hair-cut and shave!"

Keith runs his hand across his face, smooth and soft as silk.

"I guess maybe I should call you Keith. Come to see the old homestead?"

"And to say I'm sorry."

"Ain't no sorry, man. No harm, no foul. Everybody's got their thing to work out. You ain't no different than nobody else." Kitch looks around the thinned-out camp. "Things ain't much the same here these days."

"Where is everyone?"

"Oh, man. Well, you know Carolyn and Harold are a couple now? Crazy, huh? Kinda perfect too. So they moved up to the Valley, and Harold's working with Aki. Enzo and Emmy are in school. Carolyn's trying to get a job."

"Aki is still working?"

"Oh yeah!" laughs Kitch. "He's kind of like a boss. But he's still short!"

"And you?"

"Yeah, man. Kitch got a job, too!" Kitch laughs loudly. "I got the perfect job. Moving out of here today, just picking up my stuff."

"That's great. I'm happy everybody ... found something."

Kitch puts his hand on Keith's shoulder. "Your songs, man. They were good for people. Music's got power."

Keith nods. He's thinking about the one person he'd like most to see.

"And—"

"Ben?" says Kitch.

Keith nods his head.

"Well, you can just ask for yourself."

Kitch looks over Keith's shoulder and nods. When Keith turns, he sees Ben towering over him, wearing a smile that's complementary in size.

"Ben!" Keith moves quickly into Ben's open arms for a big bear hug. "I'm sorry, I'm so sorry."

"Sorry for what?" Ben pushes him away in mock anger.

"For lying, and—"

"No sorry. I know everything I need to know."

"Yes, he does," smiles Kitch.

Keith begins to explain his transgressions again, but Ben interrupts with a swipe of the hand.

"We're done with that. New verse, new song. You talk to that manager of yours?" asks Ben.

"No. He's been calling, but I don't want to see him."

"You might want to. He's probably got some money of yours."

"Yeah, that's what he says in his messages."

"You know what you're gonna do with it?"

"Well, I can't lie. I've been thinking. It won't be much, but I have some ideas."

Keith's biggest question still hangs in the air.

"Do you know where ... where Jane is, Ben?"

"I see that snake bit you good!" Ben laughs. "No, I don't know. Ain't seen old Jane since that night."

Keith frowns. He expected Ben to have that answer.

"You know, I might be able to help you with that," says Kitch.

Riding a bit of a high, Keith begins to think about Ben's question on his way home. Keith does have an idea of what he wants to do. Now he begins to form that idea into a plan in his head. It's a path that incorporates what he's learned with who he knows and what he can do. And it feels right. Walking helps his mind sort the jigsaw puzzle of ideas.

This also brings him around to thinking about Harry. It's time to face that situation. And if there is any money left from his posthumous earnings, he'll need some of it to finance his plan. Keith resolves to give his old manager a call when he gets home.

But as it turns out, there is no need to, because when Keith arrives to his mother's house, Harry is there waiting for him in the kitchen.

"These are so good, Joyce," says Harry, swallowing up the last of the waffle cookies. "Sweet, but not too sweet. Just like you."

Joyce blushes. "Oh, stop that, Harry, you're embarrassing me."

Keith is sure that she actually doesn't want him to stop. But there are things to discuss, so he clears his throat, and Joyce, to her credit, picks up on the message.

"Well. I'm going to leave you boys to your business. Let me know if you need anything." She gives Keith a kiss on the cheek as she leaves the kitchen.

It's an awkward silence between Keith and Harry. Keith is used to not talking much when he's around Harry. He isn't used to Harry not talking, and it is clear his manager is struggling more than a little.

"So, good to be alive?"

"Good," Keith nods.

"Could have been worse. You could be managing Candy."

Keith smiles a bit, and that seems to loosen Harry up an equivalent amount.

"So, business. I guess we need to go over that. You're going to find I'm not such a bad manager after all. Maybe just a flawed human being."

"Harry, I never said—"

Harry raises his hand and waves Keith off.

"I know, I know. But I did a pretty good job by you – and me – even if I do say so myself."

Harry sets the briefcase beside him on the table and opens it up. He pulls a fat manila folder out and begins going through the papers inside it.

"You weren't dead long. We released two singles, three Eps, and one full-length record. As I said, we sold a lot of physical product because of your unusual demographic. But we also broke records on streaming product. Plus, we have all the merchandising – tee shirts, hoodies, coffee cups, mouse pads. We even had Keith-themed coffins." Harry smiles morbidly. "That was my idea."

Keith isn't smiling. His poker face reveals nothing. So, Harry continues.

"As I promised, songwriting and publishing credit for 'I Remember You' have been completely reverted back to you. And it is almost as big of a hit as your own records."

Keith nods.

"By the way," says Harry hesitantly, "Candy came out of all this without much mud on her face. Everyone thinks she was a victim, and she's not setting the record straight. You know, she can barely play a G-chord, let alone use one to write a song. So, she wants to cover some of your songs, older ones. You can do what you want, but it would bring in a big revenue stream going forward. Very big."

"I'll think about it."

Keith looks at the mass of papers and knows he wants to get to the root note.

"What's the bottom line? What are we looking at here?"

"Well, there were expenses. Plus, I get a percentage. The label gets theirs. The streaming companies take a cut. I got you a great deal, but they still get to make their money. And it should be mentioned that your sales have been pretty dead since Keith Day. It all eats away at the total."

"Okay, Harry, I get it. Now, how much money do I have?"

"Well," Harry grimaces. "I'm sorry, but you better hold on to your chair for this."

Keith stares at him steadily, except for a brief flicker in his eye.

"Just tell me."

"You're—a millionaire."

"A millionaire?" asks Keith, not quite comprehending.

"A multi-millionaire."

"A multi-millionaire?"

"Well, technically, a multi-MULTI millionaire, but who's counting? In your dead months, your posthumous releases outsold everything – Taylor Swift, Justin Bieber, Foo Fighters, Beyoncé – you name it, everybody. Baby, you're a rich, rich man. Rich, rich, rich, rich."

Keith is stunned, barely able to comprehend.

"The money is in a trust, in your mother's name, but it's all going to revert to you. Just sign some papers, then you can open a bank account and start spending, And unless you spend like an NBA player, you'll never have to work again for the rest of your life. Or the next one."

"Wow," is all Keith can manage to utter.

"There's one other thing. Remember I told you your sales were as dead as the 80's since the Keith Day thing?"

Keith nods.

"Well, before the Keith Day thing, I licensed your new song, "Back Again," for use in a trailer. It's a new sequel of this old movie, *Poltergeist*. It's playing non-stop in the theaters, and the song is blowing up. They just recut the movie to include it in the actual film, and we're having a music video made. It's a hit! Brad's calling for more songs."

Keith doesn't respond. He leaves Harry's surprising news hanging in the air, suspended by uncertainty.

Harry nods, then lays some papers out on the coffee table between them. He pulls a pen from his pocket.

"Look it over. It's legalese, but I had it made simple, so it's understandable. It gives you all your money."

The pen dangles in the air for a long moment. Slowly, Keith reaches up and grasps it. He looks down at the documents and then puts pen to paper.

"Man, I hope there are no bad vibes from all of this. I'd really like to keep working together."

"Work? On what?" asks Keith as he looks up. "I'm finished."

"This is America," Harry says, his smile broadening into a laugh. "Second acts are more profitable than the first."

Keith thinks of his life of fame and its price. He also thinks about his plans for the future. All plans need money, more than you expect they will.

Then Keith looks at Harry's broad smile, his parted

lips, and his mouth, slanted sideways, as it opens wide when he laughs. He looks down into the deep, dark chasm, that endless canyon that lies inside Harry's mouth. And for a moment, he teeters on the edge.

Jane shifts in her seat, unconsciously moving her backside around like it's mashing potatoes on the chair.

Sometimes, when something confuses her, she likes to move her tush around until it stirs up an answer. Of course, she doesn't know that's what she is doing. She just knows that when a solution does come, she can finally sit still and focus.

Books and papers are spread out across the desk of her office. Today that office is the Panera Bread Company in Beverly Hills. Endless coffee, and a power outlet next to the booth, help make it the perfect spot. Plus, the friendly ex-Marine manager, David, lets her stay as long as she wants.

The contract is confusing. And daunting. It's a lot of money, she thinks, and I'd be on the hook for all of it by myself.

While she is confident, she is also conservative. Her father taught her well. She's not afraid to take a risk, but she wants to know what that risk is before taking the leap.

The leap. That reminds Jane of Brian. Keith! Oh, it's

hard getting used to the name change.

She tried forgetting. That didn't work. There were all the stories on TV, news people wanting interviews. Even when she wasn't watching the TV, it seemed that everyone around her was talking about Keith.

And now that people aren't talking about him anymore, the silence only makes all the thoughts of him in her head grow louder and echo so that they threaten to swallow up all her other thoughts.

Jane feels betrayed and abandoned. She thought she knew him, but what did she know? A shadow? A character in a play? Was it just love's illusion? She didn't really know him at all.

And yet, the thought nags at her that she did, in fact, know him. That Brian wasn't a character Keith played, but rather a mirrored reflection of the real thing.

She shifts in her seat again, leans to the left. I have to stay more focused on what's in front of me, she thinks, these papers on the table. This is my dream, held for many years. Brian ... Keith, that was a moment in time. A moment whose time has passed.

And a good thing that it has, she thinks, because I never want to see him again. Of that, I'm sure!

"Jane?"

Jane stops shifting. Her breath catches in her chest. Slowly she lifts her head, knowing all the while what she will find.

He is clean-shaven. His scraggly long hair is now

somewhat tamed, clipped below the collar, bangs hanging loosely across his forehead. He is wearing a clean, green Henley shirt over a pale yellow tee shirt, and his jeans are clean. She notices the shoes - new Chukka boots.

Jane takes it all in - he looks different; he looks the same.

"Am I bothering you?"

Jane shakes her head, not quite ready or able to speak. She tries to look cool and disengaged.

"Can I sit down?"

Keith points to the chair opposite her. She notices that his hands are clean, nails manicured. And trembling a little. No, you cannot sit.

She nods.

Keith sits down. She looks at him across the narrow table, which is a vast divide. He does seem different, more... confident. Definitely cleaner.

Keith settles into the chair, and they sit quietly for a moment. He lightly drums his fingers on the table. He's nervous too, she thinks.

"I've been looking for you. Everywhere. You ... you kind of disappeared. I guess I can't blame you. You probably think I was a jerk, and I was."

She doesn't answer. Keith nods and assumes that she agrees with his self-appraisal. It's quiet for a few moments, neither of them quite sure what to say. Jane senses that it's her volley.

"How did you find me?"

"Oh, I have my ways." He smiles as he looks over her shoulder. Jane follows his gaze, and there she sees Kitch behind the kitchen galley line, smiling and waving maniacally. Jane laughs.

"You have spies."

"I have friends."

Keith gently puts his hand on hers, but Jane moves it back. He retreats.

"What are you working on?"

"An application," she says, looking down at the papers. "For my coffee shop."

"Your coffee shop?"

"I found a space, so I have to sign for a loan to pay the security deposit, opening expenses."

"That's great!" Even Jane can see the obvious delight he gets from her success. "That's really great. It's your dream. You must be so excited."

"Yes. I am. And a little scared too. Actually, a lot scared! I can't decide if I'm doing the right thing, or if...you know. It's a lot of money. Luckily, I have great credit, but I don't want to take a bad risk. I've made mistakes."

Jane looks up at Keith, and he is stung. She takes a moment before speaking again.

"I want to be sure. As sure as I can be."

The next pause seems so much longer than it probably is. Whether the space between them is the distance of a creek or an ocean, neither is sure.

"I'm sorry. I'm so, so sorry." Keith blurts out,

emotionally. "I never meant to hurt you. That was the last thing in the world I'd want to do. God, that sounds like such a cliché, but it's the truth, I swear. I just didn't ... I wasn't ... I wasn't who I am now. I was on the road here, from another place, a different place, to here. But I just didn't know it. Does that make any sense? I had to take that path until ... until it led to another one."

He reaches his hand back to hers, and this time she doesn't move it. But she doesn't return the squeeze he gives it.

"I feel a little stupid." Jane looks down at the table, but then she lifts her eyes to meet Keith's. "A lot stupid. Like there's a big joke, and I'm the punchline."

"There was no joke, Jane. Except me. I didn't like the path I was on, and I didn't know how to get off it. But I learned."

Jane gently removes her hand, pushes her hair behind her ears.

"I learned from you," says Keith.

Jane looks surprised, then a smile creases her lips. She shifts slightly in her chair.

"Where's the new coffee shop going to be?" asks Keith as he looks over at the papers.

"Hollywood," she answers. "Further east. It's kind of out of the zone, but I keep thinking they're gentrifying everywhere, so it'll probably move that far out soon enough. Still ..."

"What?" asks Keith, relieved that the conversation

is moving to more comfortable ground, which is anywhere that's far from him and his mistakes.

"I don't know," Jane shakes her head. "I'm not sure I feel it. I want a business, but I liked where I was at. I liked the people, the ones who were on the edges, who needed help. I miss Ben and Harold. And Kitch." She laughs with a quick look over her shoulder. "I should do something that helps people. I think that's what I'm good at."

"I think it's what you're good at too."

Keith looks at his watch, then at Jane's pile of papers.

"Can you take a short break? From the papers?"

"Why?" she looks at him suspiciously.

"Nothing bad. I just want to show you something. Is that okay? It's not far."

"Okay." Jane doesn't sound fully committed or entirely sure. "But not long. I have to finish these papers. I'm on a deadline, or he's renting to the second applicant."

"Don't worry, it won't be too long."

Keith helps her pack her things. Several times their hands touch, and tingling electricity surges with each contact, sending vibrations up each of their arms.

They walk outside, waving to Kitch as they leave.

"See you tomorrow, Kitch!" calls Jane.

"Not me," he smiles and raises a thumb up. "I got me a new gig!"

They walk out the doors and onto the sidewalk of

Beverly Drive. Keith's beat-up Dodge Dart is parked right in front. He opens the passenger door, which drops a couple of inches once released from the side of the car—Keith motions for her to get in.

It's not lost on Jane that Keith now has plenty of money. But he's still driving this car.

"It's safe, right?"

"As long as we go slower than light speed," answers Keith. Jane climbs into the passenger seat as Keith lifts the door up two inches, then shuts it.

The drive from Beverly Hills to the Westside is made longer by the traffic. But the time goes by fast as they both loosen up, and the conversation glides along on newly greased wheels. Jane asks about his mother, his dog, his lousy driving skills. She finds herself again feeling the ease of being in his company, part of what she found so attractive about him in the first place.

But they really don't know each other very well, she realizes. Not in the details, the true-life stories, the everyday things. To Jane, Keith is mostly a mystery. What little she knows is from TV news and magazines, and little of that is true, she is sure. But still, there is the feeling that they do know each other in the most genuine sense.

Keith pulls down a side street in Santa Monica. Or Culver City. Maybe it's Mar Vista. Jane isn't sure. She doesn't drive so she never comes to the Westside, and all these streets seem the same. Where one town ends and another begins is a rolling mystery to her.

The street has a residential feel, though it's right off the main avenue. On a considerable lot, just past the corner, sits a large house with workers buzzing around like bees. Two of the workers pass in front of them, carrying a door frame with milky smoke glass in the center.

Keith pulls over and parks.

Hopping out of the car, he hurries over to the passenger door, just in time to help Jane open it. She climbs out and looks at the building. Arching over a doorway without doors is a sign that reads: Lennon's Lair.

"What is this place?" she asks. "Isn't Lennon—"

Before she can finish the sentence, Lennon comes running through the door, barking. He jumps up and puts his paws on Keith's chest, and begins to smother his face with wet kisses.

"Okay, okay, boy," laughs Keith.

"Damn love affair going on out here."

Jane looks up to see Ben standing in the doorway. No longer dressed in rags, he wears clean jeans, a button-up shirt, and construction boots.

"Ben!"

"Well, how you doing, Miss Jane?" he smiles at her. "You're one tough girl to find." Ben gives her one of his big bear hugs.

"I have to say I'm not surprised to see that you two are together," says Jane. "But I'm a little confused. Is this your house?"

"Could be," Ben replies, giving Keith a look. "Yes, it could be. More like the people's house."

"Come in," says Keith. "It's easier to show you."

They walk through the front door, which opens into an ample space that looks like a vast living room. Obviously, some walls have been removed to enlarge it. The glass sliding doors along the back wall, coupled with the skylight above, flood the room with light. Several couches are situated around a rectangular coffee table. At the back of the room is a long dining table and several smaller tables, each with chairs. Jane can see more tables, chairs, kids' toys, and a play area outside the glass doors.

"This is the 'family room," says Keith. "We have board games, books, other stuff. The idea is that people talk, or do things, preferably together."

"Fosters communications," says a voice behind them.

Jane turns to see Aki coming in from another room, holding and eating a bowl of cereal.

"*Community*, not isolation. Hi Jane!" He reaches out his hand and warmly shakes hers. He then slides the top off the table, and a quarter panel moves, revealing the books and board games held inside.

Keith walks to the back of the large open room. He stops at the little tables.

"Ben built these and most of the furniture in the house. The tables are made so you can join them together into a large table for group dinners. Or you can separate them for smaller groups. Really smart, isn't it?"

Keith motions for Jane to follow him. He leads her around a corner and into an open kitchen. Adjacent to the kitchen is another sitting area. This sitting area is also furnished with a couch, a couple of chairs, a table. The kitchen is clean, bright, and modern-looking.

"You and Ben live here?" asks Jane, her head tilted. "You too, Aki?"

"No. Well, yes. And no," Aki laughs.

"I think we can put it on the counter, next to—"

Carolyn comes through the back door, trailing her voice by a second. She is followed by two workers carrying a large sliver machine with a glass top.

"Hi, Jane!" She gives Jane a hug. "I'm going to have them put the pancake maker here on the counter for right now. Is that okay?"

Carolyn looks to Keith, who shrugs.

"It's your kitchen," he replies.

"Are you joining us, Jane?" asks Carolyn.

"It's a group house?" asks Jane, who is now totally confused.

Carolyn looks at Keith sternly.

"You didn't tell her?"

"I'd still rather show than tell," says Keith.

He takes Jane by the arm and leads her back through the living area to the other side of the house. Enzo and Emma run past them, screaming and laughing. Ben, Aki, and Carolyn follow behind Keith and Jane as they walk through a large open door.

On the other side of that door, they enter another world. A barista counter stands against one wall, glass doors are along an adjacent wall. The other walls are covered in bright, colorful murals. A big built-in bookshelf occupies part of one wall, with some books strewn along its shelves, several boxes of books sit on the floor. Tables and chairs are placed randomly around the room. Other tables and chairs are similarly placed outside, in a lushly landscaped area with flowerpots and green bushes.

"What is this?" Jane asks, already in love with the beautiful space.

"It's your coffee shop," says Keith. "If you want it. We don't have hair styling chairs, but we can get them."

"My coffee shop?"

"Harold did the murals," laughs Carolyn with evident pride. "Can you believe it? My man is an artist!"

"Can someone please tell me what is going on here?" says Jane. She turns to Keith, whom she expects to be that someone.

"Okay, I can do that. This isn't 'our' home, but it is a group home. It's a home for homeless women and their children. It's a cooperative - Ben, Aki, Harold, Carolyn, me - we're all in it together."

"Kitch, too. Harold and I are part-time," says Aki. "For now."

"We intend to provide a temporary home for mothers without one," says Keith. "A safe place for them and their kids until they can pick up the pieces and start again, a new life. We bought the property next door, too. We plan to expand."

"We're going to have a drug test policy," explains Aki. "If you have a drug problem, we'll accept you. But you have to be committed to kicking it."

"It ain't just about the women," elaborates Ben. "It's about the *kids*."

"We're going to provide tutors," nods Keith. "We're talking to different faith groups about spiritual guidance for those that want it. And we're trying to figure out how to place kids in schools once they're caught up with schoolwork. Carolyn is the point person for all the residents, and she's designing the kitchen. Kitch will run the kitchen. Aki does repair, plus our accounting and planning. Big Ben does design, building, and interim spiritual guidance."

"And what do you do?" asks Jane, looking at Keith.

"He's Mr. Deep Pockets!" exclaims Ben. The rest of the group laugh loudly.

"And coffee shop entertainment!" Keith corrects him with a smile.

"But where does the deep pockets money come from?" asks Jane.

"Well, you see Jane, you might not guess it by looking at me, but I was once a huge rock star, and I made a lot of money. But I died before I got the chance to spend it on liquor and drugs. So..."

"You're using that money to help people?"

"Trying," replies Keith. "But it's more than just me. Everyone who lives here has to pitch in, including residents. That's part of our philosophy - build community, grow self-reliance. The whole point will be for people to get stable, and move on, to be independent. We hope once they leave, they'll continue pitching in. People helping people. We're even creating an organic garden in the back."

"But we got one position that ain't been filled," says Ben.

"The coffee shop is our main social center," says Keith, turning to Jane. "We're also hoping to make some money here, give employment to the residents. Plus, some mothers or kids may have musical talent, and we can give them a place to showcase. We need a coffee shop entrepreneur, someone to do all the ordering, bookkeeping, be a barista. Someone to bring the imagination."

Jane is shaking her head from side to side.

"But most importantly, we need someone with soul and sunshine, someone to give support and guidance, someone to help other people help themselves."

Keith looks directly at Jane, and the rest of the group stands expectantly behind him. Jane realizes what's coming.

"Oh no, I have my own dream, my own place to open. I'm putting my application in today!"

Keith smiles. "In life, you have to choose paths. You have to choose the one that leads to your truest dreams."

Jane looks around at all the happy, smiling faces looking at her in anticipation. It's all so fast, she has other options, and this has so many uncertainties.

"What do you say, Jane? Do you choose this coffee shop?" asks Keith.

EPILOGUE

The dog is barking at her. It is no dream, and it won't stop.

"He claims this new venture will help those who are less fortunate to help themselves. The first residents are moved in, and so this experiment has started."

Vondy's smile seems painted on, mirthless, cracked. She stands in front of Lennon's Lair, which now has doors, a beautiful exterior, and rich green landscaping. Several women with young children walk in and out of the doors behind her.

"Like the horror film villain who will not die, the tale of Keith Unger has risen again, taking yet another strange turn. With his new song sitting high atop the pop music charts, it seems his latest ambition will have no trouble with financing. And Unger certainly hopes this effort will not go flying off a cliff."

Lennon barks. He stands just a few feet from her. Vondy tries to ignore him.

"I'm Vondy Wells reporting from Lennon's Lair in Los Angeles."

The fake smile disappears as Vondy drops the mic to the grass and walks straight to the van. She pulls a cigarette out of the pack in her purse on the passenger seat floor and lights up.

Smoke blows out of her mouth like a Victorian chimney as she mutters something indecipherable to herself. Lennon stops barking and just stares at her, daring her to come back out onto his grass again.

Skip wraps his equipment and pats the top of Lennon's head as he passes him. After closing the van's rear doors, he walks around and hops into the driver's seat. Vondy settles uncomfortably into the passenger seat.

"Where to now, boss?"

"How the hell should I know. We might as well stay here until there's a new Keith Unger story. Why get our hopes up."

"So In-and-Out?" asks Skip, brightly, as he puts the van into gear and drives off.

Lennon watches them leave, making sure Vondy is gone. Then he turns and runs towards the door, opens it with his head, and rushes into the house. He runs through the house, all the way to the back.

The little coffee shop at the other side of the house is abuzz with activity. There is a crowd of people, primarily women and children, lazing on this sunny afternoon, enjoying pastries and drinks. Keith stands with Ben, Aki, and Carolyn in the center of the room.

"Do you hear anything?" he asks, and Aki shakes his head.

The sound of the front door opening is followed by the fast staccato clicking of nails on the hardwood floor.

Lennon comes running into the room, tail wagging in excitement. He rushes up to Keith, who reaches down to pet him.

Harold follows the dog into the room. He is wearing jeans, a Lennon's Lair tee shirt, which is soiled with dirt and sweat, and a red bandana around his head. His glasses hang on the front of his nose.

"Okay, it's all wired up and ready to go. I think. The problem was you had the wrong feed going in, so it was cutting out the power. I'll show you. Excuse me, Jane."

Jane steps out from behind the barista counter. As she does, Lennon rushes to her and jumps up, putting his paws on her chest. She laughs and hugs him.

Harold walks over to the shelf behind the barista counter and turns on the stereo equipment. The speakers crackle, so Harold fiddles with the wires. Then he hits the play button on the front panel and turns to the group, with a nervous smile, fingers crossed on both hands.

From the speakers above, the opening chords of "I Wanna Be Rad" come blasting through, clean and crisp. Harold does a little leap in the air.

"Yes! Total sound!" he shouts over the music, smiling broadly.

"Great job, honey!" Carolyn gives him a big hug.

When the chorus kicks in, the whole coffee shop is up and singing along to the silly lyrics, with joy and conviction, dancing to the beat, bodies releasing, arms flailing.

"Oh baby, I feel so bad/I don't know, but I think you're mad/I can't help feeling sad, but all I want is to be rad."

Harry walks in with a dirty white kitchen apron on and stands in the doorway. He looks at the mad dancing people with a puzzled look on his face.

"Did I miss something?"

But no one hears him because all are lost in the blissful release and mad delirium of another big, fat pop song.

ACKNOWLEDGEMENTS

It only takes one person to write a book. But it takes a small village to write a good one.

The head of my village is my wife, Hilda. She supported this project like she supports every other project of mine – completely and without reservation. Without her love and support, Keith's story would never have been told, and I would be just another guy who was one day going to write a book. Hvala, Hilda.

My mother Olga always told me I should write. She insisted as only a mother would and knew as only a mother could. It took years for all my writing to finally become a book, and I'm grateful that she stuck around long enough to see her efforts pay off.

My late father, Nedjeljko, was an excellent writer who self-published a marvelous book about his experiences during World War II. Its distribution was limited, but its impact was broad. When he told me I was a better writer than he, it became both my greatest compliment and my primary motivation to be better.

I am grateful to Fritz Hollenbach, who gave Keith

Lives! its first read and its first edit. Fritz brought skills learned editing books by his talented late father, Karl Hollenbach, a pioneer of self-publishing who remains an inspiration to this writer. Fritz was a pillar of support in all things, at all times. Thank you, friend.

An excellent writer himself, Andrew Robles chose to take time from his own project to edit mine. He understood that I was intentionally breaking some grammatical rules, and he helped me do that without sounding entirely illiterate. This book is immeasurably better for his contributions.

Deanna Barber gave generously of her time and talents, many of which were honed as an educator, librarian, and champion of the elementary school Battle of the Books program. Every writer should be so lucky as to have a Deanna.

My friends Emily Bice, Matt Powell, and Steve Shearsby generously helped me with many fine details, from blurb assessment to critiquing possible book covers. Many other friends took time to give me feedback on the evolution of this book's cover. Thank God for friends.

I would also like to thank, for help big and small: Andy McLenon, Donald Spicer, Bryan Lafaye, Dan Wall, Kevin Benton, Kathy Nolan, Jack Emerson, Tony Marsico, David Jenkins, Brad Raisen, John Tomko, Thomas Jewett, the late and always great Rick Field, and of course, John, Paul, George, and Ringo.

Last, and most importantly, thank you to my daughter

Maja. To accomplish anything significant in life, one must first learn to show up every morning and get to work. I've tried to get up (almost) every morning with Maja, and while she home-schools, I write. Teaching is learning, and I have learned a lot from my daughter. I love you, Maja.

Actually, that isn't the last, because I'd also like to thank you, dear reader, for taking a chance on a book by an author you didn't know. Thank you for sticking with it to the end, or at least skipping forward to the acknowledgments so all the lovely people above can get some recognition. I hope you'll be joining me for future adventures in print.

Now, please go back to Chapter One and read it all over again. You probably missed things, and there will be on the quiz.

Did you enjoy this book?
You can make a big difference

Reviews are the most powerful tool I have in my arsenal when it comes to getting attention for my books. As an indie writer, I don't have the financial muscle that a big publisher would have. I can't afford to put ads in the newspapers or put posters on buses and subways. (Well, not yet, anyway).

But I do have something much more powerful and effective than that, and it's something that those publishers would kill to get their hands on.

You.

Honest reviews of my books help bring them to the attention of other readers.

If you've enjoyed this book (and I hope you have) I would be very grateful if you could spend just five minutes leaving a review (it can be as short as you like) on the book's Amazon page at:

https://amzn.to/3Ptgttw

Thank you very much, dear reader.

ABOUT THE AUTHOR

Bodie Plecas started writing professionally while attending Louisiana State University, an institution honored in song by Randy Newman. His stories have covered music, film, travel and politics and have appeared in newspapers, magazines, and on the internet.

Bodie has seen over 1000 concerts, owned over 10,000 vinyl records, and travelled to over 50 countries. But who's counting. When not writing fiction, he writes and records music under the name of Picnic Tool.

Having lived on the edges of rock and roll, Bodie now lives on the edge of America in Southern California with his wife and daughter, surrounded by his guitar collection. He is currently plotting his next record, planning his next trip, and writing his next book.

Please sign up for Bodie's newsletter and continue following his writing adventures at: https://bodieplecas.com.

You can find his music at: https://www.picnictool.com or https://picnictool.bandcamp.com or http://bit.ly/PicnicTube.

Connect with Bodie on Twitter at @BodiePlecas, and on Facebook at www.facebook.com/bodieplecasauthor/